KEYHOLE MYSTERIES
Witness 5

by B. ULENA

Publisher
Treasure Fleet – 511 Latitude Lane – Osprey, FL
34229
NTB.Promotions@gmail.com
941 468-9039 Text only

ISBN: 978-0-999-8993-3-5

Dedication

To Mark, Joy, Leah, and John
for all their patience and assistance with
printer problems, complex computer care,
and just fueling me with Sunday morning coaching,
and Wednesday night cultural marathons.

Acknowledgements

A special thanks to Leigha Buscher,
Clarissa Thomasson, and Adam Cherier
for their help with the research and advice,
also, to Mark Tancey and John Gotthardt
without them this book could never be written.

Happy Reading
2020

B. Ulena
a.k.a. Nancy Busaker

Sunday, June 14, 2020

~ 1 ~

Dixie rolled off the redheaded man and lay quietly staring up at the ceiling, her head resting on her hands. She took a deep breath and sighed.

"A penny for your thoughts," he said, turning over on his side.

"I'm wondering if we should stop."

"What? Seeing one another?"

"Everything is going to change."

"You've fallen for him!"

"Oh, don't be ridiculous. This is just another rung on daddy's ladder to success. I told him I didn't want any part of this scheme, but he threatened to cut me off without a cent. What could I do?" She sighed deeply. "Surely, he won't want to live here. Wherever we go it will be smaller than here. There will be new people around—mostly his friends. We'll never be able to meet like this."

He reached over and cupped her breast. "How can you even think such a thing? He'll have to go to work, and you can get away. We could still meet here. This house is huge—there must be hundreds of secluded places." He leaned closer to suckle her, but she pushed him away.

"Stop it, I'm serious!" She got up; her lean, thirty-four-year-old body still moist from the workout. She walked to the window and pulled back the curtain.

The Florida sun cast shadows on the lawn. The bougainvillea and hibiscus were bursting with color and the mockingbirds and scrub jays flew about calling to one another. On a day like this Venice, Florida, was at its best.

"We don't have to stay here. We could go away and make a new life for ourselves.

"And live on what?"

"I have some money saved. It isn't much, but it's a start. We could buy a little house someplace where no one knows us. I'd get a job and we..."

She sighed again. "Can you see me in jeans and a sweatshirt, running a vacuum... cleaning toilets! Are you insane? My hair, nails, and wine bills alone would bankrupt us. No, Darling. I'm stuck here."

Walking over, he put his arms around her. "We'll think of something. It will be all right. I love you. I won't lose you." He turned her around and kissed her gently. When he opened his eyes, he saw a single tear roll down her cheek. "Come back to bed and let me hold you. No matter what the future brings, we have this time together."

She smiled and took his hand. "You always seem to know just what to say to make me feel better."

He pulled back the sheets, and they crawled back into the warmth and safety of their nest. He put his arms around her and pulled her close. They lay quietly for a few minutes before she broke the silence. "What are you thinking?"

He laughed. I was thinking of our first child; a little girl with beautiful chestnut color hair—like her mama."

"Oh, children. I hadn't thought about children."

"What? You don't want children?"

"I don't know," she paused, "Maybe I shouldn't have children. My mother..."

"You aren't your mother. Are you looking for reasons because you really don't want children?"

"Well, no. I don't mean *no*. It's just that I never... Kids—you know, changing diapers, squalling day and night. Kids throw up all the time. Is that what you want?"

He laughed. "I have to admit I had not thought about it in quite the same way."

"You'd better. I've seen pictures of older children in highchairs, rubbing their hands in their food and smearing it on their faces and in their hair. Ugh!"

He forced himself not to laugh again. He didn't want to hurt her feelings or make her angry. "Actually, we have a lot of babies in our family and, you're right, those things do happen. I've noticed, though, that when they're first born, they fit like a little ball in the palm of my hand. When you look, you'll see are how small their hands are—yet their tiny fingernails are perfectly proportioned. When babies look at you, you see it's pure love they have for you."

"You're right, I haven't seen many babies."

"As they get older, they go from a *Weeble* to sitting up on their own. They quickly learn to crawl; then they stand; and before you know it, they're walking and running. They're little miracles."

"I hear you, but aren't they dirty and messy?"

"Sure. Aren't we all at times? What I see is a little girl who follows her mother around the house mimicking what she sees because she wants to be just like her mama."

Dixie burst into laughter. "Oh, no! You want a mini-me, with long dark hair, a glass of Beaujolais in hand, and an attitude to torment everyone!"

He could no longer hold back the laughter. "Just you wait. When the time comes you will see. It's a rare mother-bear that would not kill to defend her young."

"Enough talk about the distant future. I want you to hold me now. I need you to fortify me so I can make it through the next twelve hours.

A powder blue Saab convertible sped along one of Florida's sun-drenched roads. It curved to the right, pulled off, and headed for the guardhouse. The little man inside waved it on. The gate rolled away, and the convertible rushed forward onto the immaculately landscaped grounds of the Bedwick Mansion. The tree-lined path curved majestically toward the opulent nineteenth-century estate. The home's somewhat gothic style merged with a few oriental motifs—resulting in a structure both distinctive and original. It had been the winter home of J. Harrison Bedwick until he leaped from the 10th story window of his New York office in October 1929. The complex was then purchased in the early 1930s and since that time has been home to three generations of Weinbergers.

The Saab pulled around the Japanese boxwood hedge that framed the drive and stopped at the front entrance to the home. A uniformed attendant opened the door and Autumn Mariiweather, a charming, thirty-something blonde stepped out. Her white on white seersucker suit rode up a bit—accentuating her long tan legs. When she brushed the short skirt down, her bracelet made little tinkling sounds.

"Good afternoon, Adam. Am I very late?" She brushed back a strand of hair that caught a gentle breeze.

"Not very, Ms. Mariiweather, guests are still arriving." "Have you seen my brother? We were going to come together, but he wasn't home when I got there."

"I haven't seen him, but three of us are working. One of them might have. Should I ask them?"

"Oh no, thank you, Adam. He'll show up."

The attendant slid behind the steering wheel of the convertible. His hand caressed the wheel only a moment then he quickly pulled away. Autumn smiled to herself. Young boys love cars. She headed for the open front door.

The din of voices melded with the instrumental music played by a small ensemble in the solarium at the left of the grand foyer. People milled around conversing with friends, sipping champagne, and sampling exotic hors d'oeuvres offered by strolling caterers.

Autumn looked around the grand foyer. She knew many of the guests who live in Venice as well as some of the out-of-towners. Governor John Whimple and the Attorney General, Clifford Duncan; Disney's president/CEO, Kelly Smart; Lily Williams from Disney's young adult cable channel; and there were many more whom she didn't know.

Carol Tanaka strolled up with two glasses of champagne. "I saw you pull up," she said handing one to Autumn.

"The Weinbergers certainly know how to throw a party." Autumn took a sip as she glanced around. "There must be close to 200 people here."

"Well, it isn't every day the spoiled brat daughter announces her engagement." Carol pointed beyond the foyer. "A violinist is playing in the library, and there are bars set up in the wine room, solarium, and living room. When I get married, I'll be lucky to have Kool-Aid and a kid playing a kazoo."

Autumn laughed. "Well, your daddy doesn't own half the farmland in the county. Kool-Aid? Not grape, I hope."

Carol shook her head. Her auburn hair, cut in a long bob, swayed, and her smile reflected her Asian heritage.

"Glad you could make it. What kept you?" the female voice asked, more out of boredom than criticism, as she stepped out of the crowd and joined the two women.

Autumn recognized the tone even before she turned to smile at Dixie Weinberger. The three women had gone to school together. They had been cheerleaders for the same team and ran with the same crowd. Dixie's family had money, she wanted for nothing, and arrogance was her strong suit.

"What a marvelous turnout," Autumn said.

"Of course, it is." Dixie took a sip of her Beaujolais and flicked a strand of hair with a long, manicured nail. "Daddy wouldn't have it any other way. When he snaps his fingers, everyone jumps." She took another very long drink.

"Where is your Mr. Right?" Carol asked, dramatically craning her neck to look around. "Surely you remembered to invite him." She didn't look at Dixie but nonchalantly swirled the champagne in her glass.

Dixie's expression turned stone cold. "You're not funny, Carol. Of course, he's here. Daddy's introducing him around. My god, his future son-in-law *must* know all the right people."

"She's just teasing," Autumn said quickly. "We're both happy for you and Jacob, and it's a lovely party. I haven't seen this many people since Michael Bublé came to the Van Wezel." She took a sip from her glass. "You must be excited. Have you set a date?"

"Around Christmas—maybe. I haven't decided." Dixie started to say something when she noticed someone signal her from across the room "I believe I'm being summoned." As if to fortify herself for what was to come, she took another sip of her wine. "I'd better see what he wants." And she disappeared into the crowd.

"I'll bet you money he's not here. She probably forgot to tell him."

"Carol, you're heartless," Autumn said, but she couldn't help but smile and leaned in conspiratorially. "You wouldn't be a little jealous, would you?"

"What? Of her? Hardly!" She drank the rest of her champagne and looked around to see where she might get another. "Why would I be jealous?"

"Well, she's about to get married."

"Seriously? Can you see Dixie as a happy little *hausfrau*?" Carol rolled her eyes; then continued. "Marriage will be a whole different lifestyle for her. It's a sacrament, you know. Ideally, it's supposed to involve sharing, tolerance, patience, openness, honesty...and chores. Dixie has never even chipped a fingernail."

"Oh, Carol, she won't do the housework. She'll hire it done. As for all the rest, she may fool you. When you love someone, you want to make that person happy."

"I just can't imagine her doing the *'til death do us part'* routine. And if she promises that at the wedding, you can bet that he will die of some mysterious disease within a short time."

"We must have faith, my friend." Autumn put her empty glass on the tray of a passing caterer. "I'm going to see if I can find Jeff. He's probably somewhere in this crowd. Have you seen *your* brother lately?"

"No, he left home and joined that awful gang. We don't see him anymore."

"I'm so sorry." Autumn turned to leave.

"Wait, I'll go with you. There must be food somewhere in this place. I'm starving." Carol hurried to catch up.

The two women made their way through the crowd toward the living room. Popular love songs from the 1980s filled the air. The music came from a white grand piano nestled in a corner of the room. The beige walls and carpet made the white coral fireplace the main focal point. Triple crown molding encircled the tray ceiling. Fifteen-foot columns flanked the fireplace, and even larger crowned mirrors above them came in a close second. The architecture was designed to grab the attention of any visitor. The elderly woman at the piano concluded the melody and transitioned into "Kiss You All Over" made famous by the group Exile before Dixie was born.

Carol was quick to notice a buffet that sat conspicuously along the right-hand wall. "Wow!" she exclaimed. "What a spread, and look, the food is labeled. Here are peanut butter chicken wings, jalapeño poppers, and popcorn shrimp." She picked up one of the Dresden plates and began helping herself.

"I think I'd like to sample some of the smoked salmon and Beluga caviar." Autumn took a plate and cocktail fork. "Did you notice, the napkins are imprinted with their family crest? The Weinberger's seem to have thought of everything."

~ 3 ~

The small wine room across from the butler's pantry had a 3-stool bar and a crowd of any size would be elbow to elbow. The fat man took a 32-oz souvenir etched glass of beer that read "Dixie and Jacob – 2020." When he took it from the bartender, he nearly spilled some on the man seated on one of the stools.

"Sorry," he mumbled to the man, and as quickly as he could shuffled his girth out into the less crowded hallway. Here, at least, he could catch his breath and take a drink. Just then a woman approached.

"Nate," she said, tugging on his sleeve to get his attention. A smile came to his lips when he recognized the young woman. "I need something," she said, looking around the hall. "Where can we talk?"

His smile broadened. He took several more swallows of the beer and watched her squirm. "We can talk here, Fran. What is it you need?"

Her face contorted, and she replied through clenched teeth, "You know *goddamn* well what I need, you inflated fuck!"

Nate laughed out loud and then leaned right into her face. "If you want anything from me, you cumslut, you'd better show some respect." He turned and walked away.

"Wait, I didn't mean anything. Shit, you know me. I just get nervous and overreact. I didn't mean anything."

He kept walking.

She hurried after him and took his arm, not as a friend, but to avoid losing him in this crowd. "Come on, Nate."

The man opened a door on his right and peered inside. "In here." The woman followed him, and he closed the door. He turned to her. "What do you want?" He asked in a less than friendly tone.

"Just a taste. I don't have much money right now, but my credit's good. You know that, right?"

He reached into his pants pocket and pulled out a small white package. "A gram for 40."

"Jazus Cryst, Man! 40 bucks! It's usually 26! What the fuck!"

"That's the price. Take it or leave it!"

He turned to leave but she grabbed his arm again. "No, wait. I have something you'll like. Maybe we could make a trade? Come on, Nate. What do you say?"

He watched as she fumbled in her large handbag.

"I don't have all day."

"Here it is." She pulled out a scabbard and handed it to him. "Pretty nice, huh? It's at least worth $40 bucks."

He pulled out the knife and looked it over. "It looks new, where did you get it?"

She looked away coyly. "Let's just say it's a little thing I picked up."

"Is it hot? I don't want any stolen merchandise."

"Hell, no. It was... uh, given to me by a dumb fuck kid."

"Did he steal it? If I find out you've handed me..."

"No. No. I know the kid. He's clean. What do you say? We got a deal?"

"All right—but just this once. In the future, it's cash only, got it!"

She grabbed the packet out of his hand. "Yeah, Nate, I got it. You're a good man."

He replaced the knife in the scabbard and slipped it into his pocket. Then, beer in hand, he walked out the door.

~ 4 ~

The music stopped, and a hush fell over the room.

"Ladies, gentlemen, and guests," the distinguished white-haired man said into a hand-held microphone. "Welcome! I trust you are enjoying yourselves. You've all been invited to Bedwick Mansion to share the good news."

Dixie slipped through the crowd to join her father and the man who stood at his side. As she stood facing the crowd the man reached over and took her hand. Autumn noticed Dixie's startled reaction at his touch, but the rest of the crowd saw only the quick smile that followed.

"Some months ago, I talked to one of the most inspiring young men I've ever met." David had a way of crooning to crowds. He knew how to get their attention and holding it until he was finished. "He relocated from Atlanta where he was a successful investment broker. Shortly after arriving in Venice he joined our firm and has become my right-hand man. He's quick and aggressive, and he's making immense strides in improving the areas of Asset Allocation, Risk Management, and Simulation Tools at Weinberger, Inc. At this rate, I envision a partnership for him in the near future.

"You're here at this festive occasion at the Weinberger's to celebrate the engagement of our daughter Dixie to Jacob Crawford."

A round of applause and shouts of approval filled the air. David Weinberger paused a moment to let the commotion die down. He was a master at reading a crowd. He, himself was a man of many moods. He could go from the cut-throat businessman to a loving, although unavailable, father in a matter of seconds.

"Thank you," he said, holding up one hand for silence. "The wedding will take place next month, on Sunday, July 5th in the south garden.

Autumn saw the flicker of surprise before Dixie again quickly covered it with a smile.

"You are all invited," he said with flair. You will soon receive the official invitation by mail." He put a hand on Jacob's shoulder to signify the bond, and the younger man turned to Dixie and kissed her on the cheek.

"Please. Eat. Drink. Enjoy the rest of the evening." Weinberger handed the mic to the pianist and walked out of the room.

Another round of applause gradually morphed into friendly conversation, and the music began again.

"Well, what do you think of that?" Carol asked, taking a bite of liver *pâté*. "Now it's official. Our Dixie is really going to marry that guy. Whoever he is, Daddy David is certainly smitten. I don't know him, do you?"

"No. Why don't we go over and congratulate them?"

A line of people was forming to shake Jacob's hand and extend well wishes to Dixie. As they got closer, Autumn recognized Dixie's painted smile, the one she displayed when it was expected; the false one.

"Mr. Crawford," Autumn began as they reached the couple. "Congratulations. We look forward to getting to know you. Dixie is an old friend, and we wish you both much happiness."

"Likewise," Carol added shaking his hand before turning to Dixie. "You did invite him. Nice move."

Dixie glared at her. Old friend or not, Carol could always push Dixie's buttons. But Jacob, nonplussed, just turned to the next person in line.

As they walked away, Autumn asked, "Carol, why were you so hard on her?"

Carol's look was one of surprise. "Was I being hard? I thought I complimented her."

"Autumn!" called a voice in the crowd. The women turned to see a young man in blue jeans and a dark T-shirt working his way toward them in the crowd.

"Boatman!" she called and waved as the robust, swarthy young man reached them a bit breathless— but smiling.

"I figured you'd be here, but I didn't think I'd ever find you in this swarm of bodies.

"Boatman, this is Carol Tanaka. Carol, this is ..."

"Boatman—I take it," Carol said, looking him up and down. "Nice to meet you," she paused, "I think."

"I'm surprised to see you here—knowing your lack of *fondness* for the family."

"Well, that's true enough, but actually, I'm looking for Don." He glanced around searching the crowd before turning back. "My gosh, it's been ages, Autumn. I never see you anymore. What have you been up to?"

"Well, I had a bad time after—you know. But I'm back. It's getting better, and I'm writing again. I need to stay busy. I recently met Mrs. Wilburn, and she's come to live with me." Autumn laughed. "She seems to think I need a housekeeper and she's determined to take on that role. But really, her company is what I needed the most. Thanks to her I am doing much better."

"I'm happy to hear it. You have a rosy glow." The man smiled. "It looks good on you."

Carol saw a caterer with a tray of champagne and slipped away into the crowd.

"A lot has happened since I saw you last. I quit the job I had with Smallwood. Don and I bought a fishing boat. We named it the *Able Seaman*." He chuckled and ran a hand through his mass of black curly locks. "We're doing pretty well, too. We're averaging a steady four clients a week.

"Is Don still working here as a gardener?"

"For the time being. He's really caught up in the new business. He continually comes up with new ideas to improve things. In the meantime, he spends all his spare time thinking of ways to drum up business. He's amazing. Oh yeah, he's even mentioned marriage."

"Really? I didn't know he was seeing anyone. That's great news. He's a wonderful guy."

"Autumn's getting a reputation as a pretty good mystery writer. She's even beginning to make money from it," Carol announced, as she pushed her way to their side.

"You should write a book that takes place on a fishing boat," Boatman noted. "You could charter the boat for a day. Don and I know a number of great locations you could use. You know the kind, overrun with bushes, trees, and snakes. That could be very mysterious."

"What a good idea. Let me check my calendar, and I'll give you a call."

"Great. I'll wait to hear from you," he added, glancing around nervously. "I need to find Don, so I can get out of here. This place gives me the creeps."

"Gives you the creeps. What do you mean?" Carol demanded.

"I sense a black cloud hanging over this house. Something bad is going to happen. I don't know what or how, but mark my words, it will happen soon." He nodded to Carol then turned to Autumn. "Do call me. I have to go." He quickly kissed her on the cheek and slipped away into the crowd.

"Well, he was *interesting*. He'd be cute if he'd comb his hair." Carol uttered. "If you ask me, I'd say his bad feelings about the place might be partly due to his ridiculously casual manner of dress for such a swanky party. He must come from the sticks or else he's just plain antisocial."

"Carol, Boatman comes from a very affluent family in Tampa. He wanted a less materialistic lifestyle, so he went to study at Cave Hill, the University of the West Indies. The school fosters a culture and work/study environment that welcomes different ideas and perspectives. As a result, he got in with a group that practiced voodoo. That didn't suit him, but he discovered he has clairvoyant abilities. He lived in Jamaica for several years, got his degree and a *non-degree* in the supernatural. His powers are amazing. Don't be too quick to judge him.

"Hmm... you certainly couldn't tell by the way he's dressed."

"The slogan "the clothes make the man" was probably coined by Brooks Brothers to drum up business. The truer phrase is 'don't judge a book by its cover.'"

"Okay, okay. I get it!"

~ 5 ~

The south garden was bursting with color from the grand Magnolia with pristine white petals, striking Crape Myrtles, and Bird of Paradise. Favorite trees that flourished were the robust Jacarandas and the tropical elegance of Christmas, Ponytail, and Foxtail Palms. Bougainvillea hedges showed their mulberry colored blooms, while the promise of future blooms were on the climbing vines of Confederate Jasmine, the more robust purple Wisteria, and the trumpet-shaped yellow Jasmine. One would have thought the Almighty Himself had laid His hand on the ground to reap such splendor. Everywhere one looked in this park-like oasis were the white and bright blue, funnel-shaped African lilies; dwarf Mexican petunia; Plumbago shrubs; and islands of Juniper ground cover—all laced with brickwork paths and subtly placed lawn ornaments.

People strolled about the grounds; here and there small groups chatted quietly. The garden was less crowded than the house, but the opulence was spared in neither.

Boatman was not put off by the glares from the guests he passed, but from the time he had spent searching for Don. He checked his watch. 3:45 pm. He had been stuck here for over an hour.

"That's it, I'm leaving," he muttered out loud. He headed for the gate that would lead him to the area where all the cars were parked. Eager to get away, he walked swiftly. Ahead he saw a man whose features, even from behind, he recognized; a man he would like to avoid. He turned—hoping to lose himself among the few trees and parked cars.

"Never expected to see you here," the man called out, his words slurred and his balance in question.

Boatman saw the man was holding a turkey leg in one hand and his souvenir glass of beer in the other.

"I'm in a hurry, Smallwood."

"What? Too busy to talk to an old friend?" The man scoffed and took a drink of his beer, oblivious to the drops that dribbled and darkened his pale blue shirt.

Boatman continued walking with the hope of avoiding a confrontation. Smallwood was argumentative by nature, but drunk he was abusive.

"Did you come to pay your respects to the Weinbergers? Oh, that's right. You don't respect them, or anyone else for that matter. Boatman only respects Boatman." He began walking toward the younger man. "We had a pact, you bastard. Business was good; money was rolling in. Everything was going smoothly until you got a burr up your ass and quit."

When there was no reaction, the fat man continued, bent on getting his attention. "Was that your idea or your girlfriend's? No, wait. Maybe you're the girl! I get confused, you are both so *pretty*." The last word spit out like venom.

Boatman walked faster, but the barb was beginning to get to him. Smallwood, sweating and determined followed at a trot, his beer sloshing and his belly bouncing.

"Which is it, Sally? Who gets it from behind?"

Boatman turned so quickly Smallwood almost plowed into him. "I don't want any trouble. Don't take it personally. I wanted to be on my own; that's all. I quit. It's done. Get over it!"

Smallwood's face went beet red, and his jowls quivered. "You son of a bitch," he raised the turkey leg and brought it down on the younger man.

Boatman stepped aside deflecting the blow with one arm and coming up with a hard fist hitting the man just below the sternum. Smallwood's eyes bulged. He gasped for breath, and all color drained from his face as if someone had pulled the plug from a tub of water. He dropped the turkey leg and beer, fell to his knees, and puked up his last meal.

Boatman wasted no time leaving the scene, but he heard Smallwood gasp, "I'll get you for this, you son of a bitch. Hear me? I'm gonna' hurt you bad!" The man wiped his mouth with the back of his hand. "*You better believe it. It'll happen when you least expect it.*"

6

Jeff held his glass up indicating he'd like a refill when the bartender looked his way. The Stage Right was a neighborhood bar adjacent to the Venice Theatre. It was quiet now, but it would fill up around 10 p.m. when the Saturday night performance ended, and the actors stopped in to review their final performance and grab a burger and brew.

"Make it another round for my friends," Jeff called out with a bit of a slur. He turned to Sojoe and Henry Chen, who sat to his right. "My good friends," he leveled his empty glass in a toast.

"Buddies. Chums," Sojoe added, leveling his own glass.

"Comrades!" Henry called out in a terrible German imitation, as he laid a finger under his nose to indicate a mustache.

The other two burst into inebriated laughter. The bartender sat three new Scotch and sodas before them as the laughter died down.

"Do you think," Sojoe began, "we should head out? The party started a while ago. We're late."

"We *are* late," Henry said, reaching for his drink and spilling at little with the effort. He brushed the drops off his shirt.

"We're late, we're late, for a very important date," Jeff chimed in and another round of laughter followed.

"Let's take a vote. All in favor…"

"Wait a minute, Jeff," Sojoe said raising his hands for emphases. "Roberts Rule of Order demands a discussion before we can vote."

"He's right," Henry agreed. "Discussion first; then we vote." He took a drink and rapped his glass down like a gavel. "This court will come to order. Sojoe has the floor."

Sojoe sat up straight on his stool—pausing as he tried to focus. "Your honor, in my opinion, we should refrain from leaving this fine establishment. Uh, and save the gas needed to make the drive… and continue to get snookered right here."

"Jeff, what are your thoughts on the matter?"

"I'm thinking we stay. The hell with Whinebugger's soiree, or banquet, or bash; oh shit, whatever you call it. Who votes to stay?" he asked—as the others 'ayed' in agreement. "I never liked the pretentious bastard anyway."

"Yeah, but he's got a mighty fine daughter," said Henry, lifting his glass.

"She's as bad as him," Jeff added, leaning his elbows on the table to keep the room from spinning. "Everyone in that house is depraved… even the servants."

Henry scoffed. "You must be drunk. Just because the man is richer than dirt doesn't mean that he …"

"I know what I'm talking about!" Jeff answered—attracting the attention of a couple at the bar. Lowering his voice, he leaned close to Sojoe. Henry leaned in too, not wanting to miss any of Jeff's forthcoming gems of wisdom.

"Remember that waitress they found dead about six months ago? The guys at the firehouse said she had something on old man Whinebugger," he confided—checking to see if anyone was listening. Finding none he continued. "The autopsy revealed that she was pregnant, you know. How do you suppose she got that way?"

"Well, I think we all know how to get a girl pregnant," Sojoe said, with a lascivious grin--as Henry snickered.

"Shut up and listen, smartass." Jeff leaned in closer. "If Whinebugger got her pregnant and she wouldn't get rid of it ... and maybe she threatened to tell someone—his wife maybe or put it on Facebook or Twitter. The man is known world-wide. Sure, he'd deny it, but would he want that kind of press? Hell no! I heard he quietly solved his little problem once and for all, and all that was found was a pregnant dead girl who drowned in the Osprey State Park."

"Oh, come on," Sojoe grinned and took another drink of his Scotch. "You've been reading too many Stephen King books. This is Venice, for god's sake. That kind of thing just doesn't happen here in Sleepy Hollow."

"Don't be so sure a' that, Sojoe. Since learning those 911 terrorists trained here, I figure anything can happen," Henry said, with a burp.

"I don't care if you believe me or not. I'm just saying – *Man of the Year,* or not—he didn't get where he is because he's a damn eagle scout," Jeff concluded—downing the rest of his drink.

Henry sat back on his chair. "I think that's enough discussion. It's time to vote. All in favor of going to Weinberger 's, raise your hand."

Sojoe and Jeff chuckled.

"What's so funny?"

"You are drunk, man," Jeff answered. "We already voted."

"Okay, but I still have a question. You said the daughter's as bad. Don't tell me she kills people, too." He asked—looking at Sojoe. "Maybe like the praying mantis—who eats her lover after sex?" Henry asked in all seriousness as he swayed on the seat.

"No, asshole, she's pompous, arrogant, stuck-up, and she's a slut!" Jeff tried to toss down another drink but found his glass empty.

"That bad, huh?" Sojoe glanced at Henry and tried to cover a grin. Henry picked up on it and both sputtered in glee. Jeff gave them the evil eye, which only made it worse.

"Long live the sluts!" Henry gasped between fits of laughter--as he and Sojoe gave high-fives.

7

The movie on the television droned on. It was something about Alaskan fishermen catching crabs, but Boatman was too tired to get up and search for the remote. He shook the beer can on the table beside him. It was empty. He sighed. It would take only a moment to get up and get another from the refrigerator, but he was just too tired. Instead, he relaxed and eventually nodded off.

A fog, so thick it might have been smoke, billowed and swirled silently behind his closed eyelids.

As the fog began to dissipate, he could barely make out a rowboat approaching the shore. A man jumped into the water and pulled the boat up onto the shore far enough to prevent it from floating away.

The man reached in and withdrew something. As he came closer, Boatman could make out that he was carrying a single fish on a stringer. The fish bucked and squirmed. It needed water and its gills fanned open and shut in an attempt to breathe.

The man came to a tree with a wooden shelf, and the fish was tossed on it. The eyes of the fish showed no sign of fear; not even when a hand grasped it and a knife appeared.

The knife pierced the fish behind its gill. It contorted, flipped its tail, and writhed under the cruel hand. The knife was thrust up into its brain and twisted. The fish bucked one last time and slumped on the wooden shelf.

The scene began to ooze crimson and threatened to cover everything until only the eye of the fish was visible—and it morphed into a human eye.

Suddenly, there was an explosion, and—like the breaking of a piñata—debris completely covered the fish.

The gray fog returned, and the man could be seen walking away. The human eye of the fish grew until it completely filled the view and a single bloody tear spilled from it.

Boatman woke with a start. He rubbed his eyes and swept perspiration from his forehead.

"I'll have to be more careful about what programs I watch," he said out loud.

Monday, June 15, 2020

Autumn sat at the desk in her Harbor Point home. The morning sun streamed in through the windows of her small Scottish-themed library. Shelves filled two walls of the room. There were novels by her favorite writers Diane Gabaldon, Jean M. Auel, Brenda Spalding, and RJ Coons; trade books included Writer's Market for 2016 and 2017, which she kept for the articles. Now she preferred to subscribe online—as the information was updated daily. There was her collection of magazines: *Writer's Digest, National Geographic, Architectural Digest,* and *FMER*; local newspapers: *Venice Gondolier, Herald Tribune,* and the *Observer.*

Time seemed to drag as she sat at the desk, her pen poised over her legal pad. She liked to write the first drafts in longhand before typing and developing each segment on the computer. A soft knock at the door broke her passivity, and she laid the pen down.

"Come in, Mrs. Wilburn."

"I thought you might like a cup of coffee." The frail eighty-five-year-old woman entered with a steaming cup. "How is your writing coming?"

"I seem to be stuck at the moment." She took the cup and cautiously sipped the hot brew. "Mm... just what I needed, thank you. Have a seat and stay a minute."

Mrs. Wilburn sat in the matching plaid chair beside the desk facing Autumn. A cloud of thin white hair framed her stern face. She adjusted her frameless bifocals.

"I want to thank you for all you are doing for me. It's been a pleasure having you here."

"I'm the one who should thank you. I don't know what I would have done if you hadn't offered me a place to stay. I have no more family. I would have been on the street." She paused, thinking, and began again. "I had a good life and wonderful family, but one by one they all died. I've never been very good with money and after nursing some and then paying for their funerals, I woke up one day alone and broke and creditors beating on my door." She took a deep sigh. "Well, you see—the little I do for you is all I can pay to live in your fine house."

"Meeting you at the bookstore that day was a godsend. I had been having periods of depression and had even considered suicide."

"Oh, my dear, you are too young to suffer so much. Do you want to talk about it?"

"I don't know. Talking about it only brings it all to the surface and the pain and grieving begin anew."

"When you're ready, you can always talk to me. Life can be so difficult, but it helps to have someone to talk to. That is what you've done for me."

Autumn sat the coffee down and went to the woman. She wrapped her arms around her and gently kissed her on the cheek. "You are quite welcome. It seems we have both found the situation rewarding."

Nate sat holding his throbbing head as if to keep it from bursting. He had awakened when the sun poured in through the showroom windows, reflecting off the waxed terrazzo floor, and into his office where he had fallen asleep after the party.

"If I survive this day, I will never drink again." Even when he groaned it hurt. He gently massaged his temples and prayed for relief of this god-awful headache.

Most of what had happened last night was a blur. He remembered the woman and what she wanted, which prompted him to check his pockets. It was there. He pulled it out and laid it on the desk. The leather scabbard had sown edges and was secured with rivets. He pulled the knife out and laid it beside the scabbard. Looking more closely, he realized the handle was of birch and some kind of bone or maybe hoof or antler. He turned on his computer, impatient to research it. "This is more than a $40 knife."

The monitor lit up—revealing the wallpaper. Nate hit a couple of keys, and he was quickly on the Internet.

"Where are you, baby?" he asked aloud. A page of knives and scabbards came into view. He scrolled the page and hit "next," and another page appeared. Suddenly there it was. He blinked, his eyes growing wide as he read. He quickly knocked three times on the wooden desk.

Breathlessly, he read aloud the words on the computer's monitor. "Marttiini Witch's Tooth Collector Fillet Knife. $120.49!" A nervous laugh escaped. "Fran, you stupid puss, you didn't even know what you had!" He gasped. "Or did you?"

He continued to read, "Finnish folklore says that a witch's tooth is locked inside..." Nate jumped out of the chair and backed away.

"She did!" He vigorously wiped his hand on his pant-leg as if to rid it of any witchy residue. He began sweating. "That's what it means, it's a witch's curse! She cursed me!" He looked at his hands. "Oh god, I had the wicked thing in my pocket all night! How does it work? Maybe something will activate it, and it'll ruin me... destroy me! I have got to get rid of it."

He carefully picked up the knife with the edge of his shirttail preventing his thumb and forefinger from touching it. He slid it back into its scabbard and tossed it. It slid across the desktop and came to rest against the desk lamp.

Just then he heard footsteps in the showroom. Nate had forgotten to activate the alarm on the double doors that were opening. He watched a silhouetted form move steadily toward him. The bright sun reflecting off the floor made it impossible to see who or what was coming. Step by step it advanced, the sound of its shoes reverberating throughout the building. Nate gasped. There was no way out of the room without coming face to face with the evil demon. He couldn't run. He watched as it drew closer. He held his breath as the apparition reached the door. Nate shrank back until he hit the back wall. He was perspiring heavily. His hand shot to his mouth to hold back a scream...

"Smallwood, I never expected to find you open this early, but I'm glad you are."

It was a man. He looked familiar, but for a moment Nate couldn't remember. The man entered and took the seat beside the desk.

Nate wiped his brow with the sleeve of his shirt. He took a deep breath as he realized this was a customer who had been in once before.

"Mr. Black. I'm not open yet, but... what can I do for you?"

"I'm still considering whether or not to get a boat. I'm finding more free time, and I'd like to spend some of it on the water. It's relaxing, and my job is very stressful."

"Please excuse me a minute. I'd like to wash up. Look around and see what we have in the showroom. I'm sure we can find exactly what you need."

David Weinberger angrily tapped his Cartier pen on his Palais executive desktop as he listened to the caller on the phone.

"You can stop right there," he said in a tone that made people sit up and listen. "I will not agree to those terms." He paused as a bitter frown formed on his forehead. "Stop sniveling!" He shouted. "Go back, and this time, quote the offer exactly as I told you! Tell that pucker-headed buffoon that this is my final offer, and unless he wants it all to go up in smoke, he'd better take it!" A cruel smile came to his lips. "He'll *know* what I mean. And don't call me again until you have his signature on the contract." He slammed the receiver into the cradle.

There was a soft tap at the door.

"Come in," he said, much more crossly than he intended.

Dixie entered with a wine glass and sour expression on her face.

"What is it?" he asked, his manner still reflecting the previous conversion. He walked to the window and looked out.

"You're not making this wedding deal any easier for me."

"What is that supposed to mean?"

"You told everyone the wedding was set for July 5th. Don't I have anything to say in the matter? Am I not a part of this arrangement?"

"Dixie," he said, turning back to face her. He paused for a moment and his tone became gentle, that of a doting and long-suffering father. "You told me you didn't want any part of this *scheme* as you called it. Does this mean you've changed your mind?"

"Well, I..."

"Are you ready to take on the responsibilities of a wedding—the duties of a future bride and the commitment of a wife to make the marriage work? Is that what you're telling me?"

"I... I don't..."

"If not, then step back and let me handle it," he paused, "as I've always done." He moved toward her and a loving smile came to his lips. "Haven't I always taken care of you? Haven't I always bailed you out when you got in trouble? Nothing has changed. It's just that I've found a man who can take care of you. He has money, so you will never want for anything. What more can you ask for?"

"I want to marry the man I love. I want..."

"Oh, Dixie, be serious! Yesterday you loved a drunken gambler. Today you love a penniless dreamer. Tomorrow it will be some other worthless excuse of a man."

"No, I..."

He put a fatherly arm around her shoulders and walked her to the door.

"Just relax, Honey. Daddy knows what's best for you." He reached down and took the wine glass from her hand. "It's too early to be drinking. Now go shopping or something and let me get some work done." He nudged her out of the room and closed the door behind her.

Dixie wiped the tears that were building and walked toward the dining room—knowing that the wine bar was just beyond. As she approached the far side, a dark shadow reached out and grabbed her around the waist. She would have screamed, but his lips muffled any sound she might make. Then she recognized the red hair.

"What are you doing here?" she whispered and looked to see if anyone was near.

"I was working outside, but I had to see you. I saw you go into the study, and I waited."

She started to say something, but he kissed her again. She took a deep breath and allowed herself the pleasure of the moment. The kiss was long and warm and made her tingle.

"I love you," he said but didn't release her.

"I love you," she whispered and then opened her eyes. He listened when she talked. His calmness brought her peace. She smiled up into those brown eyes that were even darker than her own. She felt she could see into the very soul of this man who was so caring and tender. She had no doubt of his love for her; nor hers for him. If only they could marry and live forever like this.

"Your love for me is the keyhole of my heart. My love for you is the key that invites you in."

The man coming through the gallery saw them and stood back watching. The pair kissed a few more times and then left through the kitchen. The man stepped out of the shadows. Jacob Crawford was not pleased. His fingers drew up into fists. "We'll see about this," he said and stormed out the way he'd come.

David Weinberger sat at his desk rubbing the spot between his silver brows. The pain was starting again—the onset of another migraine. He covered his face with both hands and took deep breaths.

He reached into the top right-hand drawer of his desk and removed the little white bottle with its blue lid. Migra-Eeze™ was the best treatment he had found. He was on a monthly regiment, and though the migraines were easing, the medication was not irradiating them.

He left the study and was crossing the living room on his way to the kitchen for a glass of water to take the pill when he happened to look out the plate glass windows. He saw Dixie and a red-headed man running hand in hand across the lawn.

David froze on the spot. "What the hell?" He thought the man looked familiar, but from this distance, he couldn't be sure. One thing was certain, it was not Jacob Crawford. "No doubt this is another of her self-centered, carnal mongrels after her money. It won't last long. I have a quick solution to problems like this." He rubbed his forehead frowning and walked on.

11

The clock had indicated 10:25 p.m. when he left her. The man hurried through the gate of the south garden and along the area that only yesterday had been full of cars. His truck was parked on the street at the edge of the Bedwick property. The surrounding area was still overgrown, although some of the property was being cleared for the construction of additional housing.

The smell of rain filled the air. Lightning had been threatening in the night sky for some time. Now it flashed in one blinding bout, and a few seconds later thunder boomed.

Don looked into the sky. Lightning flared again, immediately followed by a clap of thunder that made him instinctively duck his head. With the sound of cracking wood and the distinct smell of ozone, he knew that one was close. He realized he should have left earlier, but leaving Dixie was getting harder and harder to do. He was confident that one day soon they would break away and he'd never have to leave her again.

The first drops began to fall with a splat. Three, then six and soon it was raining hard, and then it became a deluge.

The redheaded man pulled his hood over his head, more out of habit than anything. The rain didn't bother him as memories of Dixie filled his thoughts;

her smooth white skin when he opened her blouse, the lacy pink bra that fell away so easily with a flick of the hook, and her firm round breasts that tumbled free.

He wiped the rain from his face. There were no streetlights as he made his way along the tree-lined road to where his truck was parked, but the frequent lightning made it easy to see.

He had avoided parking on the Weinberger property to prevent being discovered by the household. Additional care must be taken now that the engagement had been announced. His job with the Weinbergers was critical. He knew that if they were discovered he'd be fired, and access to the property—and Dixie—would be cut off. He wanted more time to convince her that she didn't need them. They loved one another, and it wouldn't be long before she got the courage to leave and they would be free of Bedwick and all its inhabitants.

Lightning flashed again, and he clearly saw the truck through the trees. He absently fumbled in his pocket for the remote, but his thoughts were of her. He loved how her mouth curved up into a smile, her chocolate brown irises that grew darker when they made love. He remembered the smell of her hair that cascaded over him and the whimpering sounds she made when she climaxed.

He drew a deep breath as he approached his 2016 Big Horn Ram and worked the keyless entry. Another flash of lightning turned night into day.

The redheaded man noticed how the truck appeared black until lightning brought out its true-blue color. In that split second, he saw the reflection of a form behind him; a dark figure wearing a short-brimmed hat. The redheaded man turned but he was hit hard in the stomach and fell to the ground on his hands and knees.

The intruder jerked the hood off just as thunder boomed and echoed across the town. As the dark of night returned, Don felt something pierce his neck. He felt the strike move up, heard a crunch, and felt something break. He felt the sharp thing move higher. He knew he'd been hit, but what he felt was confusion. It had hit him hard; a gray haze enveloped him, and he became disoriented. His last thought was Dixie's smile just before everything went black.

Tuesday, June 16, 2020

~ 12 ~

Tancey and Daniel were walking her Chihuahua, Mojito along a tree-lined section of Honore. As she brushed back her long brown hair, she noticed a clump of yellow flowers across the road in the field.

"Daniel, look! See those yellow flowers? Let's take a closer look." She started across the road. "Come on, Mojito. Let's go this way."

The area was filled with tall grass, weeds, and the yellow stalks dancing in the early morning breeze.

"Those are Coreopsis. Oh, my gosh! I've never seen one up close."

"Are you talking about these daises? They grow everywhere. What's so special about them?" He hurried to catch up.

"I was just reading about them." She made her way through the high grass to the colorful patch of wildflowers. "They aren't just daisies; they are *the* Florida state flowers! You know—the flower on my license plate."

"So?"

"Well, for one thing, you don't usually find this variety so far south. You'll only find the ones with the red centers in northern Florida. That's why I chose that plate, because the flower had a red center."

"I thought you liked the depiction of the sun. You know, white billowy clouds, exotic birds squawking overhead; sunny Florida."

"Well, yes. I do like that part." She rolled her eyes. "But there are no clouds or birds on the plate." Tancey plucked one and studied it. "I recently read that they're a member of the Aster family and birds and butterflies love them."

Mojito moved closer, lifted his leg, and watered the plant.

"Mojito doesn't seem to like them, if I get his message right."

"Whether he does or not, their seeds have little hooks, and if one catches on his fur, he might accidentally plant one in our yard. Oh, wouldn't that be nice!"

"Yeah, I guess." He wiped his brow and glanced at the sky. "Let's get going. It's too hot to stand out here in the sun."

Tancey picked a small bouquet before they crossed to the shady side and continued down the road where the trees shaded the walk. Up ahead they spotted a blue truck parked along the berm. Mojito lunged with such force he pulled the leash from her hand and ran toward it barking. The two dashed after, calling him back. Barking continuously, the dog ran to the collapsed form in the road on the driver's side. Tancey retrieved the leash and pulled the dog away when she noticed the pool of blood.

She and Daniel looked at one another, too shocked to speak. She reached for her phone and dialed 911.

13

Boatman had just finished his shower when the doorbell rang. He looked through the peephole but didn't recognize the two men outside. However, one wore the uniform of a Venice policeman. He slipped on his white embroidered towel wrap and opened the door.

The younger man in uniform stood behind a swarthy older man. Boatman thought he might have stepped right out of the Mickey Spillane stories. His image was complete with a fedora and a light-weight trench coat.

"What can I do for you?"

"This is Officer Brian Kincaid with the Venice police. I'm Sylvan Bradshaw with the Sarasota County Police force. Sir, may we speak with you?

"Certainly, come in," The young man stepped back and held the door open. Bradshaw entered the room and Officer Kincaid followed.

"Do you know a Donald MacKenzie?"

Boatman felt a tension building in his gut, and a picture of Don flashed in his mind. He felt a heat rising in his body, and he immediately sensed death. "Yes, he lives here."

"I am the homicide detective, Sir. We are investigating the murder of Mr. MacKenzie."

"Oh my god!" His hand went to his forehead as a vision flashed in his mind. Don smiling, a dark figure, a flash of lightning, a fish squirming under a knife, then a dark pinpoint spiraled backward until it became a wall of black. Boatman had to sit down before he passed out.

"Murder? How? When?" He looked up, confused; his mind was racing. "Oh, I'm sorry. Please, have a seat."

They sat. Bradshaw studied the young man's reactions as he relayed the details. "A young couple found the body in the road beside a truck registered to a Donald MacKenzie. A photo ID of Mr. MacKenzie was in the glove compartment."

"When did this happen, Detective Bradshaw?"

"The coroner says he died between 10 p.m. and midnight. The truck was parked along Honore, just north of Laurel Road."

"Of course, it would be. Don worked as one of the gardeners for the Weinbergers. Their property is right there."

"Do the Weinberger's gardeners usually work that late?" He made a note in his cell phone. "Any idea what he'd be doing there at that hour?"

Boatman chuckled. "Oh yes. I imagine he was seeing Dixie Weinberger. But her father would not have approved." A vision of Dixie asleep flashed across his mind. "Have you talked to them—the Weinbergers?"

"No, we've just begun our investigation. Did MacKenzie have any enemies? What kind of a guy was he?"

"Enemies? Not likely. Don was a gentle soul, a real St. Francis. You know—the kind birds flock to."

"He was gay then," Kincaid said, nonchalantly. There was no missing his strong southern drawl.

"Did anyone give him trouble about that?" Bradshaw asked.

Boatman chuckled. "Gay! Is that what you think? Oh, hell no. He grew up in a large family, and they owned greenhouses. He learned to appreciate beauty, handle tender plants, and such. You know, he was raised that way, went to mass on Sundays, phoned his mother every day until she passed, and he's still close to his siblings. Well, *was*. They all live somewhere in Oregon. I can get you his sister's number. You'll want to notify them, no doubt."

Boatman crossed the room and fished in a drawer until he came up with an old battered address book. He went back and handed it to Bradshaw.

"Thank you," he said. He looked it over, handed it to Kincaid, and asked, "You aren't planning any long trips, are you?"

"No," Boatman swallowed hard and for the first time, sadness crept into his voice. "Don and I recently purchased a boat, and we charter half-day and full-day trips. The business is building steadily. I wonder how much this will change things, but then we often took charters out alone if one of us was busy. Time will tell, I guess. It never occurred to me that I would have to work it alone." He paused—thinking. "To answer your question, I am always accessible by phone unless I'm somewhere in a dead zone, but you can leave a message, and I'll get back with you as soon as I can."

"I'll keep that in mind."

"I wouldn't say Don had enemies exactly, but there are a couple of things. I used to work for Nate Smallwood, owner of that boat dealership on the bay. Nate didn't take it well when I quit. I ran into him at the engagement party at the Weinbergers. We had words, and I hit him. He was furious and said he'd make me sorry. Nate's a boorish SOB, but I can't imagine he'd murder anyone."

"You're referring to Jaguar Boat and Supply, I take it?"

"Yes, sir."

"How about this girl, would she be the jealous type?"

"Oh, I don't think so, but I don't know her very well. David Weinberger, on the other hand, is not a man to fool with. I'm sure you know him; if not personally, then by reputation." He paused before continuing. "Don expected to quit gardening and handle chartering full time." He paused again as if thinking and a smile crept to his lips. "He felt there would be a wedding down the road."

"Ms. Weinberger?

Boatman nodded. "However, on Sunday the Weinbergers hosted a huge party with easily over a hundred and fifty guests. David announced the engagement of his daughter to some out of towner.

"How did Don react to that?" Bradshaw continued to make notations.

"I don't think he was there. At least, I couldn't find him when I looked. He got home late that night and left early on Monday. I never saw him, but that wasn't unusual. He was always on the go."

"Okay," Bradshaw made another note on his phone. "You've been a big help, thank you. If you think of anything else, you can contact me or Kincaid at this number." He handed him a card, and Boatman walked them to the door. "I think that's all we need for now, but we'll stay in touch until this is cleared up.

As they left, Boatman closed the door and leaned back against it as the full impact of the tragedy hit him.

14

Traffic had stopped for the light. Venice was settling into a quiet period since all the seasonal "Snowbirds" had gone back north. The light turned green, and everyone moved forward. Fran made a right and raced past the drug store and businesses on East Venice Avenue. When she reached Valenti's, she was going 60 miles an hour, ran through the yellow light at Pinebrook, and kept going.

She turned the rearview mirror toward her to check her reflection and ran her fingers through her dishwater blond hair.

"Shit! I look like a fuckin' scarecrow. Angela had better take me, or I'm really gonn'a be pissed. Goddamn it!"

As she approached the Jacaranda roundabout, she slapped her turn signal and pulled into the turn lane in one quick movement—cutting off the black Nissan Altima already in that lane. The driver slammed on his brakes and laid on his horn.

"Fuck you!" Fran yelled and flipped him the bird. She sped ahead and took a right with a slight skid. She jammed her foot on the accelerator and turned left at the T. She raced along the aisle and pulled into a vacant spot in front of Lime Time.

The man in the Nissan sped past her still honking and yelling. She thumbed her nose at him as she exited the car. She was still annoyed as she strolled through the glass door into the beauty shop.

The U-shaped complex welcomed clients into a waiting area with product displayed on white shelves next to the check-in/checkout station. Chrome chairs with lime-colored backs and seats lined the four floor-to-ceiling windows overlooking East Venice Avenue. Fran breezed through to the second room where four stations were surrounded by floor-to-ceiling mirrors and manned by three other beauticians. Three sinks sat along the back wall.

"Where's Angela?" She didn't wait for an answer and headed around the corner where one door led to a large room divided by a curtain. One side was for microdermabrasion and the other for manicurists and pedicurists. Another door led to a utility area/snack room and restroom.

Angela was coming out of the utility room with an armload of lime-colored towels and almost bumped into her.

"Oh, Fran, what can I do for you?" she asked as she strolled past her heading for the towel cabinet.

"I didn't come to buy opium! It's my goddamn hair," she said tugging at it with both hands.

Angela laid the towels on the shelf, closed the door, and looked at her. "I see what you mean." She reached up and ran her fingers through Fran's hair. "Let Lateefa wash your hair n' I will take you now."

The shop looked huge reflected in so many mirrors. Almost everything was chrome and white— except for the chairs, stools, and dryers. Wide, lime-green panels were reflected in the mirrors, and the floor was a pickled whitewash laminate.

Angela smiled to each of the girls wearing their lime green smocks with the embroidered "Lime

Time" as they busily combed and coiffed the customers. As she quickly prepared her station, the mirror reflected a beautiful young businesswoman in her early thirties. She wore her own magenta dyed hair in Bantu knots that complimented her caramel skin tone.

"Angela, I'm not shit'n you, this hair is driving me crazy!" Fran called as she returned.

"Well, you ha'b come to da right place," she said in her gentle Creole accent. She swiveled the chair around and motioned for Fran to sit. "How would you like it--shorter? Sculptured? Dreadlocks?"

"Shit no! What do you mean dreadlocks! You gotta be fuck'n kidding me!"

Angela laughed heartily. "Yes, Fran, I be kidding you. Do you want it cut? Do you want it styled?" She removed the towel from the woman's wet hair and patted it to remove more of the water.

"I don't know. What do you suggest?"

"How 'bout a short pixie? It would add a touch of pizzazz."

"Would it be a lot of work to keep it looking right? I don't want to have to screw around with a bunch of shit. I just want short hair that I don't have to fuck with."

"Okay, maybe a short, a spiky cut dat's easy to manage but is still stylish."

"Yeah, that sounds good. Let's do that."

"Would you like to change da color?

"Oh no, I don't think so. Too freak'n fussy. I'm no girly-girl. Save your color shit for one of your prissy customers."

That drew a look of scorn from the woman in the next chair, but when Fran caught her eye, she looked away.

Angela draped the towel over Fran's shoulders and tied a waterproof cape around her neck. "We'll gi'b you such a cut dat even Jamie Lee Curtis will be jealous."

Good. I like her, she's one bitchin' broad."

Carol pulled into the only space in front of Lime Time, turned off the motor, and slipped the key into her purse as she stepped out of the car. A click of the remote drew a short beep—announcing that the car was locked. She pushed the salon's front door and entered the beauty shop.

Lateefa had just finished scheduling a caller and hung up the phone. "Good morning, Ms. Tanaka. Do you have an appointment?" she asked, thumbing through the pages of her appointment book.

"Yes, with Valerie, at 11. I'm a little early." She took a magazine and a seat near the window.

"I'll tell Val you're here," Lateefa said with a smile and hurried into the next room. The front door opened again, and two women entered talking.

"It's true, Joanie," the chubby brunette said, holding the door for the older woman. "My sister was driving to work and passed it. Police, an ambulance, a fire truck, emergency lights flashing all over the place, and one policeman was cordoning off the area with that yellow tape that reads 'POLICE LINE DO NOT CROSS.'"

"Oh, yes. I heard about that too," remarked a woman who had been quietly waiting her turn. "Don MacKenzie," She rolled the name over with her tongue. "I don't believe I knew him."

That got Carol's attention, and she listened more closely. Before long the whole shop was buzzing with the news.

Fran came up to the reception desk following Angela. She handed her card to the owner, who quickly ran the payment and tip through the machine.

"He'd been comin' here for years. I always cut his hair. What a nice guy. Why would anyone do such a t'ing?" Angela asked, handing the card back to Fran.

"No one in Venice would!" the chubby woman added. "It had to be someone from Sarasota or maybe Bradenton."

"Do you suppose it was about drugs? A lot of young people are into drugs these days." The older woman shook her head in disapproval.

Fran turned to leave and noticed Carol. "Tanaka, you here for a blow-job?"

"If you mean a style and blow-dry, then the answer is yes." Carol's tone and blasé expression displayed her dislike of the woman. "I see you got your head sheared. Oh my, Angela forgot to
color your roots or was that on purpose?"

"Very funny, Bitch. It's a fuckin' pixy cut, done in the latest style. I wouldn't expect a China doll to know anything about American styles."

"*China* doll? She's not Chinese." Angela interrupted with a quizzical look.

"That's an empty-headed plaything, of course," Fran said with a sneer and a confident toss of her head.

Val motioned to Carol from the other room. Carol started to leave but turned back to Fran. "If you talk really nice, Angela might give you your money back; unless of course you prefer to look like an orphaned house boy." She turned again and walked off.

Fran thought for a moment, but a witty comeback escaped her. "Fuck you!" was all she could manage and stalked out of the shop.

~ 15 ~

Dixie took a sip of her morning Beaujolais, sat the glass on the Persian taboret beside the NordicTrack 2950 treadmill, and switched on the tri-fold wall monitor. In a blink the room filled with light and a view of Scotland's Three Sisters mountains. She stepped on the belt, secured herself, and started walking. The push of another button started the gentle rendition of Bolero. Little by little the speed and climb increased pushing her to a trot. Her heart rate rose, and she began to perspire as the beat of the music increased.

She felt as if she were running along the many ridges and peaks as the climb extended to Glen Coe. She could lose herself in this imaginary world— where soon the red headed-man was at her side, smiling as he kept pace with her. She wanted to stop running and sit with him on the grassy glen and catch her breath. She closed her eyes for a moment and imagined his arms around her and his warm breath on her lips. She wanted to shed her clothes and lay with him in the cool air forever.

The wall of mirrors to her left reflected her in the real world of the gym with the Bowflex Trainer and elliptical machine on mats to protect the bamboo hardwood floor. She did not notice. Nor did she notice the reflection of the man standing at the double doors even when he stepped quietly into the room. It wasn't until he stopped the music that she was jolted from her reverie.

"We need to talk," he said, as the machine slowed to a stop. "We will be married in a few weeks, and we need to get a few things straight."

"What?"

"Well, Dixie, we haven't had a chance to get to know one another, and there is no better time than now." He sat on one of a pair of straight back Polywood chairs, his legs looking tanner against his white shorts. He brought his fingers to a peak and rested them against his mouth watching her expressions change from placid, to puzzled to annoyed. A subtle smile crossed his lips, almost evil.

She didn't appreciate his interference or his expression. She pulled a towel from the rack and wrapped it around to shield herself from that look.

"What do you mean? What do you want? Can't you see that I'm busy?" She stepped over to the taboret, picked up the glass, and took a long swallow.

He was up and out of the chair in an instant. He slapped the glass from her hand, and it flew across the room and crashed into the wall of mirrors. Then he seized her wrist and twisted it 'til she cried out.

"You will not use that tone with me, you tramp."

She wrenched her hand away. "Who do you think you are? What's the matter with you, Jacob, and why are you acting like this?" She turned to get away from him, but he grabbed her again. Dixie lashed out; he caught her hand before she could claw him and shoved her into the treadmill. She fell hard. Shocked and bruised, she slid to the floor.

"I'll tell you who I am. I'm the man you are going to marry, and you *will* act like I expect my wife to behave!"

She rose to her feet. "If I marry you, it will only be to please Daddy. But then again, I may not. I may just leave you both."

"You think you'll leave with another man? Never! You and I are in this for the long run."

"Well, we'll just see about that!" She picked up the towel that had fallen during the struggle.

He snatched the towel from her and threw it back on the floor.

"You need a lesson in loyalty, and you *will* take me seriously." He grabbed her by her hair and threw her to the floor—dropping beside her. She fought, but he held her arms up with one hand and with several strong tugs wrenched her Jojo skirt off. When she tried to scream, he slapped her hard. The struggle excited him. The more she fought, the more he was aroused.

Nimble fingers unzipped his Chinos, and he quickly had his tool out, hard and ready. When he thrust it inside her, she screamed, but her tears only kindled his pleasure. There was no love here, nor was it hate. His determination to control empowered him as he thrust again and again—and with each, she cried out.

When he finally climaxed, he let out a groan, not unlike the sound of an ape, and collapsed. His full weight on her pinned her to the floor. She lay unable to move. Tears soaked her hair. As she struggled to breathe, she thought she might pass out.

He finally roused and got to his feet. He adjusted his clothes, took a deep breath, and ran his fingers through his steel-gray hair. He looked down at her.

"Well, my dear, was it as good for you as it was for me? Now you know what's in store for you. We *will* marry, and you *will* be a good wife," he chuckled. "No one will know what happens once the doors close."

When she started to get up, he kicked her in the stomach. Picking up the towel, he threw it at her. "Clean yourself up. You look terrible." He turned and strolled out of the room.

The two-story building set back from the road in the shade of five mature magnolia trees. The owner, Nate Smallwood, had chosen the name "Jaguar Boat and Supply," when he had opened the business four years ago. He told his bookkeeper at the time that he wanted his business to have the same name as his new car. Smallwood would never say what he actually paid for the XJ, but he intimated that it was exorbitant.

Jaguar Boat and Supply sat on Dona Bay in Nokomis. A two-story pole barn had many bays for seasonal storage, a large service/repair area, and fuel pumps near its two boat ramps. The store displayed Bertram, Boston Whaler, and Mikelson Yachts in various sizes and a storeroom of parts and accessories.

A disheveled man vaulted from the old truck as it rattled to a stop. He entered and went straight to the office. Smallwood finished going over the previous day's sales, jotted a few notes on one, and slipped them all into the open safe and closed it. He sat down with a cup of cold coffee in one hand and opened the newspaper with the other just as Matt rushed in.

"Did ya hear? D'a found a body over on Honore. Durndest thing! I jus' drove by d'ere on my way here. Cops all around. Blue n' red n' yellow lights aflashin'.

Cops a'flaggen, cars try'n ta turn off a Laurel. It's a real mess!"

"What'd I tell you? Didn't I tell you?" Nate was absorbed in reading his paper. The only movement was the fat Bolivar Belicoso Fino cigar he rolled from side to side when he talked. "Extending Pinebrook past Laurel was an accident waiting to happen."

"No, sir. D'at tw'eren't no car accident." Matt leaned closer resting his fists on Nate's desk. "For sure, t'was murder!"

"You're crazy, old man. This is Venice; we don't have murders here." Nate did manage to glance at him before turning back to the paper. "If there'd been a murder, it would be all over the news."

"I'm tellin' ya, Nate, d'ere's a big crowd n' police have d'em yellow tapes strung all 'round. A guy was walkin' past me, an' I rolled down my window an' as't if anyone was hurt, an' he said he heard da cops say t'was murder!"

Nate finally put the paper down and turned to Matt. "Why don't you fix yourself a cup of coffee? You're getting too excited."

"Naw. I figure I'll go back an' get a look f'er myself. I never seen a murder before." With that he turned and hurried out the door, his stiff arms flapping at his sides.

Nate sat and watched the old man get into his battered pickup truck, start the engine and drive off, smoke rolling in his wake. Nate turned back to his newspaper, a broadening smile on his lips.

~ 17 ~

The cell phone rang. Autumn gave a deep sigh. "Just when I'm on a roll there's another interruption." She pushed the green button. "Hello," she said—holding the cell phone between her shoulder and ear as she continued typing on the computer. In a moment her fingers stopped, and she looked off in the distance listening. She took the phone in her hand as the caller continued. Tears welled in her eyes as she sat back listening.

"When?"

"Late last night around midnight. Autumn, would it be all right if I came over?"

"Of course, Boatman."

"I'll be right there." The call ended. Autumn turned, staring out the window for a long moment and then laying the phone on the desk. There would be no more work on her novel today.

She rose and headed down the hall to the kitchen where she put on a fresh pot of coffee. She was standing at the counter lost in thought when Mrs. Wilburn came in carrying clean, folded dishtowels.

"What's wrong? What's happened? You look like you're about to cry." She put the towels in a drawer and went over to Autumn. "What is it, dear?" She put her arm around the woman's shoulders.

Autumn turned, tears falling quietly. "It's Don MacKenzie, an old friend. Someone murdered him."

"Murdered?"

"Oh, no. How could such a thing happen?" Autumn pulled a paper towel from the bar fastened to the cabinet and dabbed her eyes. "Boatman is coming over. He must be devastated. Don was his closest friend and business partner. They even shared a house together."

"What about you? Will you be all right?" The old woman looked her in the eye. "Will you?"

Autumn forced a smile. "I'm not sure. I... Well, this isn't about me, is it? I have to be strong for my friend."

She patted Mrs. Wilburn's hand and walked across the room to another cabinet where she pulled out coffee mugs. Mrs. Wilburn took flavored coffee creamer from the refrigerator and napkins from a drawer. Just then the doorbell rang.

"Mrs. Wilburn, would you mind getting that?"

"Of course, dear," she said and walked away.

The girl went into the half bath off the kitchen. She studied her reflection and quickly wiped away any trace of tears. "You can do this, Autumn," she said in a whisper, but the image in the mirror did not reflect confidence.

A silver Dodge Ram spun into the drive and stopped with a jerk.

"What's Boatman doing here?" Jeff asked aloud as he put the truck in park, pulled the keys from the ignition, opened the driver's door, and jumped out in one single flowing motion. He reached the front door of Autumn's house and entered without knocking.

"Hey, where is everyone?" he called.

"We're in the study," came the response.

"Hi," he said as he entered the room. There was a moment of silence. "Am I interrupting something?"

"No," Autumn said. It was obvious that she had been crying. She sat with her elbows on the desk rubbing her temples, another sure sign that she was upset.

Jeff looked at Boatman sitting on the edge of his chair; his arms resting on his knees as he rubbed his hands together.

"Something's up," Jeff pulled up a chair. "What is it?"

"It's Don. He's been murdered."

Jeff wasn't sure he had heard her right. "Don? What happened?"

Autumn closed her eyes and waited as Boatman relayed what he knew.

Jeff sat back in the chair and let out a deep breath like a hard fist to the gut. "Oh my god! Do they have any idea who...?"

"There were no witnesses. The detective didn't know anything when he talked to me." Boatman rubbed his forehead. "How could this happen? Why didn't I get a warning? I should have felt something."

"Maybe you're too close," Autumn offered "although you were upset at the Weinberger's party on Sunday. You said you felt something."

"Yes, I couldn't get away fast enough. Wait a minute. I ran into Nate Smallwood that night. He was drunk and obnoxious as usual. He threatened me— me—not Don. "Surely, he wouldn't..."

"Oh hell, I wouldn't put anything past that piece of shit," Jeff said and pounded the arm of his chair. "He's as mean as a snake, and he's been pissed ever since Boatman quit."

"Could he have been caught with Dixie? Maybe he got in a fight with someone over that. Oh, I can't imagine killing someone for that... Still, things could easily have gotten out of control if it was Jacob."

"I wouldn't be surprised, Autumn. Those Weinbergers can't be trusted—especially the old man. What do you think, Boatman?"

"I don't know. If I could think straight, I might be able to learn something, but my mind is in overdrive. Maybe I am too close to this as Autumn says." Boatman stood. "I've taken way more of your time than I planned, but I wanted you to hear this from me rather than on the news."

Autumn went to him and put her arms around him. "I am so sorry, Boatman. It's a shock for all of us. In time we'll all be able to think more clearly." She looked into his eyes. "Who will handle the arrangements?"

"The police will contact his family. I imagine they'll come down and do it. There will be an autopsy, of course, and I don't know when they will release the body. I gave the address book to the detective. I imagine the family will contact me, but if not, I'll see them when they get here."

"I'm sure they'll call. Oh my god, this is such a nightmare!" She released him and wiped away a tear. "We will just take it one day at a time."

"Let me know if there is anything I can do, Boatman. If you just want to get drunk, I'm well-practiced in that department," Jeff patted the man's shoulder companionably.

Boatman turned to Autumn. "I'm sorry to put this on you, too. I know how it must be affecting you."

"It's okay, Boatman, really."

He smiled and nodded. He couldn't think of anything else to say, turned, and left.

"Autumn, are you all right?" Jeff watched her go to the window. She raised one of the slats of the Venetian blinds and watched Boatman walk to his truck. "Is there anything I can do?"

"No, Honey. No one can help. It's something I have to deal with. It's just that this brings back all the grief. Sadly, Boatman must be having the same wretched feelings. A word, a sound, a smell... Just when you think it's getting easier something happens to open that wound, and the grieving begins all over again."

She watched the man open the door of his beloved 2006 Ford pickup. It had been a beauty in its day, but the once shiny upper half was covered with dirt and pockmarks that went all the way to the metal. One hub cap was missing, and the whole body dipped from the weight of the man as he climbed in behind the wheel. They could hear the motor struggle when the engine started. As it backed out of the drive and pulled away, blue exhaust trailed.

Autumn took a deep breath, dropped the slat, and turned to her brother. "Jeff, I'm surprised to see you. What happened to you Sunday? We were going to Dixie's together."

"Something came up."

"A girl or a bottle?"

He chuckled, "You know me too well," he cleared his throat. "Autumn, I just couldn't make myself go. Those people... Dixie's okay, I guess. I know she's your friend, but I can't stand being around those pretentious... I'm sorry. Not sorry I didn't go, but sorry I disappointed you."

"You didn't disappoint me, little brother. I know you're not comfortable around them, and that's okay. Is that why you didn't come around for two days?"

"Well, kind of. But, I met a guy, a film producer." Excitement built as he talked. "He's really something; he makes movies. He was telling me about a project he's working on. He had the script, and there's a director lined up. Brad Pitt and Chris Pine are already signed to go and... and all he needs is a little start-up money." As he saw her expression, he quickly added, "I'd be one of the producers. You know, above the line."

She shook her head. "How much 'above the line' money are we talking about?"

"Not much. You know, these movies make millions! And when they go to television it just keeps paying. My name would be one of the first listed. Producer! Can you imagine? I'd be famous. With all the money I'd make I would pay you back and have enough left over to invest in another movie."

"How much?"

"Not much."

"How much?"

"Well, to be perfectly honest..."

"Honestly, how much?"

"$150,000."

"Ouch!"

"Come on, Autumn. 150K now and mega-thousands down the road. What an investment!"

"Who's the director?"

"Well, you probably haven't heard of him, but he's one of the rising stars in Hollywood!

"His name is...?"

"Adam Cherier. You may not have heard of him, but he's been in the business for ages. He's a screenwriter with films to his credit. He's amazing!"

"I'll think about it. I've just got so much on my mind right now. I'm only now getting over the loss... and now Don. I can't do this right now." She kissed him on the cheek and turned to leave the room.

"But you'll think about it, right?"

"I'll think about it, Honey."

~ 18 ~

Dixie was curled up on the seat of her glass-enclosed tiled shower with the hot water from the double head spray pulsing against her naked body. She had tried to scrub his seed and smell away, but she could not wash away the memory. Hot tears mingled with the heat of the water, and her sobbing seemed endless.

She could picture the red-headed man. What would he think? She knew he felt a pang of jealousy when it came to Jacob. How could she tell him? How would he react now? How could he even think she had feelings for this monster? Surely her father didn't know when he'd arranged for this man to marry her. These thoughts only brought more tears.

Dixie took a deep breath, walked over and turned off the water. She closed the door of the shower behind her and walked to the double tile sink. The strong lighting and the reflection in the mirror revealed the slice on her cheek where his ring had cut her, and a discoloration was building. Turning, she could see three bruises from the fall.

Her feelings of helplessness grew with the realization of her situation. There was no way to hide this from the man she loved. How could she cover it? Could she? No. Would she be able to lie to him? And her father, could she lie to him? *No*, she thought. *That's what I have to do. Tell father! Then he'll cancel the wedding and remove Jacob from the house and our lives.*

Bolstered with new confidence, she wrapped herself in a towel and reached for the hairdryer. It was then she saw the bruises on her wrists.

Sometime later, dressed in jeans and a tank top, Dixie headed down the hall to the study. Airbrushing her makeup had completely covered the bruise on her face, but she couldn't hide the cut. Airbrushing makeup covered her wrists, but to be safe, she wore bracelets on both arms.

When I tell Daddy, he will see what a monster Jacob is. I can't wait to see the smug expression of confidence melt and turn to surprise when Daddy turns on him. I will try to contain my happiness when it happens, but inside I'll scream with delight!

She reached the door to the study and didn't bother to knock. She walked into the room and strolled right up to the desk where David sat typing something into the computer.

"Daddy, I'm sorry to bother you, but I have something to tell you."

David looked up. When he saw her, he rose from his chair. "Darling, are you all right?"

David rushed to her. "My poor dear, let me look at you."

"What?" Dixie was confused.

"Jacob told me how you slipped on the treadmill. Are you hurt badly? Should I call the doctor?" He brushed a strand of hair from her face to look closer at the cut.

"What?"

"Sweetheart, I simply explained how you fell in the gym and cut yourself."

She whirled around.

"Cuts like that can be dangerous if not treated right away. You were lucky. A few inches higher and it would have been your eye. Wasn't it lucky I was there?" Jacob walked over and put his hand on her. "I have to take care of my wife, don't I? You can count on it, Sweetheart. I will never let you out of my sight. I'll always be there for you." He leaned over and kissed her on the cheek.

"Thank you, Jacob. I don't know what I'd do if anything happened to my little girl."

"Daddy, I need to talk to you!" She pulled away from Jacob. Her hands were shaking and her voice trembling.

"I can see you're upset. Are you sure I shouldn't call the doctor?"

"Yes, I'm upset, but it's not that. I... I don't want a doctor..."

"Well, all right then. Why don't you take a long swim? That will help you relax. Jacob and I have a lot of work to do." David kissed her on the forehead and went back to his computer.

Dixie was stunned. She looked at Jacob and saw that smug expression that she hated. But now there was much more to hate. She turned and ran out of the room.

She ran blindly down the hall as tears of frustration filled her eyes. Her whole life had been a sport, a match of wits. She had learned very young that if she wanted something, she had to play the game, and she almost always got her way. She had a whole treasure trove of tricks that would get people to do as she wanted, but these would not work on Jacob. This game: being forced to marry a man that she didn't know—or have feelings for—was different.

A new factor had been added. One with which she had no experience—Fear. She ran down the hall hoping she would make it to the nearest bathroom before she threw up.

19

Soft footfalls hurried through the grand foyer, where two men waited at the front door. Mary sensed something was very wrong. Why would a homicide detective want to speak to Mr. Weinberger? And why would he bring a policeman? "Oh, if I were a mouse," she whispered as she knocked softly on the study door.

"Yes, come in."

"Mr. Weinberger, there are police at the door, and they want to see you. Should I bring them in here?"

"No, Mary. Give me a minute, and I'll see them in the library."

She gave a quick nod and hurried out of the room.

"Let's continue this later, Jacob. I'll see what they want. I'll still need to make a few calls. After lunch why don't you go to the bank and pick up the paperwork on the Carmichael property? Make sure everything's there. I'll look it over later tonight."

David closed his briefcase, sat it beside the desk and, shut down the computer. He reached over, pulled the thumb drive out, placed it in his shirt pocket, and walked out into the hall.

Jacob didn't move. He raised his hand to his mouth, perhaps to cover that very expression that Dixie hated so much. When he took the hand away, he was smiling.

David walked the short distance to the library where the two men were waiting. "What can I do for you gentlemen?" he asked as he strolled in.

Both men were seated and quickly rose when he entered. "Mr. Weinberger, I am Detective Sylvan Bradshaw with the Sarasota County Police, and this is Officer Kincaid.

"It is nice to meet two men of the law," David reached out and shook their hands. "To what do I owe this visit? My daughter hasn't been doing anything stupid again, has she?"

"Sir, I'm a homicide detective. We're investigating a murder that took place late last night."

"A murder? Around here?"

"Yes, sir. I understand the victim was an employee of yours—a gardener. Do you know a Don MacKenzie?"

Weinberger took a seat, and the men followed suit.

"Yes, of course. He's been one of my gardeners for the last few years. He's a quiet fellow but a good worker. He was murdered, you say?"

"Yes, sir. What were you doing between ten and midnight last night?"

"Me? Let me see... I had dinner, and then I believe I was swimming laps in the pool. Sometimes I can't sleep, and spending energy wears me out so I can relax. Where exactly did this happen, may I ask?"

"On Honore—just past Laurel. I understand that's pretty close to your property. Did you hear or notice anything strange?" Bradshaw tapped a note into his phone.

"You mean a shot? No. I didn't see or hear anything strange."

"Mr. Weinberger, was everyone home at that hour?" Bradshaw tugged at his earlobe, an unconscious habit when he thought someone was lying.

"As far as I know. But you may have noticed, this is a pretty big house, and seriously, I don't keep tabs on the comings and goings of the household."

"It *is* a big house, that's for sure. How many people live here?"

"My daughter, of course; Mary North, our maid; my wife; she has a suite of her own upstairs. She suffers from dementia and requires 24-hour care. Two full-time nurses are with her around the clock. They go by to a very strict schedule."

"How well did you know the victim?"

"Like I said, he worked here. How well do you get to know your gardeners?" he paused and then continued. "What I mean is—they come; they do their work; they go. They don't live here; they're just hired help."

Weinberger was getting peeved with this line of questioning, and it was beginning to show in his tone. "Detective Bradshaw, am I under suspicion? I'm a busy man, and I have a lot of work to do. Why don't you get to the point?"

"I'm sorry, Mr. Weinberger, but a man was murdered last night—a man who worked for you— and it happened practically in your back yard."

"I have told you all I know. And I don't know about any murder."

Bradshaw started to speak, but David interrupted. "This discussion is over, gentlemen. Mary will see you out." He left the room, and the two men just looked at one another. The detective was making a note when Mary entered. Without a word, the men followed her out of the library and into the grand foyer.

"Thank you, ma'am," Kincaid said, as she opened the door, and they walked out.

David returned to his study. Jacob was there working on the books and looked up when he entered the room. He could tell by David's posture he was upset. "What was that all about?"

"One of our gardeners was murdered last night."

"Imagine that," Jacob said, and turned again to his work, but his lips turned up in a cruel smirk.

20

The late morning sun spilled through the six floor-to-ceiling windows of the circular morning-room. Mary North adjusted the blinds to lessen the glare while Dixie poured a cup of coffee from the urn on the buffet and took a seat at the table.

"How did you sleep, Peaches?"

"Not well. I ache all over, especially my back." She took a quick sip of the coffee, found it too hot, and set it down. She added a dollop of cream and stirred the steaming brew.

"I'm not hungry, Mary." She stretched her shoulders took another sip before putting the cup down again. "Have you seen Daddy?"

"No. He and Jacob had been working in the study before the police came." She put a few slices of bread in the toaster and pushed the lever down, then filled a footed bowl with fresh sliced strawberries and blueberries and placed it before the girl.

"Really, I'm not hungry."

"Shall I fetch the morning paper? It's been a little crazy today. I brought it in but haven't had a chance to look at it. You need something nourishing. You're a little peaked."

The two pieces of toast popped up, and Mary spread them with butter and strolled to the table.

"You say the police came? Why?" She took the plate of toast from Mary and sat it in front of her on the table. "What did they want?"

"Oh, it's awful." Mary began. She pulled out a chair and sat across from Dixie. "There was a murder last night." She leaned closer and lowered her voice. "I can hardly believe it. A murder here, and close to the house! I know I shouldn't listen at the door, but it isn't every day the police come calling."

"How terrible! Was it a robbery? And why did they come here?"

"It apparently happened along the road outside our south gate. They wanted to talk to Mr. Weinberger. They had a lot of questions—like where he was last night, and who was in the house?"

"I don't understand. Why would they question Daddy?"

"Because of who it was that was killed; it was one of our gardeners, Don MacKenzie. I can't believe it. He was such a nice man."

Dixie froze. "Who?"

"The gardener. They found him outside this morning next to his truck. I didn't hear how it happened but..."

"Don!"

Mary reached for the girl's hand. "Oh, Peaches, are you feeling all right?" Mary started to say more, but Dixie stood up so quickly that her chair fell over, and she ran from the room.

She ran blindly down the hall. As she passed the wine bar, she grabbed a tin of Bruichladdich Classic from the shelf and ran to the garage. From the rack of car keys beside the entry, she grabbed one from the hook and hit the button to raise the overhead door.

The red Porsche backed out of the garage before the door was completely up. Dixie backed out in a huge arc, slammed the car forward into first gear, and sped down the drive. The car squealed around the turn and swerved onto the road heading north.

Her mind raced; her breathing heavy and forced. Her head ached, and she felt drunk, as though her vision was milli-seconds behind her thinking.

When she reached the intersection, she could see a line of cars and people milling around. The police had cordoned off the northbound lane, and cars had to pull into the southbound lane to get by. There was no ambulance or body, but several unmarked vehicles were there with blue and red lights flashing. The line of cars inched along as curious onlookers tried to see what was happening. Don's truck was not there. A young officer was directing traffic, and just behind him, she could see a large dark stain on the road and the chalk outline of the body's position.

Dixie watched the scene as if it were a slow-motion movie. The Porsche had slowed to a stop, and the officer rapped on the hood and jerked his thumb to signal her to move on. She pulled ahead, and once she was able to get out of the parade of cars, she left the scene.

Breathing heavily as though she'd run for miles, and lightheaded, she sped along the country roads. The car swerved on gravel and left a trail of dust. The roads lead through acres of brush, fields of cows grazing, open spaces with ponds, cluttered orchards, and fields of crops she wasn't familiar with.

Gradually she calmed, her breathing slowed and when she looked around, she had no idea where she was. Her hands were shaking, and her mouth was dry. She pulled the car onto the berm and put it in park. She ran her fingers over her temples and down across her eyes, but the thought/vision was still out of sync.

The whiskey lay on the passenger seat, and without a moment's hesitation, she pulled the top off the tin and removed the bottle. In the center console, she retrieved the matching red corkscrew she'd been given by the salesman when she purchased the car. She quickly uncorked the bottle and took three full swallows.

For several seconds there seemed to be fireworks going off in her throat and head. At first, it felt hot, and then quickly turned cold. Dixie looked at the bottle's label. She had heard that there was a bit of black magic in the making of the brew, and she had to agree. With the motor running she took two more full swallows. She sat in the red Porsche somewhere in the country for a very long time.

~ 21 ~

As Boatman drove away from Autumn's house, he was consumed with guilt. *I should have sensed this coming. If I had I might have been able to stop it. What good is this gift if I can't use it for the people I care about? Gift. Yeah, right! Whoever coined that phrase certainly didn't possess one."*

At the intersection, he turned onto Beach Road that would become Airport Road. The old Ford pickup rattled and whined with every bump in the road. Boatman's father had given the 2006 Ford Ranger to him as a going-away gift and paid for its delivery to Barbados that first school year. 'B'man had cherished the gift like no other.

Boatman passed the 30 mile an hour sign going 50. With all he had on his mind, speed didn't matter somehow. He passed the airport and flight center.

The café is doing a good lunch business if the number of cars in the lot is any indication. Don and I had breakfast there a week ago and I spent most of the time listening to his plans for a future with Dixie. I wonder how she's taking this. Bradshaw must have contacted her and Don's family by now. So many people will be touched by this loss.

He turned onto Avenida Del Circo. His mind was chirping at such a rate he felt he probably should not be behind the wheel of a car. He sped through the green light at US-41 and turned left onto Golf.

In a matter of minutes, he pulled into the driveway of the house that he and Don shared. A squirrel chattered in the oak tree as he went up the path. He slid the key in and unlocked the door. Boatman was immediately struck by the void he felt when he entered. It was as if the house itself knew Don would never be back.

The refrigerator light glistened off the bottle as he pulled it out and twisted off the cap. He chugged-two thirds of the cold brew before he stopped to take a breath. Suddenly, he felt exhausted and flopped down on the couch—his legs splayed out before him.

The bottle was emptied on the next three swallows, and he sat it on the floor. He took a deep breath and closed his eyes, but he could not relax with his thoughts screaming like a runaway subway car. Memories of Simka and Don were a marathon of memories that seemed unending. When pacing didn't help, he tried deep knee bends and push-ups. That did help. He took a seat on the floor—legs crossed Indian-style; hands placed loosely on his thighs. He closed his eyes and cleared his mind.

"My Lord, my God, I firmly believe that You are here, that You see me, that You hear me. I adore You with profound reverence; I beg Your pardon for my sins and the grace to spend this time of prayer fruitfully. My Immaculate Mother, St. Joseph my father and lord, my guardian angel, intercede for me." The words were barely audible, and then he sat quietly listening to the sound of his own heartbeat. There was no interfering wind or sounds of clock or fan or traffic.

In his mind's eye, he saw himself walking through a fog that lifted slowly over a rolling green and grassy meadow. A short distance away was a two-story building with wrap-around porches on both levels and a gray mansard roof with a central dormer. There were many floor-to-ceiling windows, each with 12 panes of glass and shutters. He recognized the façade from his time in Barbados—where it had represented a safe place to visit when meditating. He climbed the steps to the front door and went inside.

He stood in a circular gallery with closed doors flanked by the tall windows. There was a large, beveled glass-top table in the center of the room. A strong sun shone in through the windows. It was so bright he couldn't make out the item on the table. He moved closer for a better look. The object was a birch handled fishing knife that Boatman recognized as a Rapala® brand. On the blade near the handle, he could make out two letters. Then he saw blood on the blade. It was pooling on the glass top table and dripping onto the floor. The floor quickly filled with blood.

Suddenly, one of the doors opened, and a dark figure brushed past him, through another door, down a hall, and out of sight. Boatman chased him. The hall ended at a wall, but a window appeared before him. He saw the dark figure at a great distance. The figure turned and looked back at him, but the runner was too far away to be recognized.

The hall dissipated, and the fog once again encircled Boatman. He opened his eyes. "Oh my god," he said, and he rubbed his forehead as he digested the message he'd just received.

Wednesday, June 17, 2020

~ 22 ~

Bradshaw handed a glass of water to Mary. "Thank you for coming, Miss North. Please, don't be nervous. You aren't in trouble. I just wanted to talk to you away from the house."

"I'm not sure I should be here. He might fire me if he finds out I was here." She took a sip of water with shaking hands.

"You can always tell him that you had no choice. That would be the truth."

"What do you want to know?"

"Tell me about the family—Mr. Weinberger, for instance."

"Well, he's a very private, fastidious man. What I mean is he lives by rituals."

"I don't understand."

"When he wakes each morning at precisely 6:15, he works a crossword puzzle before getting dressed. After brushing his teeth, he showers, shaves, and then dresses. I always arrange his closet. You know, in order of length, slacks first, white shirts next, jackets, coats, and so on. They are all on walnut hangers. That's what he likes. I organize his accessories in the top two drawers of the bureau, followed by colored shirts in the next drawer, sports shirts next, sweaters next. He expects them all to be neatly folded." She took another sip of the water.

"Fastidious, you say. It sounds more like obsessive."

"Wealthy men seem to be very particular. Trofeo is his favorite brand of clothes and Open Walk in shoes, but he prefers Pelle Tessuta Tizano in sneakers."

"What does he do for fun? Is he a sportsman?"

"Well, no. He is an avid reader with two libraries. There's the large one on the south side of the grand foyer, and he has a private one in his master suite. The main library has a variety of leather-bound and timeless classics; the *Rembrandt Family Bible*, a keepsake Bible illustrated with Rembrandt art; *The Philosophy Bible, The Definitive Guide to the Last 3,000 Years of Thought*; and whole collections of books by current adventure writers like Clive Cussler, Dan Brown, and many more. His private library however has mostly books either by or about Napoleon Bonaparte, including collections of books on The Life of Napoleon Bonaparte. He's convinced that he's the reincarnation of the man. But please, Mr. Bradshaw, don't ever tell him I said that."

"He won't hear it from me. Go on."

"Each morning at 8:45 I take him a tray of two poached eggs, three crisp sausage patties, two slices of dark toast with butter on the side, a four-ounce glass of orange juice, and a pot of creamed coffee. He prefers to eat alone and glances through the newspaper before leaving his..." she smiled shyly, "his 'personal sanctuary' to take on whatever the day holds."

"Miss North, does he fish?"
"Oh, no, I don't think he ever gets his hands dirty. He'd more likely hire someone to do it."

He jotted a note. "Does he have any hobbies? Is he a golfer or a gambler? Does he own a boat?"

"No. Mr. Weinberger doesn't have time for such things. He's a very busy man. He seldom takes lunch and doesn't eat dinner until after 9 p.m."

"I take it he isn't into sports either?"

"No. He feels baseball is boring and football is too violent. He does swim," she said as if to justify it. "You could call that a sport, right?"

"Is there a Mrs. Weinberger? Who else lives in the house?"

"Mr. W. and Dixie, of course. Jacob Crawford, her fiancé has a room on the second floor. Mrs. Weinberger is gravely ill. She has a suite on the third floor and never leaves it. Don't get the wrong idea, she's not locked away, or anything like that. It's just that she isn't herself. Her mind is gone, you know. Mr. W. refused to have her institutionalized. He'd rather have her home."

"Is that because he can visit her more often than if she were farther away in some facility?"

"Oh," she paused, choosing her words more carefully. "No, I suppose he felt she'd be more comfortable in a place she knew."

Bradshaw tugged at his ear and asked. "How often does he visit her?"

She was suddenly quite nervous. "I should probably get back. I will be missed."

"All right. That will be enough for today, but I may have to speak to you again. Officer Kincaid will see you out."

Mary North grabbed her handbag and hurried past Kincaid in her rush to getaway.

Mrs. Wilburn watched Autumn as she stirred her coffee mindlessly and stared off in the distance. The old woman sat across from the girl, opened her napkin, and placed it on her lap. She blew into the cup and then sipped the hot brew. She found it still too hot and sat the cup down. The girl seemed mesmerized. She took a bite of toast and laid the rest down on the plate.

"Are you all right, dear?"

"I didn't sleep well. I had another of those horrid nightmares."

"Oh, I'm sorry, Dear. Does it help to talk about it?"

"I don't know. Maybe." Autumn took a sip of her coffee and set the cup down. "There was no moon, and it was pitch black outside, but I opened the back door and went outside. I didn't have any trouble staying on the path since it was so familiar to me. It was tree-lined, and in places, I occasionally had to brush the branches out of my way. It was very quiet. There were none of the usual sounds of crickets or other nocturnal creatures. I came to a clearing, and in the distance, I thought I saw a light. Someone had lit a candle. Its light shone on a small body of water— a pond. I noticed something in the pond. When I got closer, I realized it was a body floating face down.

"Without warning, there was a flash of lightning that lit up the scene. When I reached for the leg to pull it to shore, it came to life. The thing stood and walked toward me. It had no eyes and no teeth, but I knew immediately it was Jeff. I didn't want him to touch me. He frightened me. I turned and ran back toward the path. He followed. The tree branches blocked me. I couldn't get past, and he was coming closer. I saw an opening and ducked through it. A lot of people were milling around on the other side. I saw Don MacKenzie, and when he saw me, he started toward me. His head lopped to one side—as if it were almost severed and was hanging only by a tendon. I wanted to scream but couldn't. I turned and ran in a different direction, and all those people started toward me.

"I couldn't catch my breath, and as I ran my feet were sticking to the ground as if I were running ankle-deep in tar. I was on the verge of panic when a hand reached out and pulled me to safety. It was Richard, my husband. I fell into his arms and we kissed.

"Where have you been?" I asked.

"I told you I was going to Canada," he replied.

"Oh, Richard," I said. "You have been gone so long and I've missed you so much. Why, darling, we even had a funeral!

"Suddenly the scene began spinning and quickly swirled to a pinpoint. When I found that I was alone in the blackness, I screamed."

Autumn took a deep breath and reached for a napkin to wipe her eyes.

"Oh, my dear! That was a terrible dream." Mrs. Wilburn got up and put an arm around her. "But it was only a dream. You're safe now. Nothing can hurt you."

Autumn patted the woman's hand. "Oh, you are so wrong. Having him with me for that moment and holding him in my arms..." She closed her eyes for a moment and when she opened them again Mrs. Wilburn saw tears forming.

"Now the wretched mourning begins anew," Autumn sighed. "When will this grieving ever stop?"

"I do understand." She rose and started to leave but stopped. "I'm sorry, dear. It must be all the dying and drama in your life at the moment. Why don't you lie down and get some rest? I'll call you in a couple of hours." Mrs. Wilburn turned and walked out of the kitchen.

Autumn rose and headed to the bathroom. In the medicine cabinet, she found the small bottle. Melatonin had become a frequent sleep aid; she took one. Without it, there would be no sleep and even so, there were no guarantees.

~ 24 ~

"How did it go?" David sat on the corner of the desk in his study. It was almost eight o'clock, and the sun was waning. It would be dark in another half hour, and he was ready for a drink—followed by dinner and a swim. He enjoyed nothing more than an evening swim to settle his nerves after a hard day. He took a sip of the Johnny Walker Blue he kept in the study as part of his closing of business each day.

"Are you sure no one saw you?" This was not really a question, and, of course, the response had better be yes. People who did business with him knew what was expected of them and knew the penalty for failure.

"Good." He rose and swirled the ice in his half-filled glass. "You'll find your money in the usual place. I'll be in touch." He laid the receiver in its cradle and walked to the window. David preferred the tethered phone over his cell phones. He felt they were more secure. He had two in the house—one in his study and one in his bedroom. No one in the household—neither family, nor service help, nor colleagues—were allowed to use either.

He pulled back the curtain and surveyed the property. "Why is it, when one problem is solved, and another always seems to raise its ugly head?" He was still watching and hoping when there was a knock and the door opened. He turned, "Oh Jacob. Any news?"

"Nothing. The police have put out an *all-points bulletin* issued for the surrounding counties. They're bound to find her soon. I mean, where can she go? Her purse is here with her cell phone, credit cards, and money. We've checked all the hospitals, airports, and even the bus lines."

"She'd never take a bus," David said, his voice barely audible. "Maybe she's found a new boyfriend. They swarm around her like hornets. Did you try her friends? Does anyone know where she might be staying?"

"I phoned everyone on her phone list. No one knows anything." Jacob scratched his head thinking. "Could she have been kidnapped?"

"Kidnapped! Who would dare! He stalked across the room, poured another drink, and took two full swallows before continuing. "Maybe kidnapped," he offered after another pause—thinking. "No, there have been no threats or demands for money. My guess is she's probably holed up with some low-life."

"Oh, I doubt that. She must know better by now..."

David turned on the younger man. "Why would you say that? Have you done something? If I find out you've done anything to my daughter...!" His tone and threat came so quickly Jacob was caught off guard, especially when David bolted toward him.

"Whoa, wait a minute." Jacob threw his hands up to block the hit he expected and backed away. "How did I suddenly become the cause of her disappearance? I didn't do anything. I'm the guy who's going to marry her."

David stopped cold. He ran his fingers through his hair and tried to calm himself. "You're right. Sorry.

It's just that I'm so worried." He took two more gulps of the Blue and sat the glass down. "Go find something to do. I want to be alone."

"Sure, David, I understand," Jacob answered. He backed away, and quickly left the room. Out in the hall, he took a deep breath, wiped his forehead, and realized he was sweating. Jacob turned back and looked at the closed door of the study. "So, that's how it's going to be, old man? I see I'm going to have to be more careful. You gave me the prize, but once we're married, I'm taking over. You're going to find that I'm the better man, and in the end, I'm going to have it all and you will have nothing. Nothing! And you will soon *be* nothing."

That afternoon the door of the police station slammed shut behind them as Detective Bradshaw and Officer Kincaid headed for the small cubical, they called an office. Kincaid carried the bag lunch they'd picked up from the local greasy spoon. Bradshaw stopped at a shelf where a half-empty coffee pot sat. He picked up the pot and smelled the contents. He paused a moment as if considering then poured some into a grimy coffee cup that read "World's Best Dad" before taking a seat behind a well-worn six-drawer desk from maybe the 1950s.

"Go through that address book and notify MacKenzie's family. They won't release the body for several days, and that will give his folks time to get here." Bradshaw asked—reaching for the bag of food. "What did you think of Weinberger?" He opened the bag and pulled out a hamburger and fries and slid the bag to Kincaid.

"Well, he's short on patience, or could be he don't like cops."

"Do you remember some time ago; a body was found in a lake at the Osprey State Park? Turned out she was pregnant. A sad story—a young woman, quite a looker. We found no trace of the killer, but there was some scuttlebutt in which Weinberger's name floated to the surface a few times. But with no witnesses, no leads, and no clues, nothing ever came of it and it's now just become another cold case.

Kincaid took a bite of his sandwich and shoved in a few French fries while chewing. "He may be an egg-suckin' dawg, but he's got one kicker of a house," he added, still chewing. "What are you thinking?"

"I'm thinking he's one lying son of a bitch. He told us he was swimming in his pool about the time of the murder and didn't hear a thing. Only a man with a death wish would swim with lightning flashing all around him. If you'll remember, it was a hell of a light show that night even after the rain came."

"Why would he lie about that?"

"Exactly." He took a bite of his sandwich and chewed thoughtfully before swallowing. "That's what we're going to find out."

Bradshaw put the sandwich in his mouth and held it there, so he could use both hands to open the box containing MacKenzie's items. Inside he found the folder of pictures from the crime scene. He took the bite and put the sandwich down, opened the folder, and studied the pictures. "It appears that MacKenzie was on his knees, maybe he'd fallen before he was struck. From the angle of the thrust, the perp would be right-handed."

"More than likely a man than a woman," Kincaid added, taking the last bite of his burger. "It was curious how the knife was all but hidden under the hood of the guy's jacket. Maybe he turned a bit... maybe he sensed the perp and started to turn."

"Maybe. We'll never know. The kids who found him didn't know he was stabbed, just that he was lying in a pool of dried blood." Bradshaw continued to shuffle through the pictures.

"Funny how those kids weren't creeped out by what they found. You'd think kids like that would have freaked out, but they were pretty calm."

"Kids that age have seen everything imaginable on TV. With all the news broadcasts, reality shows and CSI... And movies are even worse. I read that kids by age five have witnessed more than 400 murders thanks to television. *That* should be a crime."

Bradshaw threw the last quarter of his sandwich in the trash and took a sip of his coffee. He winced, then set the cup down. "Times have changed. It takes two incomes to get by these days, so with both parents working kids are left alone in front of the television. TVs are raising this next generation," he put down the photos and paused. "Hand me the weapon."

Kincaid reached over, picked up the bagged knife and handed it to Bradshaw.

"Did they find any prints?"

"No, at least nothing they could use. There was a partial print on the underside, but it's pretty small. Still, they noted there was a little triangular mark on it, maybe a scar. Otherwise it was clean as a whistle. The perp probably wore gloves. Is that a varnished handle?"

"Birchwood, I believe, and a stainless-steel blade. It's a Rapala® brand, you know for filleting fish," Bradshaw said, hefting it from hand to hand testing its weight.

"Yeah, pretty common brand—nothing special about it. It looks like any other fishing knife."

"You're almost right. Rapala knives are common, probably due to their price, but this one is top of the line. The handle is reindeer antler."

Kincaid laid the bagged knife on the desk, slipped the pictures back in the manila folder and dropped it in the box with the other items.

"You young bucks, when will you ever learn?"

"Huh, learn what?"

"Okay, here. Look it over again and tell me what you see." He handed the bag to Kincaid, sat down on the battered office chair—probably the same vintage as the desk—and propped his feet up.

Kincaid looked it over. "What? A handle—birchwood, you said. The inscription on the blade says 'J Marttiini Finland, Hand Ground Stainless', so what? Probably every fisherman in the state of Florida has one of these. They aren't expensive. There's nothing special about it."

"Actually, this one is considerably more expensive. Turn it over and look at the other side of the blade, college boy. Then tell me what you see."

Kincaid turned it over. He moved closer to the window where the light was better. "Well, flip me over and call me flap-jack! There are tiny initials lightly engraved up near the handle. I saw it earlier, but I took it to be just a fancy design, you know, made at the factory. I can barely make out the elaborate script, but it looks like J and M."

"And who do we know with the initials J and M?"

Thursday, June 18, 2020

~ 26 ~

Bradshaw turned to see Kincaid stroll in with a bag in each hand. "Why the quirky grin?"

The younger officer sat the two bags on Bradshaw's desk. "Well, I've been running around like a chicken with its head cut off. Maybe now I'll be able to sit and relax for a while. I spent most of last evening reading, made a few calls this morning, and I'm feeling all right as rain with the world."

So, what were you reading, *War and Peace?*

Hell, no. I took MacKenzie's address book home and read it from cover to cover. I called Mrs. Davenport and gave her the sad news. She was sadder than a one-car funeral. She gave me the names of her kin, but she said she'd pass the word. I gotta admit that was not a call I enjoyed."

"Are they coming to Florida?"

"Janie Davenport—that's MacKenzie's sister— said some might. Mary Ellen Frankenwalter, that's her older sister, is laid up with something called *lumbago*. She said Uncle Hiram and Aunt Betty were at the farm in the mountains and don't have phones and the mule that brings the mail died last week. I take it they're some kind of hermits. Freckle and Pickle, they're the twins. Well, they are on a church camp revival trip in Scotland and won't be back till the middle of next month."

"Did she say when to expect them?"

"Well, no." He scratched his head thinking. "She said she was deeply saddened by the news; said she'd call Boatman about the arrangements. I imagine they'll stay in touch with him."

"Anything else?"

"Well, she did say Uncle Hiram and Aunt Betty probably wouldn't come down."

"Why is that?"

"Seems like old Hiram is so cheap he wouldn't give a nickel to see Trump ride a bicycle."

"What's in the bags?"

"I'm hungrier than a raccoon at midnight, so I stopped at Yummies and picked up a couple of donuts and coffee." He opened one bag and took out two piping hot paper cups of steaming coffee.

Bradshaw opened the other and pulled out a square donut that would easily measure eight inches per side with a round knot in one corner. "Those folks sure know how to bake," he said, taking a bite and pushing the bag back to Kincaid.

The younger man took the other treat, a dark glazed delight that could feed a family of three. "These are my favorite: apple fritters."

"Well, eat up and get your traveling shoes on. We're going to see a man about a knife."

~ 27 ~

Inside Jaguar Boat and Supply Nate sat with a cup of coffee as cold and bitter as its owner. As he looked around the empty showroom, the clock on the wall read 4:47. A few months ago the place would be packed with customers eagerly comparing brands, styles, and features of this year's models, and asking questions to the point that Nate would have to stay open an hour longer to accommodate the crowd. Now it was so quiet that setting the coffee cup down would create a tiny echo in the room.

Nate reached into his shirt pocket and pulled out one of his Cuban cigars. He lined up the cutter to the shoulder of the cigar and snipped the cap in one smooth motion. He brushed a finger across the freshly cut edge and took a test draw before lighting it.

Sarah Ann, the cashier, watched from the window of her office. The guy was a slob, but when it came to his cigars, he was an aficionado. She watched as he slowly rolled the freshly cut edge above the flame and then lit the center. As he took a puff or two, she might have imagined that here was a man content with his business and looking forward to tomorrow—another day of selling to happy boat owners and counting all his dough.

It would never occur to this post high school girl—as it did to Nate—that sales had dropped drastically this past quarter. After all, she'd never met Boatman, who had left before she started this job. Her job was to take and record all the money that came in for boat sales as well as parts and supplies and answer the phones. That kept her busy. At the end of the week, she would turn over all receipts to the bookkeeper who would record them.

The old bookkeeper, Bernard Copeland, had been with Nate from the opening of Jaguar Boat and Supply, and he knew the true situation very well. Contentment was the farthest thing from the truth. Sarah Ann would have quit on the spot if she had been able to read Nate's mind.

Nate took his cell phone from his pocket and poked a series of numbers with his fat middle finger. It began ringing as he raised it to his ear.

"Hello," he heard the familiar voice on the other end, and purposely waited before responding.

"Hello?" The seconds ticked away. "Hello? Who is this?"

"I just heard the news." Smallwood wanted to laugh out loud, but he controlled himself. "Poor Don. Cut down in the street like roadkill. How sad."

Boatman knew by the sound of his voice that Nate was smiling when he said it. "What do you want, Smallwood?"

"My dear boy, isn't it obvious? I'm expressing my sympathy for the passing of your girlfriend, or business partner, or whatever he was."

"You're a heartless bastard."

"Well, I may be, but I wanted you to know I don't hold a grudge."

"What the hell are you talking about?"

"Have you forgotten so soon that night at the party when you struck me? Didn't I say you'd be sorry? Well, you are sorry, aren't you? Sorry, you no longer have a partner."

"If you've got something to say, say it, or I'll hang up!"

"I imagine right now the coroner is opening him. They have to do that, you know, in homicide cases. He's probably right now slicing your girlfriend up. They peel away the face, you know. He's not so pretty without a face. All you can see is muscle and tissue, but he isn't bleeding any longer. Then they'll open the chest and poke around..."

Boatman punched the red icon on the face of the cell phone disconnecting the call. He threw it against the wall, bounced on the couch, and slid to the floor. The young man covered his eyes with both hands and let out an anguished cry.

Walmart is always busy, and today was no different. He drove past without a second look and headed north toward Sarasota.

The Venice Mainstreet had planned big events to pump up the downtown business at this usually bland time of year. The past two months had been unusually poor for those merchants, so Erin Silk and her team had scheduled a June Festival that included a downtown parade, themed cookouts at the various parks: 1/ Puppy Fashion Show & Hot Dog Bonanza. 2/ Police & Firemen picnic with rides and sirens. 3/ Bike Tour of the city—followed by pizza and beer bash on the island. 4/ Gambling Cruise and family games near Marker 4, and 5/ Fireworks scheduled at the South Jetty.

Nor did this entice him, so he kept going. Luck was with him as he made the lights from Center Road all the way to Blackburn Point. Ahead, he turned right on red and then left into the Osprey Walmart's parking lot.

There was a steady influx of teens in ragged jeans, men in flip-flops and baggy shorts, women in mismatched clothes, and sweaty, crying children parading through the entrances, while others exited toting swimming noodles, bath towels, portable grills, carts loaded with groceries, bags of ice, and coolers of beer, and other assorted beverages.

He pulled into an open parking space and strolled into the north doors.

No one noticed the man in Ray-Ban sunglasses, a tight-fitting black T-shirt, black slacks, a baseball cap, and running shoes as he strolled through the crowd. He walked past the produce and stopped at the first aisle. A biker carrying his helmet and a case of Bud stopped for a second to admire the man's tattooed arms. But when the man turned and looked at him the biker rushed off to the checkout aisle.

The man in black stopped and appeared to be looking at sale items on an end rack. He looked like any other festive shopper. On a closer look, one might think that he was neatly dressed. Even the baseball cap was worn with the bill in the front. There was no gun protruding from his waistband because it was neatly strapped to his right ankle. Nor did the knife strapped to the left ankle show. The man in black slacks turned toward the deli and stopped at the island filled with sandwiches and salads prepared earlier in the day by the deli staff.

Behind the hot case, a blonde with short hair neatly tucked into a blue baseball hat with a Wal-Mark logo was waiting on a line of customers. She smiled and said things like "Have a nice day" and "Catch you on your next visit."

When the last customer left, the man stepped up to the hot case. It was filled with several kinds of chicken wings, mashed potatoes, gravy, corn, macaroni and cheese, and other fried finger foods.

The blonde smiled up at him. "What can I get you?"

He noticed the name tag dangling from the thick seam of her V-neck cotton shirt, and his lips turned up in a slight smile. "Hello, Fran."

"That's me," she responded in a bawdy laugh. "What can I get you?"

"I'm thinking about that." He looked away pretending to search the hot case before looking at her again. "Maybe I'll have some fried okra."

"Sorry—no fried okra."

"Are you sure?" he asked, with an almost friendly smile on his lips.

"You're probably thinking of Publix."

"Maybe you're right." He smiled again, and his eyes held hers in what might be mistaken as flirtation, then he turned to leave. "I'll see you later," he said in passing and headed out the exit into the heat of the day and the busy parking lot. Shoppers passed him on both sides, but no one even glanced at him.

He pulled the remote from his pocket and pushed the button to unlock the car door. He slid in, started the engine, and put the car in gear. The motor came to life immediately. He backed out of the space and turned right. At the end of the lot, he turned right again heading West. When he reached US-41, he turned left, and the black Nissan slid smoothly into the traffic.

~ 29 ~

David swirled the drink in his glass. It was not his habit to drink at 10:30 in the morning, but he wasn't himself today. Sleep had been fitful; he had tossed and turned all night. Where could she be? Oh, she'd had tantrums before and hadn't come home, but something ate at him. He couldn't put his finger on it. His gut told him that something was very wrong. Was she so upset about marrying Jacob? Of course, she didn't want this marriage, but surely, she must see that this was best for her.

Just then there was a gentle knock on the door.
"Yes?"

The door opened and Mary stuck her head in. "You didn't have any breakfast, and I thought you might like some coffee, Mr. Weinberger." She entered with a small tray with creamed coffee and a dish of fruit."

"Thank you, Mary. But as you can see, I already have something."

"I'm so sorry. I know you're worried." She sat the tray on the edge of his desk and started to leave.

"Mary, wait. Please, sit for a moment."

"I wish I could help."

"It's been hard for me, ever since Rosemary became ill. I miss having someone to talk to. I can't seem to talk to Dixie. It always seems to upset her. I would have thought that by now, at her age she'd understand how I feel about her." He took a sip of his drink. "When I was her age, I was married, and Rosemary was failing. I didn't know how to raise a daughter. I've done my best to give her anything she wanted, but apparently, that wasn't good enough. She picks losers. All they want is her money, and she can't see that. Jacob will be good for her. He can keep her in the lifestyle to which she's accustomed. What more can she want?"

"Girls today want love, and not so much being cared for."

"Love? Love is the stuff of movies and novels. Love! Whoever came up with that one was a dreamer. Security, that's what women want—and need! Look at Rosemary. Where would she be today without my caring for her? And Dixie, where would she be without all the things I've given her?"

"I know, Mr. Weinberger, but girls today want to be independent. They want to make their own choices, even if those choices are not the best things for them."

"That can't be right. I know women. They want insurance and the protection that money brings." He downed the last of his drink. "I appreciate your thoughts, Mary. Leave the tray, and I'll get something to eat in a bit."

Realizing she'd been dismissed Mary closed the door behind her as she left.

30

A sharp rap on the front door startled Jeff as he read. He tossed the 145-page script on the end table and went to the door.

"Jeff Markison?

"Yes."

"This is officer Kincaid, and I am Sylvan Bradshaw with the Sarasota County Police. May we speak with you?"

"Of course, come in." Jeff motioned to the chairs in the living room and went back to where he'd been reading. "What is this about?"

"Mr. Markison, do you know a Donald MacKenzie?" Bradshaw sat down and pulled out his cell phone and made a note.

"Oh, yes. I just heard that he was killed. How awful!"

"How well did you know him?"

"It's a small town, Mr. Bradshaw. I don't remember when he came to Venice, but it was maybe ten years ago. We ran into one another from time to time. Yes, I knew him. I consider him a friend, but we weren't close. Not drinking buddies, or anything like that, you know."

"Did you go fishing with him?"

Jeff chuckled. "If you're asking if I was ever on his boat, the answer is no. Do you know what they charge to take guys out fishing? I prefer to spend my money on other things."

"Are you a fisherman, Mr. Markison?"

"No, sir, are you, Mr. Bradshaw?"

Both men chuckle, but Kincaid remained pokerfaced.

"I'm not much of a fisherman. I'd fall asleep if I had to sit and watch for the bobber to drop out of sight."

"Are you a hunter?"

"Why all these questions? What is it you want from me?"

"You're right, Mr. Markison. I'm just trying to get to know what you young guys do for fun. MacKenzie had a fishing boat, and I just wondered if you ever went on it with him? You say no, so maybe you went hunting together?"

"Sorry, I can't help you there. I knew him, but we didn't hang out together."

"Can you tell me where you were from about 10 p.m. to midnight on Monday?"

Jeff sat up at this. "You mean Monday night when he was killed? Am I a suspect? Is that why you're here?"

"It's just a routine question, Mr. Markison. We ask it of everyone we talk to." Bradshaw looked over at Kincaid, then back to Jeff. "By any chance do you own a Rapala® fishing knife?"

"A what? A fishing knife. I just told you I don't fish..." Jeff hesitated. It was only for a split second, but Bradshaw picked up on it.

"Yes. It's about so long," he opened his hands indicating the approximate length. "It has a bone handle. Does that sound familiar?" He watched Jeff closely for a reaction, but he already knew he was right.

"I just told you…" Jeff fidgeted in the chair as perspiration built on his forehead. He absentmindedly brushed it away.

"Maybe you should try harder to remember. This is very important, and the wrong answer now could change your life." Bradshaw sat back and allowed the silence to grow. He watched Jeff closely. The young man didn't look at him, but he seemed to be searching everywhere else in the room. The young man's eyes couldn't seem to rest on any one spot. Bradshaw watched and waited patiently.

Finally, Jeff took a deep breath and looked down at his hands. "You're right, I did have a knife like that, but I don't know where it is. I may have loaned it to a friend. I don't remember."

"Who would you have loaned it to? How long ago?"

"I , I don't know!"

"If you don't fish or hunt, why would you have a knife like that? What did you use the knife for?"

"Well, I don't know. I think it was a gift."

"A gift? From whom?"

Jeff fidgeted in his seat, growing more nervous by the moment. "I, I don't know. I don't remember. Do you expect a person to remember every gift they get? I had it for a while, but I don't know where it is or where it came from. I don't remember. I must have loaned it to someone, I don't know. What would a person do with a knife like that?"

"That is what I'm asking you. Why would someone give you or buy you such a knife? Are you a whittler, do you carve little animals from wood?"

"No, no! I don't do any of that. Why are you asking me all these questions? What do you want from me?"

"I just want you to give me a straight answer. The knife is yours, but you don't know what happened to it. You say you don't have a reason to own such a knife. You think you might have loaned it to someone, but you don't know who. What am I supposed to think?"

Jeff slumped down in his seat like a whipped dog and said nothing. Bradshaw waited in silence for several minutes. "Well, I'll tell you what I think. I think we should go down to the station. That will give you time to get your thoughts together. It may help you remember. In the meantime, I may have other questions."

Bradshaw and Kincaid stood at the same time. Jeff remained silent, but he eventually stood and allowed them to usher him out.

Friday, June 19, 2020

31

Autumn brought a breakfast tray of orange juice, toast, and an egg with bacon on the side into the study. The sun—just visible through the trees at 7:26 a.m.—cast a golden glow through the room. She sat the tray on the desk and pulled out the chair when the cell phone in her pocket rang.

Autumn sighed deeply, annoyed to be interrupted so early. She pulled the phone from her pocket—trying to decide whether or not to answer at such an early hour. The reading on the screen simply said "Venice." She didn't recognize the number and was about to ignore it, but something changed her mind. She hit the green button and said... "Hello." There was a moment of hesitation before the male voice responded.

"Autumn."

Immediately she knew. "Jeff, what is it? Are you all right?"

She heard the voice on the line break into tears.

"Jeff! Where are you? Are you hurt?"

"No, I... I'm in trouble, terrible trouble," he said, followed by sobs.

"Tell me where you are, and I'll come get you. Are you hurt? Were you in an accident? Talk to me!"

"I'm in jail. They think I killed Don. I've been here all night. They kept asking me questions. I didn't know what to tell them. I didn't do it, of course, but they don't believe me. Autumn, what am I going to do? They are talking about the murder and asking me where I was, and about a knife I had. I'm scared, really scared."

"Jeff, listen to me. Have they formally charged you?"

"I don't think so, but I don't know for sure. They said I could make a call. I can't believe this is happening to me. What am I going to do?"

"Okay, first you have to calm down. Let me make a few calls. Where are you now?"

"I'm at the Venice jail on Ridgewood."

"Try to stay calm. It's going to be all right. You didn't do this, and once they understand that they will let you go. We will get through this, honey. Try to get some sleep. That will make you feel better. Did they feed you?"

"They said in about an hour. I don't want food. I just want out of here!"

"You need to eat something and get some rest. It will help you stay calm. Give me a couple of hours."

"But, Autumn ..."

"Trust me, Jeff. Do what I say, and I'll see you in a little while."

"Okay," there was a long pause. "I love you." The line went dead.

Autumn closed her eyes and took a deep breath. When she opened her eyes again, she realized that she still held the phone to her ear. She laid the phone on the tray and pushed it away along with the uneaten breakfast. As she sat down, she rubbed the spot between her eyebrows where the familiar throbbing promised an oncoming headache. Then she covered her eyes with her hands to hold back the tears that threatened to spill over. "Oh, my god! Where do I begin?"

32

The phone was answered on the fourth ring.

"Carmen Varzea, attorney at law. May I help you?" The stern and confident female voice asked.

"Uh, this is Autumn Mariiweather. May I speak to Carmen?"

"Ms. Mariiweather, would you like to make an appointment to speak to Ms. Varzea?"

"Do I have to make an appointment? I'd like to speak to her first."

Ms. Varzea is out at the moment. Would you like to make an appointment to speak to her?"

"When would she be available to talk to me?"

"What do you want to speak to her about?"

"It's confidential. Is she available?"

"Ms. Mariiweather, would you like to make an appointment to speak to Ms. Varzea?"

"Please, just take my number and have her call me at her earliest opportunity."

"One moment, please."

There was a click as Autumn was put on hold. Soft elevator music played in the background. Moments passed before there was a click and the receptionist's voice came back on. "Ms. Mariiweather, Ms. Varzea is on the line."

There was a click, and the soft voice of Carmen Varzea began, "Autumn, what a surprise. What can I do for you?" Her voice was like honey spread on a buttermilk biscuit in the late afternoon sun.

"Carmen, it's Jeff. He's in trouble. He's been arrested. You remember Don MacKenzie. I believe you met him at Boykin's Halloween party last year. Nice guy. Quiet. Stayed pretty much to himself. You remember? He was murdered on Monday, and the police have arrested Jeff. Carmen, he didn't do it. We're beside ourselves with worry. We don't know what to do. We need your help."

"Calm down, Sugar. Have they charged him formally or are they just holding him?"

"I don't know. He called from the Ridgewood facility. They held him overnight. They allowed him to make one call, and he called me. I don't know how any of this works, and you were the first one I could think of."

"Okay. I'll go and talk to him and see what I can do. If they haven't charged him, then they are just holding him for questioning. Why don't we meet—the three of us—say... 2:30 this afternoon in my office?"

"Oh, thank you, Carmen. I can't tell you how much we appreciate..."

"It's okay, Sugar. I hope you still feel that way when you get my bill."

Carmen strolled into the station like a woman on a mission. The men on duty turned to watch as she sauntered across the linoleum, her high heels tapping and hips swaying. There was no question about it, she strode with confidence, aware that it was a turn-on for every swinging dick in the room.

"I believe you're holding my client, Jeff Markison."

She had a way of peering under her eyelashes in a comely manner that got a man's attention. The officer at the desk was captivated and hesitated a moment or two longer than necessary. He cleared his throat hoping no one noticed and pointed to Brian Kincaid's cubicle that he shared with Bradshaw. She gave the officer a charming smile and moved away.

Kincaid looked up at the sound of heels approaching and smiled. "Well, well. You're a sight for sore eyes." Kincaid put his pen down and threaded his fingers together. "Long time no see. What can I do for you, Carmen?"

"I understand you had Jeff Markison locked up all night, Mr. Kincaid. What is he charged with to warrant such luxury accommodations?"

"Take it easy, now. We haven't exactly charged him, but the evidence is strong." He sat back in his chair trying to appear professional. She'd made him nervous from the time they'd first met over a year ago. "I suppose you'd like to have a word or two with him."

"You are very astute, Brian. That is exactly why I'm here."

"Really," He smiled and looked away for a moment. "I suppose you aim to snatch him away from us as well."

"You are on top of your game today. I'm impressed."

"I hope you can get more out of him than we did. But what can you expect from a hog but a grunt? I figure if his lips are moving, he's lying."

"If you'll kindly show me the way, I'll happily take him off your hands."

Kincaid took a ring of keys off the hook, nodded in the direction of the cells, and the two of them headed down the hall.

The officer opened the door to a small room with a large table and a couple of chairs. There was what appeared to be a medium-sized television on the wall and a cabinet underneath. Carmen knew it was a close circuit video and recording equipment that were used in police investigations. Other than these, the room without windows was stark.

"Make yourself at home. I'll bring your client," Kincaid said, and closed the door behind him.

She sat her bag on the table and took a chair to wait. It had been about six months since she'd been in this room. At that time, they were investigating a man of interest in a suspicious drowning at the Osprey State Park. Samuel Nolen was his name. A bad-to-the-bone character, tattooed from his neck to the tips of his fingers, 1 ½ ear lobe plugs, and eyes that you'd swear could see through walls. She found him disgusting. He would look at her with those piercing eyes that she knew were undressing her. He'd grin as if he could read her mind, and he'd lick his lips with his long, pointed tongue. It was so nasty it made her nipples prickle. Only once was she left alone with him, and that, she vowed, would never happen again.

They were never able to get enough evidence against Nolen and had to let him go. He might have crawled back into the hole he came from. He seemed to have disappeared, for surely, if he were still in Venice someone would have seen him.

When the knob turned, Carmen jumped. Kincaid ushered Jeff into the room. He looked awful. He had slept in his clothes, and there were dark circles from lack of sleep. His skin was sallow—from fear no doubt. It was hard to believe that this was the Markison that turned heads when he walked down the street. He was no longer the tall, confident, and happy brother of Autumn. She'd never seen him look so wretched.

Kincaid pulled out a chair and nodded for the young man to sit. He looked like a whipped puppy.

"I'll speak to my client alone," Carmen said when Kincaid started to pull out a chair for himself. He stood for a moment looking at her as if considering. Then he pushed the chair back and headed for the door.

"I'll be right outside if you need me," he said, glancing at Jeff then back to her.

"I've got this," she said, and waited for the door to close behind him before turning to Jeff. "Are you all right?"

His expression reminded her of her own brother, who when he was six, and she had found him behind the garage with a cigarette in one hand and a lit match in the other. It was the look of hopelessness. His furrowed brow, and tears building in his eyes.

"Tell me what happened," she said, and laid a calming hand on his sleeve.

For the next twenty minutes Jeff relayed what he remembered about the past sixteen hours and interjected the thoughts and the emotions he had felt at the time. When he finished, she patted his hand, excused herself and left the room.

Kincaid was at the drinking fountain when she strolled over to him.

"Are you filing charges?" she asked.

The officer looked at her as he wiped a drop of water from his chin. "Uh, no—at least not yet. Maybe I'd better call Bradshaw."

"Maybe you should. Tell him I'm leaving with my client, and if he has a problem with that, he can call me." She strolled back to the conference room. "Come with me, Jeff. We're out of here."

For the first time in many hours the young man's eyes lit up, and he quickly followed her out of the station, into the parking lot, and into her car.

"I don't know how to thank you," he said—sliding into the passenger seat and reaching for the seat belt.

"This isn't over yet, but I intend to get to the bottom of it."

~ 33 ~

Jacob looked around the nearly empty parking lot to be sure no one was watching before entering the run-down bar in the rear of the liquor store. He paused a minute allowing his eyes to adjust in the dim interior.

"Over here," a burly man called out in a raspy voice - like the croaking of a frog - which is how he had gotten his nickname. "You're late."

Jacob moved toward the sound and took a seat in the corner booth opposite the man. "I had trouble getting away. He's becoming more difficult by the day."

"That's not my problem," croaked the man.

"I don't know what you're so worried about, I'm the one who has to be on stage and dance to this piper!"

"So, how's it going?"

"I had to teach his brat a lesson, but I don't expect any more trouble from her. As for you, practice patience! The wedding takes place in 16 days. After that we'll take charge."

"It'd better. I'm not the patient type."

"In the meantime, I'll convince him that she isn't capable of handling his affairs and get him to change his will—making me executor and beneficiary as her husband, or—of course—if she should happen to die."

"Do you plan to kill her?"

"Why would I kill such a precious pussy? I had a taste of what it'll be like, and I don't mind telling you, she's a great piece of ass. The next time will be even better."

"Well, don't let your cock mess up this sweet deal!"

"You know what they say, all work and no play... well, I don't have to draw you a picture."

"Just the same, you'll have me to deal with if you screw up."

"Stop worrying, Frog. Sixteen days and we're in! You'll get what you want, and so will I."

The Saab crossed the intersection at Milan and the trail and pulled into the center lane. Traffic was sparse this time of year, and she waited only a moment before she could turn into the parking lot in front of the Tandem building. No rain was expected, and Autumn felt it was safe to leave the top down on the convertible. She did drop a small towel over the steering wheel, which would get hot in the afternoon sun.

She took the elevator up to the third floor and walked down the hall to Carmen's office. A young girl stood filing papers. The plaque on the desk read: Opel Hemmings; Receptionist. Opel laid the papers on top the filing cabinet and went to her desk before speaking.

"May I help you?" She sat, pulled the chair up, took a pink pad and a pen from the drawer.

"I want to see Carmen."

"Ms. Varzea is in a meeting. What did you want to talk to her about?" She wrote the date and time on the pink pad.

"We're working together on a case. How long do you suppose the meeting will last?"

"What is your name?" The girl was so stoic it was beginning to annoy Autumn.

"Autumn Mariiweather."

The girl wrote the name on the pad. "If you would like to wait, you may take a seat."

Autumn took a deep breath and sat in a chair along the wall. Obviously, this girl did not know that she and Carmen had known one another since kindergarten, but Autumn didn't want to talk to this girl anymore then she had to. Instead she tried to calm down and relax.

The posh office was impressive. The reception area and the hall leading to other offices, conference room, and break room had highly polished hardwood floors. The only rug she could see was an off-white Berber carpet on which sat the receptionist's desk and chair. An Italian black and chrome coffee table and two black Worthington leather chairs balanced the room. The interior wall displayed a huge C. Kett painting of a stern eagle in an ornately carved black frame. A few tall plants softened the effect, and glass walls revealed the interiors of the various rooms down the hall.

When Autumn looked at her watch, she found that she'd been waiting almost 45 minutes. Just then a door opened, and she heard voices.

"Thank you for bringing me into the loop. I'll keep my eyes and ears open and let you know if anything transpires. How long do you plan to be in the area?"

"Hopefully only a few days," the fair-haired man said. "I'm eager to get back. My docket is—as you would say—full to the brim, and time is of the essence."

When Carmen looked up and saw Autumn, her focus changed. "We'll talk again soon, Larry. Excuse me," she said, and turned to Autumn. "Have you been waiting long?"

As the man left, he paused at the door. He noticed Autumn, and she smiled. He smiled back, pushed his dark-framed glasses up on the bridge of his nose and walked out the door.

"A new man in your life?" she asked Carmen. "No, he's with the FBI and is here on a separate case. He thought I might be able to help."

"Can you?"

"I don't know; time will tell." She turned to Opel. "We'll be in conference for a while; hold my calls." They turned and headed down the hall. "How is Jeff? Is everything all right?"

"As they say, no news is good news, and since we haven't heard anything from Bradshaw—that's good news."

They entered Carmen's conference room. The tray ceiling was painted metallic silver, which reflected the lighted Minka Lavery chandelier. The six-inch-deep walnut crown molding was made even richer with the silver continuing around the ceiling and gradating into a gun-metal gray on the walls. The furniture, including the wood-trimmed straight back chairs, was walnut, while the fabric on the chairs was a deep blue—matching the carpet.

Carmen strolled to the credenza and poured two cups of coffee. "My assistant has been checking the backgrounds of some of Don's friends and acquaintances. Although everyone said he was a great guy, we're not so easily influenced. A man doesn't usually get murdered because he's so nice. Usually, there's something hidden in his background.

"I can't imagine that you'll find anything. I've known Don for quite a while, and I've never heard that first negative remark."

Just then Opel's voice came over the small intercom attached to the phone. "I know you said to hold your calls, but you were waiting for a call from Mr. Gilbert."

"You did the right thing, Opel. Transfer him."

"Coming through," Opel responded. "Mr. Gilbert, Ms. Varzea is on the line."

"Fred, thank you for calling. How did it go?" Carmen asked the caller as she reached over and hit the speaker button that allowed Autumn to hear the conversation.

"It was murder, all right. The knife Bradshaw has is probably the weapon, but you'll know more when the knife is tested for blood residue. The blade entered the greater occipital nerve behind the right ear and severed the occipital artery before plunging into the brain. To stab someone like that, from under and then up into the brain, the victim had to be facing his killer. He was probably on his hands and knees. There was a fresh bruise on his abdomen as if he'd been hit, and there were abrasions on his palms, probably from hitting the blacktop when he fell. Those were the only spots? No sign of drugs or anything?" Carmen glanced over at Autumn, who sat wide-eyed—her hands covering her mouth as if she might cry out.

"Well, there was nothing to indicate that he used drugs. He appeared to be in very good health. There was an old break in his left femur. That was probably from an accident when he was young. His blood work was good, liver and heart were good. He'd had pizza for dinner, and it appears that he'd had sex just before to the incident. That's pretty much it."

"Thanks, Fred. Can you send me a copy of your report?"

"Certainly, I'll email it right now."

"Great. Thank you." She hit the button that cancelled the call and turned to Autumn. "Are you all right?"

"I'm all right. It's just been a bad week for me. I appreciate you allowing me to hear it. There was nothing in it to indicate Jeff was in any way responsible, except that it was his missing knife that was used. I wish we could find out how someone got a hold of it."

"A lot of people are working on it. Have faith."

~ 35 ~

Bradshaw took the Venice by-pass north to Sunset Boulevard, and before long he crossed Smokey Pines Way. In time he came to the Jaguar Boat and Supply and pulled in between two cars.

"Do you know what they call the color of that car on the right?" Kincaid asked.

"I give up. What do they call the color of that car, college boy?"

"It's called *money* green." He opened his door and got out.

"Zat so?" Bradshaw said, as they walked to the building.

"Yep. Zat's so, Boss, 'cuz it takes a lot'a money to own one."

Smallwood was coming out of the restroom drying his hands on a paper towel. He looked up and saw the first man and took on the posture of an old friend. Then, when he noticed the second man was in uniform, he stiffened, and the smile disappeared.

"What can I do for you gentlemen?"

Bradshaw flashed his badge and introduced himself. He had never met Smallwood, but he'd heard rumors. Word had it the rotund man had interests besides selling and working on boats. "We'll only take a few minutes of your time, sir."

"Well, make it quick. I'm a very busy man."

"Yes, I can see that," Bradshaw said scanning the empty sales floor. "May we speak in your office?"

Without a word Smallwood gestured toward the glass enclosed room. As they entered, Bradshaw observed the desk was covered with papers, fast food wrappers and Styrofoam cups. The old, worn chair behind the desk was tattered and stained.

Smallwood sat behind his desk and gestured to the two straight back chairs in front of it. He crossed his arms and glared at them.

"We are investigating the murder of Don MacKenzie. Did you know him?"

"I did."

"He was a customer then?" Bradshaw asked, jotting another note.

"I didn't say that."

"Well, how did you know him?"

"His roommate used to work for me."

"His roommate?"

"Yes. That's what I said." Arms still folded; Smallwood adjusted his position—causing the chair to squeak.

"Who would that be, Mr. Smallwood?" Bradshaw didn't like his tone. He looked at the man directly. If he wanted a hard time, Bradshaw was just the man to give it to him. He held his gaze and waited for the fat man to reply. The silence between the men continued while the clock's ticking seemed to grow louder.

Finally, exasperated, Smallwood broke the silence. "What do you want from me? You must already know the answer to that question! Why are you here? Am I a suspect? What is it you really want? You come into my place of business—your man in uniform—now everyone knows the cops were here! Is that it? You want to humiliate me?"

Bradshaw spoke slowly and calmly. "We are investigating the murder of a young man who lived here in Venice. We are talking to people to learn more about him and why such a thing would happen. You're right. We have spoken to the man who shared a house with him. But we want to hear what you know about him."

Smallwood unfolded his arms and pulled the chair closer to the desk. "Boatman used to work for me. He wasn't much of a salesman, but he was okay. One day he told me he was quitting. He said that he and his fag-friend were going into business together." Smallwood reached into the dress box and pulled out a cigar. "I thought *good riddance*. It wouldn't be much of a loss."

Bradshaw's ear began to itch. "So, there was no bad blood between you?"

The fat man snorted, "Of course not."

"This MacKenzie—did you know him?"

"I met him one time. I don't remember when; it was ages ago." Nate unwrapped the cigar, bit the end, and lit it with a small disposable lighter. He threw the wrapper at the ashtray. It missed.

Bradshaw stood and walked to the office door. He looked out into the showroom. "This is a nice place you have here. How long have you been in business?"

"We finished the building in January of '16. Business had been good until..."

"Until what?"

"Uh," Nate stalled a second. "Oh, you know how it is... Uh, it's the summers. Everything slows to a crawl." He rose and joined the man at the doorway hoping they would leave.

"Business slow?" Bradshaw asked, although it was obvious from the lack of customers.

"Yeah, it's the summers, all right. It'll pick up again around Halloween."

Just then, an elderly gentleman rushed from a back office. He wore a suit, and his glasses were pushed up above his eyebrows. The little hair he had wrapped from ear to ear in back of his head. He studied the fistful of papers in his hand. "Nate, we have a problem. None of these figures jibe." He looked up and saw Nate was not alone. "Oh, I'm sorry. I didn't realize you were busy." When he saw Kincaid, he blanched—drawing the sheets to his chest. "I, uh... We can talk later. I'm sorry." And with that he rushed back the way he'd come.

"It looks like I'm needed. Are we done here?" Nate took a long drag on the cigar and blew it out slowly.

"Yes, for now. We may need to talk again later. Thank you for your time." The two officers made their way to the front door. Smallwood headed for the bookkeeper's office.

"Mr. Smallwood," Bradshaw called. "One more thing."

Nate stopped short. "Yes? What is it?" he asked impatiently.

"Do you know a Jeff Markison?"

"No! I don't know *everyone* in the area! Will there be anything else?" Nate was visibly irritated and turned away.

"Well, yes—one other thing." Bradshaw purposely waited for the man to turn so he could see his eyes before he asked. "Are you a fisherman?"

"Do I fish?" Smallwood was at his last thread of patience and could blow up at any moment. "Of course, I fish! It's Florida. Everyone in Florida fishes!"

"What do you fish for?"

Smallwood was now fuming, and his voice rose two octaves. "What! Grouper! Snapper! Sheep's Head! Will that be all? As you can see, I'm very busy." He entered the room and slammed the door behind him.

The two got into the car. Kincaid buckled up. "Really? 'What do you fish for?' I was sure he was gonna' pitch a hissy fit! Was that question somehow pertinent?"

"The Rapala® isn't used for big fish but more to skin smaller fish such as Grouper, Snapper, and Sheep's Head. Plus, I wanted him off balance so he might make a mistake."

"Did he?"

"We'll know soon enough. I'm also curious about the protective way the old man clung to those papers when he spotted you.

Saturday, June 20, 2020

~ 36 ~

Dixie opened her eyes. The afternoon sun filtered through the sheers at her bedroom window, which transformed the beige of the walls and bedding to a golden hue. Her throat was dry, and her stomach ached. Then her memory kicked in, and she remembered Mary telling her Don had been...

"No!" she screamed, sat up and burst into tears.

Mary jumped from the chair beside the bed and rushed to her. "Oh my god, girl! We thought we'd lost you."

Dixie hadn't noticed the woman before, but now grabbed her hand. "Please, please tell me it was all a bad dream. Tell me nothing has changed."

"I don't know what you mean, dear. You could have dreamed, I guess. You've been out of it for three days."

"What are you talking about? What are you saying?"

Mary sat on the edge of the bed and held Dixie's hand. "A Manatee County's sheriff's deputy found you in your car last Wednesday. He said the car was out of fuel, the battery was dead, and you were passed out." Tears filled the housekeeper's eyes as she stumbled on. "The police rushed you to the hospital and called Mr. Weinberger. They told him you drank nearly the whole bottle of that whiskey. Everyone thought you had tried to kill yourself. You almost did. Oh, my dear, we thought for sure you were going to die. We were so worried. The doctor wanted to keep you at the hospital, but your father insisted you be home. Nurses and doctors have been in and out ever since." Mary took a tissue from the nightstand and blew her nose. "You gave us such a scare."

Dixie heard most of what Mary had said, but her mind was replaying the woman's words from Tuesday and the drive past the site. Everything else was a blur. She didn't care. She wished she had been the one who had died. She turned toward the window. The sheers distorted the view, and she could barely make out the Crepe Myrtle swaying in a breeze. She closed her eyes, laid down, and spoke no more.

Autumn called again, just as she had every day since she had heard that Dixie was missing. Jacob's phone call had alerted her, but no one would share any news of her whereabouts.

"Weinberger residence—how may I direct your call?" Mary chimed.

"Mary, it's Autumn. Have you had any word yet?"

"Oh yes, she came to this morning. She's awake now. She dozes off and on, but she's safe and sound. They delivered her car this morning," Mary paused, "but, Autumn, she refuses to speak to any of us. She's in such a terrible state. I don't know what we will do. Mr. W. is beside himself with worry, and Mr. Crawford visits her frequently. He must love her very much, but she won't utter a word."

"Mary, may I visit her?"

"Oh, my dear, please do. Maybe a friend can bring her out of this funk. I'm so afraid that she might try again."

"Thank you, I'll be right there."

A short time later Mary saw Autumn pull up, and she opened the door as the young woman came up the steps.

"I'm so glad you're here. She needs to see a friendly face. She's been through so much, first the police finding her, then she's rushed to the hospital. The doctor wanted her to stay in the hospital for a few days, but Mr. W. insisted that she be kept here, and he's hired nurses..."

"Is she in her room?" Autumn asked.

"Yes, she might be sleeping. I think she prefers to sleep rather than be bothered by her father and all these strangers. Go on up."

Autumn took the stairs two at a time. At the landing she turned to the right and stopped at the second door. She knocked softly. When there was no response, she slipped inside.

Dixie lay facing the window bundled in the bedding and with her eyes shut. She looked asleep, but Autumn couldn't be sure. "Dixie, it's me."

The bundle moved as the girl turned over. When she saw Autumn, she threw off the covers and sat up. "Oh, Autumn," she cried.

Her friend sat on the bed, put her arms around her, and held her close.

"Don's dead. Did you know that? They said he was murdered. Who would do that? How can I live without him? Autumn, I don't want to live without him."

"Shh. Please don't say that. I couldn't stand that."

"Autumn, you know how I feel. You've been through it. They don't know; they don't care."

Autumn held her close wishing she could say something to ease the pain, but she knew there were no words. She had heard them all herself when friends and family tried to help; but no one could. Tears filled her eyes. She'd been told that time was the balm that would lessen the pain, but after five years it had not yet begun.

"They care, they just don't understand."

Dixie sat back and took a Kleenex from the box on the nightstand and dabbed her eyes. "I wait to hear his voice. I thought I heard him coming up the stairs, but it was only Daddy. I cannot stand the emptiness I feel. It's like a piece of my heart has been ripped from me." She blew her nose. "Autumn, I can still feel his touch. I can still smell him on my pillow."

She went to the window and looked out. "How can I bear to look into the yard?" Her hand went up and covered her mouth as if she might hold all her feelings inside.

Autumn sat on the bed listening. She did understand. She had felt... still felt the emptiness and longing. She also knew it would never end. In time, Dixie would realize that there were moments when she didn't agonize over his passing. Just when she could get through days without tears; when she thought it was getting better; a sound, or smell, or a dream would remind her, and the sorrow would begin anew.

Dixie stepped away from the window and crossed to the bed. "Tell me. What happened? What have you heard?"

"Oh, Sweetie, do you really want to hear that?"

"Please, I need to know. I want to know it all. Maybe that will help me get through this. Please."

"All right, but stop me if you..."

"I won't need to. Please."

"Don must have left your house around 9:30 or 10 Monday night."

"Yes, he did. We were in the theatre. It's quiet, and no one ever goes there unless there's a party. We made love. Don thought that we should go away and start a new life. But I didn't think it would work. I refused. He was so good, he'd just say don't worry about that right now, we'll talk about it later." She brushed away another tear. "Oh, I'm sorry. Please, go on."

"You'll remember how it stormed that night."

"I drove by the place where it happened. I saw the police cars and the tape. His truck wasn't there, but I saw the blood on the street." She took a deep breath to avoid crying.

"It happened when he got to the truck. Two college kids found him the next morning."

"Was he shot? Did someone shoot him?"

"No, they found the knife. He'd been stabbed from behind." Autumn paused and caught her breath. "Dixie, I have to tell you something. I don't know how to tell you."

"What is it? You can tell me anything. What do you know?"

"The knife they found... It's... Oh my god, how can I say it?" She rose and walked around the bed.

"What is it? Tell me."

"The knife... He didn't do it, but the knife..."

"What!"

"Dixie, it's Jeff's knife. He hadn't seen it in ages. He never used it, and he never even knew it was missing. But somehow the killer used Jeff's knife."

"Carmen, Jeff, and I met this past week. We laid out everything we knew or what we could remember. I had seen the knife a year or so ago when Jeff had it. We were cleaning his closet. Why is it men never throw anything out? Everything has some sentimental value. He still had a sweatshirt from high school, can you believe it? Anyway, I pulled a box from the shelf, and the knife was in it. I asked him at the time where it came from. I think he said it was a gift, but he didn't remember from whom. He didn't lie when he told the police. Anyway, they still suspect him. He's home, but he never leaves. He's scared to death that they won't believe him, and he'll end up in prison."

"Could he have taken it to Goodwill or donated it to the Habitat for Humanity ReStore?"

"I don't think so. It was a very nice one, and at the time I suggested he might give it away. It was too nice to throw out." She took Dixie's hand. "But how are you doing? Mary tells me that you haven't been out of bed. You shouldn't stay cooped up all day."

"Oh, Autumn, I hate it here. I can't do anything without remembering Don."

"I know, lying here alone with your thoughts doesn't help either. What about Jacob? Does it help talking to him?"

"He's a monster! Marry him! I'll die first!"

"Please, don't talk like that. You have to get up and move around. Why don't we go out to lunch? Come on. It will do you good."

It was almost 2:30 by the time Dixie dressed and they got away from the house. Autumn pulled out of the driveway and headed west on Pinebrook toward Venice. The girls pulled their hair up and pushed it under hats against both sun and wind. Autumn had hoped the fresh air and sunshine would help Dixie's mood, but she sat, her arm against the passenger window, her chin resting on her hand. Autumn wanted to say something cheery, something comforting but couldn't think of anything. She asked. "What are you thinking about?

"Don—of course," Dixie sighed. "Thoughts of him fill my head, and I can't think of anything else."

"I'm sure. That's all part of the grieving period."

"He wanted me to run away with him. He said we'd go where no one knew us. He thought that because we loved one another, we'd always be happy."

"How did you feel about that?"

"I didn't think that was such a good idea. When you've always had it, you don't think about it. But it would make such a change... I was afraid to be without money. I'm sure that sounds shallow, but... He asked me if money was so important. I thought so. I still do. Autumn, I can't imagine not being able to get whatever I want. I've gotten used to having someone to pick up after me; to clean my house and my clothes. I know I'm spoiled, but that's what I'm used to. It's the way I like it. I don't think I'd be happy with a different lifestyle.

"Will marrying Jacob keep happy?"

"Daddy thinks so, but I know staying with that monster would be a living hell! I could never do that. I'd kill myself first."

"Dixie, that's the third time you said that. Killing yourself is not the answer. You're a grown woman, educated and worldly. Honey, you have options. You can find another solution."

The Saab continued on before taking a right onto Venice Avenue. They drove in silence through the residential area, and past several plazas, before crossing the Intracoastal. Traffic was light, and the sidewalks and stores were considerably less crowded along the main thoroughfare. Autumn turned left onto The Esplanade.

"Have you ever been to The Glass Menagerie?"

"No. Don and I never went out for fear of being seen and Daddy finding out."

The year-old facility was of circular construction with parking wings on the north and south sides. The exterior consisted of eight white 20-foot columns tipped in gold and six 15-foot etched glass panels on the front and back. The center two opened fully, while the others pivoted to allow fresh air. Both front and back doors were crowned with arched, burgundy stripped awnings. Clusters of Fox Tail Palms and Hawthorns created cool vistas around the building.

"I haven't been here either, but I've heard nothing but good reports about the food," Autumn said as they entered the posh restaurant.

Blue and old rose 50s style chairs rested on the plush green carpet, while the blue walls and gold columns were softened by the warm lighting of the round midcentury pendants and other backlighting.

"Don't you just love the soft and calming music of the 1950s? I have always loved that period. Daddy has a collection of 33 1/3 albums. I like the one about moon songs by a singer named Vaughn Monroe.

"I don't think I've ever heard of him," Autumn said as they approached the hostess.

"Do you have a reservation?" she asked.

"No, do we need one?"

"Not now, but during the high season, you can't get in without one. Just the two of you?" she asked, and almost without an answer she said, "I have the perfect spot for you. The view of the ocean with sea birds is breath-taking."

"That's just what we need. Thank you."

The table looked out over the beach and the ocean that seemed to go on forever. The hostess left them with menus, and a young boy took their choice of beverages.

Dixie sighed deeply as she took in the view. "You were right. I needed to get out. Life has been pure hell since I learned that Don was killed. No one seems to understand what it's like. Well, Daddy wouldn't, or couldn't. He suspected I was seeing someone, but he had no idea who. Obviously, I could never have told him. I told him I was in love with someone. As usual, he didn't listen."

"What about Jacob? How do you feel about him? Is there any chance you might grow to love him?"

"Hell no! He's horrible. He's controlling. He's mean! Not just mean—he's cruel. Autumn, I truly feel that if I married him, he would kill me one day."

"Oh my," she leaned closer. "Does your father know how you feel about him?"

"I tried to tell him, but he doesn't listen, and Jacob's always around watching and waiting. I'm truly afraid of him. I believe he enjoys hurting people."

"Dixie, I want you to know that you can always talk to me. You need someone you can trust, and you know you can trust me." She took the girl's hand. "Please, I'm serious."

"Thank you." Dixie began to tear up and brushed the tears away with the back of her hand.

"Maybe we should change the subject," Autumn continued. "We're here to enjoy ourselves. What do you think?"

Dixie withdrew her hand, brushed one last tear away, and smiled. "I agree. Let's enjoy the sunshine and the beauty around us while we can."

~ 37 ~

It was late afternoon when Autumn left the mansion. She felt a headache coming on, and her stomach was queasy. She headed for the guardhouse and the small man inside waved her on. The gate rolled away, and the convertible sped along the lane. She turned left toward home. The car's a/c blended with the salty hot June air, and Autumn took a deep breath. But instead of being refreshing it made her nauseous and she swallowed hard to keep it down.

"If I can just make it home..." she swallowed again. Autumn brushed a few strands of hair out of her eyes and realized she was perspiring. Cars whizzed by, but she hardly noticed as she focused on watching the road, which appeared to be going in and out of focus. She shook her head and tried panting to clear it. She got the first three green lights, but the fourth was already yellow when she sped through.

By the time she reached her home on Harbor Point in North Venice, she could barely see. She had chills, and a black cloud was settling over her. She pulled onto the driveway of the garage at an angle and turned off the engine from habit. The driver's side door wouldn't open. She tried three times before she remembered it was locked. Her head was spinning, and she took each step slowly to keep from falling.

Mrs. Wilburn was dusting the furniture when the door opened and Autumn staggered in. She got as far as the couch before she collapsed.

"Oh, my lord!" The woman pulled her onto the couch and ran to the kitchen for a wet cloth. "Autumn, can you hear me?" She washed the girl's face and neck with the cool fabric, but there was no response. Mrs. Wilburn rang her hands, anxious about what to do, and when she touched her again the girl was cold. Mrs. Wilburn covered her with a light throw and stayed by her side.

Behind her closed eyes she saw the couple held hands as they walked along the path through the woods toward the cabin on the lake. Maple, walnut, and oak trees were just a few of the many varieties of trees in this section of the property. The sun was going down, and the path was already dark due to the heavy canopy. The cottage was out in the open and clearly visible in the crimson afterglow of the setting sun. They had planned this vacation to Eagle Lake for months and had looked forward to the cooler Maine weather. The temperature had dropped to a brisk 42 degrees overnight.

"What did you enjoy the most today?" Richard asked. "Besides the pristine wilderness and hardwood forest, I mean?" Their path was a bed of pine needles that covered the ground along with an assortment of leaves and acorns.

"That's a silly question. Being with you is what I always enjoy the most." She squeezed his hand. "But of course, I also enjoyed the Wilderness Festival. We've seen a lot of animals on television and in pictures, but it was thrilling to see them up close."

"I thought you might like the aviary the best. You seemed to be taken by those little feathered fellows."

"Actually, I did. Maybe we should get a bird. They seem so happy all the time."

"My grandmother had a canary. It chirped non-stop all day until she covered it for the night. I don't know if I could handle all that *happiness*."

Autumn laughed. "Finches are like that too. Big birds, like cockatoos and parrots, are very noisy. I was thinking about a cockatiel or maybe a budgie."

Just then they heard a commotion nearby, and two men in forest ranger uniforms burst onto the path. "Folks, you'd better take cover," the first man said in a strong French accent. "A rogue bear has been spotted in the area. We believe he's loose somewhere in these woods. Hurry now, and if you see anyone else out here, warn them too."

"Thanks for the heads-up, but we're staying in that cabin up ahead. I take it you're out to catch it?" Richard asked.

"Yes, sir. We hope to catch him with our tranquilizer-guns. But if he gives us trouble, we have orders to kill him. One way or another we'll get him." With that they ran off in a southerly direction.

"Let's hurry, Richard. I've been as up close and personal as I hope to get with animals that big."

Once inside the log cabin Richard built a fire in the fireplace and Autumn fixed a light supper of fish cakes on rice with left-over green beans. The furniture conveyed the mood of the north along with rustic decorations. As she finished setting the round oak table with its plaid tablecloth, he walked in.

"I know you drink white wine with fish, but I am in the mood for a tall glass of Port. What do you say?"

"It sounds delicious," she said, kissing him on the nose. She placed the blue petit-point napkins while he opened the bottle and took two port sippers from the shelf.

"I take it there's no such thing as a 'tall' Port glass," he said holding up the 3 ½ ounce glasses with their two front feet and straws.

"Well," she said, leaning closer. "We'll just have to have several."

"Or, we'll use these," he said, exchanging them for two champagne glasses. He kissed her and sat the items on the table. "Let's eat, I'm famished!"

They were finishing their third glasses and the fire had faded to embers when they heard a thud on the porch.

"Good grief! What was that?"

"I don't know, but you stay here. I'll go check."

"I'm not sitting here alone! We'll both go check."

They turned on the porch light and went to the window. The angle was wrong, and they couldn't see most of the porch. There was another thud, and the whole house seemed to shudder.

"Oh my god, Richard. What could do that?"

"I don't know, honey. I'll have to open the door..."

"NO! I won't let you. What if it gets in?"

"You're right. I need a weapon. I put the ax in the pantry after chopping wood yesterday. Wait here and I'll get it." He was gone only a moment and returned with the Craftsman tool. "Stand back now." Richard eased the door open just as the cabin suffered another thud. Autumn screamed.

She and Richard watched as the huge brown bear threw itself against the wall of the house. In the porch light they could easily make out the distinctive hump on its back, and they saw blood on its paws and muzzle. As the bear rocked from side to side on all fours, it made a deep guttural sound. The feathery end of a tranquilizer-dart bobbed with each movement of the bear. Obviously, that particular dart hadn't done the job. The pooling of blood under the animal suggested that it had been seriously wounded.

Autumn pulled the door open a couple of inches to watch. This slight movement aroused the bear—which rose to its full height and roared. They could see what looked like foam around its muzzle. Suddenly it charged. The storm door shattered under the weight of the 600-pound bear. The force of the blow knocked the inner door off its hinges. Richard fell against Autumn, who was shoved against a cupboard.

The bear slashed at Richard—leaving five three-inch deep gashes in his chest—as he and Autumn both cried out in terror. The bear then grabbed Richard by the shoulder and shook him. Autumn could see Richard was frantic as he pushed and clawed with his free hand—all the while trying to use the axe, but the long handle hampered any movement.

When the bear backed off, Autumn felt a spark of hope, but it was short lived when the bear went at him again. Richard's eyes showed terror. The smell of the stench of the animal and its blood filled the room. Richard blinked once, and his eyes rolled back.

Autumn was screaming. "Richard, Richard, what can I do? How can I help?"

The bear was making that god-awful low guttural growl. In the next few minutes everything appeared to be happening in slow motion. Could he hear her?

His efforts were waning. He looked over at her, but he seemed unable to focus—as his strength diminished.

The bear faltered then dove at him—his mouth open as he grabbed him by the throat.

Autumn imagined that Richard smelled his hot foul breath and knew he could feel the warm blood that dripped from it. She imagined he could only see red matted fur--as his arms relaxed and his whole body went limp. The bear had severed his carotid artery—so Richard did not see his blood mix with that of the animal and spray into the air.

The next moment brought a deafening silence. The bear stopped growling. Richard stopped fighting. Autumn stopped screaming. She got to her feet and jerked the axe from Richard's hand. As easily as chopping a length of wood, she drove the blade of the axe into the bear's neck. He reared back, dropping his prey. Autumn, fueled with adrenalin and filled with anger, flung the tool again and again at the head of the beast until both fell—the bear breathing its last as she dropped from exhaustion. Oblivious of the sticky carnage on the floor, she crawled to her husband's side. She would never have the strength to move the bear off Richard, so she curled up beside him, cradled him in her arms, and passed out.

Autumn awoke. For a moment she was disoriented. She was no longer in the cabin, but in her own home and she had the mother of all migraines.

Mrs. Wilburn rushed to her side. "Oh, my dear, you're awake, finally. I didn't know what to do or where to turn. I've been so worried." She took the young woman's hand. "Are you all right? You were crying and calling out in your sleep."

"I need some water."

"I'll get it right away." Mrs. Wilburn nodded—hurrying out of the room.

Autumn sat up and swung her legs over onto the floor. She put her hand to her head as if that might make the headache go away, but of course it wouldn't. Why did this keep happening? Why did she have to relive that night over and over? The tears came again, and she sobbed uncontrollably. "Oh, Richard..."

38

The long spreadsheet was open on the desk; the edges weighted down. A stapler and a jar of paperclips held it open. Smallwood ran his fingers through his once blond, now mostly gray hair and uttered something profane. The black numbers covered the left half of the sheet before they turned red. Nate shrieked, pushed the heavy items off the edges and crushed the paper in his fists. He dropped the wad of paper and covered his eyes—resting his elbows on the desk. Nate Smallwood sat like that for a long time. When he finally looked up and saw the rumpled survivor, he carefully tried to brush the wrinkles out.

The large plate glass doors opened, and he heard footsteps approaching. Smallwood brushed his hair with his palms and went to see if this was a potential buyer.

"Oh, Mr. Black. Hello again," he said and reached out to shake his hand.

"I've been thinking about it, and I'm ready to get a boat."

For the next twenty minutes, the two men discussed the various boats in the showroom. They moved into the office where they talked about the types, brands, engines and accessories, and poured over photos of numerous models.

Smallwood's adrenalin was on high. He hadn't smiled this much all week. He reached into the black and red cigar humidor and took out two cigars and handed one to Mr. Black.

"I think the Sea Ray SLX 230 is more to my liking," the man said as he twirled his baseball hat in his hands. "What was that price again?"

"This one ships from the UK. Taking into consideration the currency conversion fee and delivery, it's a bargain at $94K." Nate tried to keep a straight face, but inside he was doing cartwheels.

"Fine. I have an appointment and need to go," Mr. Black said, putting the cigar in his shirt pocket, "but I'll be back next week. We can do the paperwork then, and I'll bring your down payment."

"Wonderful," Nate said as both men stood up and shook hands.

Nate, thrilled with the sale, kissed the cigar before putting it back in the humidor. He walked to Copeland's office humming a little tune.

39

"I'll see you tomorrow," Fran called to the girls in the deli.

She threw her apron in the hamper in the warehouse and her hair net and gloves in the trash as she pushed through the double doors, through the area, and out the automatic doors. The mid-summer heat and humidity were oppressive as she left the air-conditioned store and headed across the dark parking lot toward her car. "Son of a bitch! I'll be sweatin' like a cock's ear before I can get the goddam car door unlocked," she murmured, and picked up her pace.

"Get the hell out of my way," she snapped at an elderly woman pushing a cart load of items."

As she opened the car door, she was assaulted by the hot air escaping. "Fucking son of a mother!" she shrieked. The elderly woman glowered in disapproval as she tottered past.

"What the fuck are you looking at? Fran bellowed and slid behind the wheel. She started the car and backed out nearly hitting the woman before shooting forward heading for the exit. The light at Tamiami Trail seemed to take forever before she could turn left and head south.

The traffic light at Blackburn Point road had turned yellow, so she stomped the gas pedal and sped through the intersection at 65 miles per hour.

Fran reached down and tapped the button that turned the radio on. Camila Cabello featuring Young Thug's song *Havana* was playing. She turned up the sound 'til it reverberated through the car and thumped the steering wheel to the beat of the music. "Havana, ooh na-na," she crooned, off key and a bit behind the singer. "...took me back to East Atlanta, yeah, na-na."

A black car pulled onto the Trail from a side street just south of Sorrento. The windows were dark, and the driver was not visible. But Fran was in the groove with the music. She bobbed her head and beat the steering wheel in time. The music was so loud she would not have been able to hear the screaming siren of a firetruck if it passed her.

"I loved him when I left him," she crooned with all her heart, rocking her new hairdo in time with the melody. "Got me feelin' like, ooh-ooh-ooh..."

The jolt was so hard she hit her head on the steering wheel, and her purse flew against the glove compartment and spilled half the contents on the floor.

"What the fuck!" She glanced in the rearview mirror and saw the lights of another car. It had fallen back but was now rushing toward her. In a flash it rammed her car again. Her whole body was jolted, and she lost her grip on the steering wheel.

"You cocksucker! What the fuck are you doing?" she shouted. She took the next right hoping to lose the tormentor, but he stayed on her tail—even when she skidded off to the left onto a gravel road.

When he hit her the third time, she lost control of the car and it jerked to the right, over a patch of wet grass, and spun till it stopped just short of an old live oak tree.

Fran was furious. In less than a minute she was out of her seat belt, out of the car, and stomping back to the car that sat idling a yard away. She marched to the driver's side window. The lights of her car illuminated a black Nissan. She hammered on the driver's side window.

"Roll down this window, you dickhead, and talk to me! What's the meaning of..."

Just then the door opened with such force that it knocked her off her feet and she fell to the ground. The man in the Ray-Ban glasses and black slacks got out of the car and stood over her.

She shook her head to clear it and eyed him closely. "Do I know you?" she asked.

"No, I don't think so. We came close a few times. Like the time you nearly ran me off the road."

"I don't remember th..."

"You should," he said, cutting her off mid-sentence, "it was quite recently. You also waited on me at the deli where you work."

"Okay, asshole, so we met. Why the fuck did you ram my car?" She started to get up, but he kicked her, and she fell back again. "Mother fucker!"

With lightning speed, he pulled the knife strapped to his left ankle and was kneeling beside her with the knife at her throat. "You have a very foul mouth," he said, pushing the knife until it drew blood.

"No! Stop!" she shrieked.

Suddenly he was on top straddling her. Her eyes went wide, and for the first time in her life, Fran was afraid. The hint of a smile crept to his mouth, and his eyes glinted with anticipation. He reached for her blouse and yanked it open exposing her white Fruit of the Loom sports bra. She wanted to say she was sorry, that she didn't mean anything she'd said, that they were just words and didn't mean anything. But he rammed his fist into her stomach and knocked her breathless. She gasped for air; she wanted to scream.

He reached into her open mouth, grabbed her tongue and sliced it out with the knife. She tried to scream, but all that came out was a most ungodly sound. Blood filled her throat. She gagged and choked when she tried to breath.

"Look at you now. You're bleeding like a pig and mewing like an animal. Is that how you want to spend the rest of your life?" He couldn't understand what she was trying to say. Her eyes were huge with fear. She sputtered blood with every breath. "I could leave you like this. You might survive... or not."

He brushed her sweaty hair back from her face almost lovingly. "But I don't think so. I try to be humane," and with that he thrust the knife into her heart. She sputtered once again and fell silent. As he pulled himself to his feet, he looked down at the woman. Her mouth was agape, and her open eyes seemed to watch him, but he knew that was an illusion. As he walked away, he reached into his pocket, and something fell from his hand.

Sunday, June 21, 2020

40

The red and blue flashing lights could be seen through the trees. Emergency vehicles surrounded the group of men and women as they worked the crime scene. The area had been cordoned off with the bright yellow tape, and the EMS pair talked softly as they waited for the coroner to give them the go-ahead and remove the body.

Bradshaw pulled up onto the dry grass beside Gilbert's dark blue Toyota and turned off the motor.

Fred Gilbert, the county coroner was on his knees giving a cursory once-over of the woman's body. He rose slowly and removed his gloves before ambling over to Bradshaw.

"Damn, Syl. This is a first for me. Brutal, to say the least," he said, running his fingers through his salt and pepper hair. "It's more like Elm Street in LA than Sorrento in Nokomis. I've never seen this kind of mutilation before. I had one years ago in Detroit, where the victim was missing a nose. I've seen missing fingers and ears, of course."

"Jezus, Fred! Is that what I think?" He said taking a step closer for a better look. "They cut... did they cut her...?"

"Sure did. We haven't found it either. What kind of person does a thing like this in the first place? What? To keep it? A souvenir!"

A female CSI interrupted the men. "Excuse me, Mr. Bradshaw. We found this—sixteen-feet from the body. It was never opened." She handed him a zip-locked bag containing an unused cigar still in its wrapper. "Her purse was in the car along with her driver's license. We've photographed and tagged everything. I think we're almost done here. We'll finish our report, box it up and leave it on your desk as you suggested."

"Thank you, Ann. Did you find a weapon?"

"No, sir."

"Okay. Thanks." He turned to Gilbert. Any idea what the weapon was?"

"Most likely a knife. To make such a clean cut it couldn't be a box cutter or razor blade. A knife would be my guess." Gilbert took a cigarette from his shirt pocket. The flame lit his features—revealing his creamed coffee skin, dark eyebrows, and sparse mustache. "I imagine you've thought about this being the second murder this month. Any chance it might be the same perp?"

"Yeah, I noticed. But we have the murder weapon from the first. Maybe it's just a coincidence."

"Of course, maybe... This, coming from a man who does not believe in coincidences," Gilbert smiled—his dark eyes twinkling. "I'm out of here. Call me if you find anything."

"It appears that this will be a long night for both of us." Fred paused one more time to look at the corpse. "What kind of person does a thing like this?"

Bradshaw turned and started to walk away. "They're called sociopaths, Fred. This one is one of the worst kinds."

One by one the teams drove off. First the truck left for the firehouse. The EMS headed for the hospital, followed closely by Gilbert. Bradshaw would stop at the station, but the real work would begin early tomorrow when Brian got to work. The CSI team had come in two black SUVs and would be the last to depart once the area had been thoroughly cleaned, as with *a fine-tooth comb* they used to say.

Monday, June 22, 2020

~ 41 ~

The clock on the table beside the staircase softly chimed nine o'clock as David made his way up to Dixie's room. He knocked gently and entered when there was no response. Dixie lay facing the window.

"I know you're not asleep, Dixie. We have to talk." He pulled the chair up to the bed and sat down. "I don't know what brought on this latest crisis with you, but I want you to know I was very worried. I don't know why you do this to me. I feel like you're punishing me for something."

He found her lack of response very annoying, and his voice rose. "I've given you anything you've ever wanted. Why do you do this to me?" He stood and pulled the blanket back. "Turn around and talk to me, damn it!"

She turned toward him. "I don't want to talk to you! I don't want to hear what you have to say! I want to be left alone. Leave me alone." She pulled the pillow over her head and covered her ears to shut him out.

"Whether you want to or not, you *will* listen to me! I thought your spoiled-brat days were behind us. My god, you are 34-years old! When are you going to grow up? Other girls your age are married with children. I just don't understand you. I've covered for you whenever you've acted up. I've done my best to raise you since your mother became ill. I don't know what more I can do."

Dixie threw the pillow on the floor and sat up. "What have you given me—clothes, shoes, a car? They don't have any meaning to me. I want a life!"

"What are you saying? I'm giving you a life. I've arranged a marriage for you, to a man who will take care of you. What more could you possibly want?"

She moved toward him. She wanted him to understand. "That's what you do. You arrange things that *you* want me to have. You never ask me what I want, and when I try to tell you what I want you don't hear me."

"What is it you want, Dixie?"

"I know you won't understand, Daddy, and now it's too late."

"Too late for what?"

"Happiness. It's too late for me to have the man I want." She was grasping to find the words that he would understand, but she knew it was hopeless. Her voice broke, and the tears could not be held back.

"It's too late for me to have the one..." She saw from his expression that he didn't get it. "Oh, what's the use? "Please, just leave me. You say you always give me what I want. I want to be alone." She laid back down and pulled the sheet over her head, so she wouldn't have to see him.

"I want more than anything to be able to talk to you like an adult, but that doesn't ever seem to happen. Okay, Dixie. Here's what *will* happen. In thirteen days, you will walk down the aisle and marry Jacob Crawford. You will go to live with him, raise his children, and be the best wife you know how to be. After the wedding I will no longer take care of you, financially or otherwise. Perhaps you will be able to speak to him, since you say you can't seem to speak to me.

"There is much to do beforehand. I will make your appointments, and you *will* go to them, even if I have to drag you!" And with that he stormed out the door.

42

Carol pulled into her driveway and hit the button to raise the garage door. She pulled inside and turned off the motor. She was about to close the overhead door when a police car pulled up behind her. As she approached the car, she saw that the passenger was in uniform. The driver rolled down his window.

"Miss Tanaka, may we have a few words with you?"

Carol's blood ran cold. Was this about Heru? "Am I in trouble?"

"No, Ma'am. I'm Detective Bradshaw. We just need a few minutes of your time."

"I suppose. Come on in."

She closed the overhead door with her remote and walked the two men to the house. They followed her along the concrete sidewalk, past a series of orange Ixora, and waited for her to unlock the door.

"What is this about?"

"I'll explain once we're inside."

Carol pulled the key from her purse, and Bradshaw noticed that she was shaking and had to try three times to find the keyhole. He realized that most people get nervous when the police come to call.

She kept the small house neat. The furnishings were sparse, possibly reflecting her Asian taste.

"May I get you anything? Coffee, maybe some iced tea?"

"We're fine, thank you," Bradshaw said. "Miss Tanaka, this is Officer Kincaid. We're here investigating the death of someone you know."

She shivered, then almost relieved said, "Oh, yes. I read about Don MacKenzie in the *Herald Tribune*. I still can't believe it."

"Actually, we're here on another case. We found a woman you know. Your name was in her cell phone."

"A *woman*? What woman?" she asked, now totally confused.

He pulled his cell phone out and checked notes. "Her name was Francis Katherine Major."

"I don't know any Francis Kather... Oh, you mean Fran! You said you're on a case. My phone number was in her cell phone... Oh my god! Fran? What happened?"

"She was killed on a side road in Nokomis yesterday. I take it you were her friend. Can you think of anyone who might have wanted her dead?"

"I wasn't her friend. Yes, I knew her, but we certainly weren't friends. I don't know anyone who liked her. She was a real pain in the..." She stopped herself. "She was rude and obnoxious, but I don't know anyone who'd kill her."

"What can you tell me about her?"

"I guess we ran into one another once in a while— that's all. We got our hair cut at the same beauty shop, Lime Time. It's out on Jacaranda at the round-about. I think she worked at the deli at Walmart. Someone there might be able to help you."

"Was she seeing anyone? Did she have a boyfriend?"

"I can't imagine that! I don't know that she ever had a boyfriend."

"Can you tell me a little about her?"

"Well, like I said, she didn't have friends—certainly, none that I know of. She was quite a loner. People didn't like her because she was an *in your face* kind of bitch. She enjoyed shocking people, and she'd say the damnedest things to make that happen. Really, I don't think I'm going to be much help."

"Thank you for your time," he said, reaching into his pocket and pulling out a card. "If you do think of anything else, please call me."

Carol walked them to the door. When the door closed behind them, she paused. "Fran dead? Murdered? What is going on?"

43

Sojoe and Henry pulled up beside Jeff's silver Dodge and got out of the car. They rushed to the door and pounded on it. A moment later the door opened, and Jeff stood there looking haggard and haunted. He was dressed only in gray boxer briefs, and an open chenille bathrobe.

"Jazus Cryst, man! You look like shit!" remarked Sojoe. Henry just stood there agape.

"Bite me." Jeff returned to his chair, the ties of his robe swinging loosely with each step. They followed looking around the room.

"Nice changes in décor. Did you hire a professional or did you do it yourself?"

"Fuck you, Sojoe! Did you come just to rag on me? If so, show yourself out."

"We came to check on you. We hadn't heard from you for a couple of days," Henry said. "We were worried."

"Yeah, I've been, uh... somewhat indisposed. Throw that shit on the floor and have a seat." He reached over the coffee table covered with empty candy wrappers, potato chip bags, Chinese carry-out boxes, and beer cans—some crushed—and picked up another half-empty bag. "You want something to eat?" He held the bag out to them. Sorry, all I have left are some marshmallows."

"I'd rather eat caterpillars, but thanks for offering." Sojoe flinched back in disgust.

"What's going on with you?" Henry asked.

"You probably read about Don MacKenzie."

The two nodded their heads but said nothing.

"He was killed a week ago Monday night. Actually, he was murdered by someone with a knife."

"Yeah, we heard that." Sojoe went behind a small armchair and pushed it forward, dumping a blanket, an assortment of dirty clothes and more empty beer cans on the floor. He kicked the items aside before sitting.

Henry looked for a place to sit and decided the floor was his best option.

"Well, it turned out, so they tell me, the knife that did the deed was mine."

"Say what!

"No!"

"Seriously?"

"Fuck a duck..."

"Did you do it?" Sojoe asked.

"No, Moron. What are you, nuts?" Jeff grabbed a crushed beer can and threw it at him. "Of course, I didn't!"

"I don't get it. What makes them think the knife belongs to you?" Sojoe leaned forward in his chair.

"Were your fingerprints on it, or something?" Henry asked.

"No," he shook his head in disbelief. "My Goddamn initials were engraved on it."

"That was mighty convenient," Henry added, scratching his head.

"How did your initials get on the knife?"

"It was a gift. Someone gave me the knife as a gift and had it inscribed."

"Uh oh," Henry uttered. "I remember now." Both men turned to him. "It was your 26th birthday. You had just gotten your degree and completed your training. You were waiting to hear if you'd been accepted. They thought you were too old to become a firefighter," Henry said, rather sheepishly.

"I remember that. Jeff, you were dancing, you were so nervous."

"I gave you the knife, remember?" Henry hurried on. "I bought it that day we spent at Service Beach awaiting the outcome. But you were so busy chatting up that chick in the white bikini that you didn't notice. They offered to engrave it, and I thought that would be cool and said okay."

"I remember that," Sojoe said.

"Me buying the knife?"

"No—that girl in the white bikini. Damn, she was hot!"

"I gave you the knife that night. 'Course, we were all so drunk I'm not surprised you don't remember."

"I don't remember." Jeff rubbed his temple as if that might revitalize the brain.

"I don't remember either." Sojoe sat back in the chair, thinking.

"Sure, don't you remember? I gave it to you in case you were turned down by the station. I told you that you'd need it to slit your wrists when you got the rejection letter.

"A fine friend you are suggesting such a thing when a guy's so miserable." Jeff tossed a half-eaten slice of day-old--or more--pizza at him.

Henry ducked and grinned. "I try."

Sojoe cleared his throat for attention. "So, where do you stand with the cops now? You're not in the slammer."

"Autumn called Carmen Varzea, and she got me out for the time being."

"Well, Buddy, if you're going down, it couldn't be better than with the illustrious Carmen Varzea, Attorney at Law." Henry chuckled at his own joke, but the other two were in a more serious mood.

"Jeff, how did your knife get into MacKenzie, if you didn't do it?"

"I don't know, Sojoe. I just fucking don't have a clue."

"Where did you keep it? Was it in a drawer somewhere? When did you see it last? Come on, you *have* to remember. It's your skin we're talking about here,"

"That's all I've been thinking about for the past three days! I JUST DON'T' KNOW!"

"Okay, okay, calm down. We're here to help." Sojoe turned to Henry. "What else do you remember about it?"

"Well, I thought it was a damn funny joke, but Jeff didn't see the humor in it. He practically threw it back at me. Hell, this was a fine knife even if the sentiment wasn't appreciated. I wouldn't let him throw it away. When we took him home, I left it on the desk in his room."

"Wait a minute. I do remember something. Autumn was nagging me to pick up my shit. When I told her, I didn't need all the stuff anyway, she suggested that I take it to the Habitat ReStore Shop on Ogden. She was hanging stuff in my closet, and this box fell off the shelf. The knife was in it!"

"Good! We're getting somewhere. Go on," Sojoe urged.

"That's all I remember."

Sojoe slapped the heel of his palm against his forehead in frustration, took a deep breath, and continued. "Okay, let's keep trying. When was it the knife fell out of the closet?"

"I don't know—maybe six months, maybe a year."

"Did you give it to Autumn? Did you put it back in the closet? Did you put it in the truck?"

Jeff's face lit up. "Yes, I remember putting it in the glove compartment of the truck. I thought I would take it to the pawnshop. They buy shit like that."

"That was not a shit-knife! That was a nice one, and I paid good money for it!" Henry barked. "It's not my fault that you didn't appreciate it."

Sojoe brushed off the comment. He didn't want Jeff to get sidetracked now that they were making progress. "You put it in the glove compartment of the truck. Did you go to the pawnshop?"

"No. I kept thinking I would, but I never did."

"Then what?"

"I don't remember ever seeing it again. I just forgot about it."

"Great!" Sojoe's sarcasm was evident.

Henry stood. "I'm getting hungry. Why don't we go get something to eat?"

"That may be a good idea. Maybe if you get some food in you, you'll be able to think more clearly. We'll wait while you change. I don't know of any restaurants in Venice that will let you in dressed like that.

"At least put on some shoes and a shirt. They're real sticklers for those."

As Jeff left the room, Sojoe looked at Henry and shook his head. "What?"

"If you're thinking of becoming a comedian, I have six words for you. Don't!"

"That's four letters."

"Don't Give Up Your Day Job!"

A short time later the three left the house. The sun was peeking through clusters of clouds, while squirrels played tag in the branches of an oak tree. Jeff and the boys were getting into Sojoe's car when they heard a car horn. They watched as Carol pulled up behind them.

"Jeff," she called as she got out of her car and rushed toward them. "I just met a friend of yours."

"A friend of mine? Who?"

"Detective Bradshaw."

"What! What did he want? Did he ask you about me?"

"There's been another murder. He asked me all about her. Were we friends? Did she have a boyfriend? Did I know anyone who might have killed her? Stuff like that."

"Her? Who?"

"You'll never guess. Not in a million years. Guess. Go ahead, guess."

"Stop playing games, Carol, I'm not in the mood. Tell me or we're going to get in this car and leave," he said, in his no-nonsense tone of voice.

"You're going to love this..."

"I mean it! You're not making sense. Why would I love to hear that someone was killed?"

"Okay, spoilsport. It was Fran."

"Fran? Fran who?"

"You know, nutty Fran Major."

"What? How?"

"He said she was killed with a knife, but he has your knife, so it couldn't be you. Get it? I rushed right over to tell you. That means you're off the hook—right? You couldn't have killed her. Now maybe they'll believe that you couldn't have killed Don, either."

"Jazus Cryst! We've got a serial killer in Venice. So much for the Living in Paradise slogan, they keep writing in the papers."

Sojoe ran his hand over his buzz-cut hair, thinking.

"I wonder, could this incident get you off?"

"Did they find another knife at the scene?" Henry asked.

"I don't know. He didn't say," Carol replied. "Jeff, how well did you know Fran?"

"Not well. I knew her, but that's about all. You know how it is in Venice, everybody knows everybody. I never went out with her, if that's what you mean."

"I didn't mean anything like that. But did you ever spend any time with her? Even if you ran into her at the grocery and people saw you together."

"I gave her a ride once. She needed to go to Sarasota for some reason. I gave her a ride, that's all."

"Just out of the blue you take that weirdo to Sarasota. That sounds fishy." Sojoe gave Henry a knowing wink.

"Don't be an ass. I had an appointment in Bradenton, and it was on my way. That's all."

"And he just happened to stop in a secluded place along the way and got himself a little piece of the pie," Sojoe added, trying his best not to burst out laughing.

"Oh yeah, Jeffrey got him some," Henry added.

"Knock it off! I told you I didn't know, or like that foulmouthed bitch!"

"So, you never stopped. Is that what you're saying?" Sojoe egged him on.

"I stopped for gas. That's the only stop I made. Now, knock it off or I'm going back in the house."

The three stifled a laugh.

"Go away, Carol. And you," he said poking each guy in the chest. "Get in the fucking car!"

~ 44 ~

The cell phone on the desk began ringing. Bradshaw turned away from the evidence box marked "FRANCIS KATHERINE MAJOR" and rushed to the desk. He recognized the number and hit the green icon.

"Hello, Fred. What have you got?"

"Not a lot, Syl. Female, Caucasian, around 36 years old. Besides the removal of the tongue, the victim was in moderate health. She had an oversize kidney and fatty tissue around the heart that would have caused trouble later in life. Needle marks indicated that she used drugs. There was a triangular indentation on her right index finger; most likely from a cut that left a permanent scar. Also, her hymen was intact."

"What?"

"Well, another word for it is maidenhead. That tells me she had never had sex—hard to believe in this day and age. That's about it."

"Okay, Fred. Thanks. Send me the report." Bradshaw punched the red icon and laid the phone down. He stood thinking for a long moment.

"What was that he said? There is something... hm. I can't put my finger on it."

Bradshaw returned to the evidence box. He picked up one item, looked it over, and put it aside before taking another. His attention was drawn to a small piece of paper. The word BOLIVAR arced over the picture of a man, HABANA, and CUBA, and it was encircled in gold. Bradshaw held it up for a closer look.

"I've seen this before; but where?" He thought for a moment before it came to him. "I've got it!" he shouted. Just then another thought came to him. "Holy Shit! It's a twofer! He found the evidence box marked DONALD MACKENZIE and rummage through it. There, in the folder was the report. Two fingerprints were found on Jeff Markison's knife— his, and an anonymous print with a triangular indentation on the right index finger.

"Kincaid, call the airlines and find out who has traveled to Cuba in the last year. We're looking for the name Smallwood."

"Wouldn't it be quicker to check who sells that brand?"

"When traveling abroad, people can bring them back into the U.S. for personal use. But if anyone is caught selling Cuban cigars within the U.S. they are subject to fines and other penalties."

A little time later, Brian returned. "I got 30 names of people in and around Venice. One is Nate Smallwood."

"I thought so. Kincaid! Get your walking shoes on. We're making another road trip!"

Once again, the pair was en route. They drove past the five mature magnolia trees and pulled into one of the many empty parking places in front of the Jaguar Boat and Supply. They pushed through the double doors and saw Nate talking to the old bookkeeper they'd seen on their last visit. Nate heard them walk in and turned expecting to see a customer. The jovial, *you've come to the right place if you're looking for an exciting new boat* expression dropped like an anvil.

"Oh, it's you. What do you want now?"

"We just have a few questions. I hope we're not interrupting anything."

"Well, you are. What is it this time?"

"Let's talk in your office," Bradshaw said, in his no-nonsense tone, and headed there. Bradshaw went directly to the Bolivar Belicoso Fino cigar dress box that sat on the cluttered bookcase behind the desk.

"How many people in Sarasota County smoke this brand of cigar?" he asked, removing one from the box.

"How the hell would I know that?" His attitude suddenly went from anger to haughty. "Those are a pretty special brand that few people can afford. Why, did you want to buy one? I'll sell you one for $25.00," the fat man said, his manner arrogant.

"Are you offering me a bribe, Mr. Smallwood?"

"What! Do you *buy* bribes these days! What are you talking about?"

"Certainly, you're aware that it's against the law to sell Cuban cigars in the U.S."

Smallwood reeled, then thinking quickly he responded. "I was kidding... I wouldn't sell you the wrapper it came in!"

"Funny you mention the wrapper, I happen to have a wrapper just like this one," he said pointing to the cigar he'd removed.

"So?"

"So, we found it near the body of Fran Major, and as you said, they are a pretty special brand that few can afford."

The man was no longer the arrogant, pompous businessman. He went white, and perspiration beaded on his forehead as he sat down hard in his padded chair.

"Why are you here? Are you accusing me of murdering that girl? I hardly knew her. I ran into her from time to time, that's all. I didn't have a beef with her, why would I kill her?"

"Only you would know that. Did she owe you money? Is that why you killed her?"

"I told you, I didn't kill her."

"When did you see her last?"

The fat man was quiet for a moment thinking. "It was at the Weinberger's engagement party. She came to me. I didn't search her out."

"Why would she search you out?"

"She, uh... she owed me money, but she said she didn't have any. Instead, she wanted to barter."

"Barter?"

"Yes, she had this knife..." He turned to the lamp, "It's right here." He shuffled the items on his desk searching. "It was right here!"

"What did it look like?"

Nate stammered as he tried to remember, and wiped perspiration from his face with the back of his hand. "I don't understand—it *was* right here. It was in a scabbard with a design of some sort. The knife itself had a name stamped along the thick edge—maybe the manufacturer—and a bone-like handle. That's all I remember."

"Did it look like this?" Bradshaw asked as he pulled a photograph from an envelope in his pocket.

Smallwood saw the scabbard. Below it was the side of the blade with the words 'J Marttiini Finland, Hand Ground Stainless,' but the print in the picture was too small to read. The third was a close up of the initials J. M.

"I'm not sure, but it looks the same. I don't know what happened to it, that's the truth, and I certainly didn't kill her."

"I'm not going to arrest you just yet. But you certainly are a person of interest in this case." Bradshaw put the photo and envelope back in his pocket. "Don't leave town, Mr. Smallwood. We might have more questions for you."

They left the building and headed for the car.

"I find that curious," Brian said.

"What's that?"

"He thought the knife killed the woman. He said nothing about the man."

"You caught that too, did you?" Bradshaw asked.

~ 46 ~

A dim flickering light from somewhere allowed Boatman to look around the dark and silent room. He didn't know where he was, but he had a strong compulsion to continue looking. The light came from the next room. He moved past an overstuffed chair and along a wall with large pictures of boats. As he approached the door that stood slightly ajar, the rays of flickering light outlining the door became intense. With each step, he grew more and more apprehensive.

When he touched the door to push it open, a feeling of dread came over him. Boatman froze. He felt compelled to continue, but suddenly he couldn't move. He wanted to run, to get out of this place, but it was as if his feet were stuck in tar. He was helpless. He tried with all his might. He grabbed his legs with his hands and tried to pull his legs free. Just then the door moved. As if in slow motion, it inched back. Little by little, it opened, and the flickering light became even more intense. Boatman could not make out the source of the light as it was impossible to look into the brilliance.

Suddenly, an ear-piercing high-pitched scream sounded. Boatman automatically covered his ears, but the screaming did not stop. The sound steadily grew louder until he could not stand it any longer, and in a fit of panic Boatman himself screamed.

Everything instantly grew quiet. He could move and backed away from the door. The bright light slowly faded, and Boatman looked around the room. It was empty. There were no windows, no furniture, no light fixtures only a book. The cover was closing on the leather-bound book that bore intricately carved symbols. As the cover closed, Boatman noticed that the last of the flickering light inside went out completely.

Boatman opened his eyes, and when he saw that he was safely in his home, he gave a sigh of relief. He sat for a moment absorbing what he had just experienced. These visions or insights, or whatever they were had meanings, but he could never figure out what they meant until something in real life happened to make them clear.

He got up and went to the kitchen and was pouring himself a drink of water when the doorbell rang. Boatman went to the door to find Detective Bradshaw.

"Well, hello again," he said.

"Hope you don't mind my stopping by unannounced, but I brought you MacKenzie's things."

"Oh, yeah, thanks." He opened the door, and the detective came in with a sealed box bearing the name DONALD MACKENZIE. "Just put it on the table over there."

"Most of it came out of the truck, but a few things were on him when it happened."

Boatman followed him to the table. "I should go through it before his family arrives."

"That's a good idea. It's been my experience that when a family member opens it, they may find something inside that brings them even more grief."

Boatman broke the tape sealing the box and opened it. Inside he saw Don's watch and picked it up. "The crystal is broken."

"It probably happened during the attack."

"Oh." He reached for the wallet. I gave this to him for Christmas last year." He thumbed through the contents. "I see his licenses and credit cards are still here."

"The attacker wasn't after his money."

"That begs the question, why? Detective Bradshaw, for the life of me I cannot think why anyone would kill Don. He was the epitome of peace and kindness."

"We have the knife and its owner. We're still investigating the case, but it looks like we've got our killer."

"I know Jeff, and I can't see him killing anyone. His sister is a good friend of mine, and if he had violent tendencies, I'd know it." He brushed through the items in the box. He spotted Don's college ring, a key ring Don had purchased in Naples from a street vendor, and the clip containing his business cards. The glossy cards bore the names of both of the owners, phone numbers, and *Able Seaman Charters* superimposed over a picture of the boat.

"I remember when he got these. He was excited to start handing them out. He had a lot of ideas for building the business, and he couldn't wait to begin."

"I cannot do anything to take away the loss of your friend but catching his killer and putting him away will help remove the stress and bring you and the family closure."

Boatman shuffled the items in the box as if looking for something. "Where is his journal? Didn't you find his journal? He always kept it with him. He didn't want to be without it in case a customer called."

"Really," Bradshaw looked in the box. "This is all we found. How big was this journal?"

"About 6 x 9 inches. It was a leather-bound hand-tooled book that I gave him when we bought the house. He kept everything in it. It was like a diary."

"Are you sure it isn't here in the house somewhere?"

"He always had it with him."

"Did many people know about this book?"

"He didn't keep it a secret, but of course, he didn't broadcast it either. I imagine it held a record of all the times he saw Dixie, and maybe even what they discussed. He kept notes on people he met, especially those who he liked or didn't like, and why."

"That's interesting. Could this be what the attacker wanted when your friend was killed? Would you happen to have a picture of this journal?"

"No, I don't think so, but it has voodoo symbols all over the dark walnut cover which overlaps, and ties holding it closed. It had belonged to a friend of mine from the West Indies." Boatman suddenly paused, lost in thought.

"What is it, Son?"

"I hesitate to tell people this because in this country many don't understand. Do you have an open mind, Detective?"

"Well, I've seen a lot in my line of work, if that's what you mean."

"When I was studying in the West Indies, I discovered that I have an ability—some call it a gift. I wouldn't call it a gift, I find it more of a curse, but I have it just the same."

"Are you speaking of the paranormal?"

"Yes. That's what I'm saying. When I was in college, the students were experimenting with mental telepathy, voodoo, and other forms of the paranormal. I have visions. I, I think I've always had them, but I thought they were just dreams. They're quirky. I see things, actions, and symbols that don't make sense until something happens like in my vision."

"For instance?"

"A while ago I had a vision that I was in a dark house. A flickering light, similar to a candle burning in another room, drew my attention. When I got close to the door of the room, the flickering grew into a blinding light. I was scared to death, and yet unable to run. It was horrible; then someone screamed. It was a high-pitched scream like that of a woman. Then the door opened, the light faded, and I saw a book hanging in mid-air. The fading light came from the book. As the book cover closed, the light diminished."

"Do you have these dreams or visions often?"

"They are coming more and more frequently."

"You say the book a hand-tooled and leather-bound?"

"Yes. It wasn't identical to Don's, but now I think it was symbolic, you know?"

"Are you aware that a woman was murdered last Friday?"

"No. Who was it? How was she killed?"

"Her name was Francis Major."

"I know a Fran Major. How was she killed?"

"She was stabbed and mutilated."

"Oh my god! How awful! Do you have any idea who did it?"

"We're investigating it. We're wondering if the attacker is the same one who killed MacKenzie."

"I wish I had a better understanding of these visions. I suspect the book I saw represented Don's journal. The screaming woman might have represented Fran, but the visions are so symbolic I can't be sure."

Well, I have to get back. I'll look for the journal, but I assure you it wasn't among his belongings. If you come up with any other dreams or ideas, don't hesitate to contact me."

Boatman walked him to the door. "Yes, Sir, I will."

Tuesday, June 23, 2020

It was another fine day in Paradise. Wispy clouds held the sun and heat at bay but could not protect anyone from the humidity or failed plans.

"I understand, Miss Oakley. She was unwell and simply forgot to notify you that she could not make her appointment. She's much better. Could we reschedule her fitting for tomorrow? Of course, I'll be happy to pay for the missed session, and you may bill it directly to me— David Weinberger. I believe you have the address.

There was a knock on the door.

"3:30 tomorrow afternoon. Yes, and thank you for being so understanding. Good-bye," he hung up. "Come in."

Jacob entered.

"What do you want? I'm very busy."

"I'm sure you are, getting ready for the wedding and all. But I have received a bill from United Wedges, International. I don't recall either ordering or receiving anything from them. I thought perhaps you did and put my name and number on the order by mistake."

"You must have forgotten it. I don't make mistakes."

"No, I checked my orders, and there is nothing for United Wedges, International."

"Well, go check again. I told you, I'm very busy."

"David, this bill is for $47,582! I would never have forgotten anything like that!"

David slapped his hands on the desk and rose to his feet. "Are you calling me a liar, boy?"

"No, Sir. I'm simply bringing this problem to your attention and assume you'll take care of it." He bit his lip and tried to stay calm, but his voice was rising. "I'm trying to tell you that I didn't order this, and I have no intention of paying for it."

David was almost always able to keep his emotions in check, but his problems with Dixie and setbacks in his secret dark side projects have him on edge. It was futile to try to talk to him at times like this.

"You will remember that I gave you this job. I agreed that you could marry my daughter, and I even promoted you with a hefty salary! Maybe I made a mistake. Am I going to regret my action? Maybe I should let you go?"

There was a long pause as Jacob considered. "No, Sir. You're right. I must have missed something in my search. I'll go back and look again. I'm sorry I bothered you."

He closed the door again as he left, and then stormed down the hall hitting his fist into his palm. "I'll pay the fucking bill AND marry your daughter, old man. Then you can kiss this world good-bye—both of you!" he sneered. "Why not pay it? I'll get my money back 100-fold when you're gone, Boy! Enjoy your wealth while it lasts. Twelve days from now it will all be mine!"

~ 48 ~

Tuesday was usually quiet at Bennett's grocery, as most customers do their shopping on Wednesdays when the newspapers ran their BOGO ads and coupons. On Fridays, homeowners come to beat the Saturday crowds stocking up for the weekends.

Autumn enjoyed the laid-back calm of going on Tuesdays. Her list today consisted of salmon, black beans, and rice; staples included bread, butter and eggs; and fresh vegetables: spinach, Romain, broccoli, cauliflower, peas, and carrots; and today she treated herself to freshly-cut long-stem roses and baby's breath.

She was checking her list when she heard a male voice.

"Well, we meet again."

The voice wasn't familiar, but when she turned, she recognized the brown framed glasses, simple mustache, and sparse beard of the man she'd seen in Carmen's office earlier. She smiled.

"Do you live around here?" he asked, pushing his cart to the side in case other shoppers needed to get by.

"Yes. I thought I was one of the few who shopped on Tuesdays."

"I'm renting a small condo nearby and figured I'd better stock up before things get busy."

"I take it you're here on business."

"Are you psychic?" He raised an eyebrow in a comical way.

"No," she laughed. "I heard you tell Carmen that you were eager to finish and get back."

"That's true, I do have cases on my desk that need my attention, but I imagine I'll be here for a while." He noticed her quick smile, lovely hazel eyes, and straight white teeth.

"Venice is quite lovely. When the snowbirds leave, the cultural events go on hiatus, but we still have the beach, good restaurants, and enjoyable nightlife. I hope you can enjoy some of it while you're here."

"Maybe we could meet for a cup of coffee?"

"I'd like that." She liked his subtle sense of humor, and she couldn't miss the fact that his brown eyes were the same color as his framed glasses.

"Now?"

"Yes, now. Unless you have something pressing that you have to attend to."

"Well," she said, pointing to her cart. "What about the groceries?"

"Do you have ice cream in there?" He gave the cart a cursory look and smiled.

"No," she said, then laughed, deciding that nothing in her cart would go bad in the time it took to have a coffee, or two. "I would enjoy a coffee-break."

Together they pushed their carts to the glassed-in break area behind the deli. Larry pulled out a chair for Autumn.

"I'll take mine black," she said, with a smile. "They have enough condiments here to make the coffee taste like hot chocolate. Just the way I like it."

"You are a unique woman, Ms. Mariiweather."

Autumn reached into her purse and pulled out a small compact that had belonged to her mother. The round silver container held a small beveled mirror. Originally, it had held face powder and a fitted powder puff. She checked her reflection. Her lipstick had long since gone away, but it would be useless to reapply it and then smear it all over a coffee cup. *Besides,* she thought, *it's too late now to make a good first impression.*

Larry was back in no time with a tray holding a Berghoff Stainless Steel Vacuum Flask, 2 porcelain cups, and two apple fritters larger than the saucers they rested on.

"Oh, my! How did you know apple fritters are my favorite pastry? She asked as she took the items from the tray and set them on the table.

"Good. They happen to be mine, too."

"My husband, Richard used to bring me some when I was under the weather or especially stressed. I've missed that."

"Oh, I didn't know you were married."

"Well, I'm not, not anymore. He died several years ago."

"I'm sorry."

"Are you married?"

"Not anymore. My wife left me and later divorced me."

"I'm sorry."

"She said that I took my work too seriously and was always away from home. I stayed late doing paperwork and got home around ten p.m. She took all her clothes and most of the furniture. There was a note, something to the effect that she couldn't live like that anymore and was filing for divorce, 'and by the way, there is dinner in the oven.' That was almost ten years ago. She's happily married to an accountant who works out of their home."

"So, are you a workaholic that can't find your way home?"

He laughed. "When she walked out, she left me with nothing better to do than work. I wonder sometimes now whether it was cause or result? I had great expectations when we got married, but little by little we grew apart. I can't say our marriage was a happy one. We were content, but I don't think either of us was happy. Enough about me, how are you doing?"

"Better by the day. I've begun writing again, and Mrs. Wilburn, a woman who came to live with me, helps me keep my sanity. I didn't think I could go on when Richard died. I had bouts of critical depression and went through many terrible months."

Larry saw that she was beginning to tear up. He reached over and laid his hand on hers. "Take a deep breath and let it out slowly. It helps. You're right, it will continue to get better by the day. You'll never forget him, but it will hurt less in time."

He knew how she felt and wanted to help, but he also knew that she would have to handle it her own way. He lifted her hand and kissed it, and then poured each of them some coffee.

For the next hour and a half, and three cups of coffee later, they talked about her pending book, his work ethic, Jeff's current trouble, his meeting Carmen, their favorite novelists, operas, and movies. They talked about his work schedule; she talked about hers; and explained what they loved and hated in the world.

As they pushed the carts through the parking lot preparing to go their separate ways, he stopped. "I have really enjoyed your company this afternoon. May I take you to dinner?"

"I'd like that. When?"

He looked at his watch. "I have to take these groceries to the condo and make a few phone calls. Would seven p.m. be too late? They have wonderful seafood at Phillippi Creek."

"Tonight?" She paused—thinking. "I could... Yes, I'd like that very much. Shall I meet you there?"

"Or I could just swing by and pick you up."

"Oh, all right." She reached into her purse and pulled out her business card. "Here's my address and phone number."

"Great. I'll be there 7ish. Do we need a reservation?"

"Not this time of year," she smiled. She had enjoyed this time with him. In her heart, she felt that they would become friends, and that voice in her head whispered, *Richard would like this guy*. "I'll see you then."

Dixie paced the floor of her bedroom in deep thought. This had once been the scene of her happiest moments. Today the sun cast bits of sunshine through the trees making living designs on the wall above the bed. She closed her eyes remembering him. In her mind she could hear his sweet proposals to leave this place, to go away where they could have peace and live happily together. She wanted to remember the warmth of that moment. She wished so badly to feel his touch, hear his voice, and smell the presence of him. Tears welled at the fact that it would never happen again. She held back the sobs that cried to be released.

Dixie took a tissue from the nightstand and dabbed at her eyes as she walked to the window. She pulled back the curtain and searched the grounds. She saw Don plucking dead flowers from the Begonias, trimming the Indian Hawthorne, watering the newly planted Juniper Blue Rug. She turned away. Of course, he wasn't there. No matter how much she wished it, he would never be there again.

She went into her bathroom, reached in and started the water running in the shower, and stripped off her nightgown. The warm water pulsing off her body was comforting. Don reached out and stroked her back as he had done so many times in the past. She closed her eyes and allowed her mind to bring back the loving memories. The water beating her brought back other memories. Jacob pushing her down, tearing her clothes, penetrating her mercilessly, defiling her, humiliating her, threatening her! She turned off the shower, wrapped herself in a towel, and got out. She was drying her hair when she heard a knock at the bedroom door. But before she could answer, it opened, and David walked in. He went directly to her bathroom.

"I see you're getting ready. Good. Your fitting appointment has been rescheduled. You don't want to be late."

"I'm sorry you went to so much trouble, Daddy, but I'm not going," she said in a tone he had not heard her use before.

"Of course, you're going. Don't be ridiculous."

"I'm not marrying Jacob, either."

"Now don't start that again. This is the best thing for you. He'll take care of you and you'll want for nothing. You know, I've always taken care of you..."

"Oh yes. You've always made me do what you wanted. You never cared about what I might want. It's always been your way." She was surprised to hear her voice rising.

"How can you say that? Haven't I always given you whatever you wanted?"

"You've always given me what *you* wanted! You don't hear me. You don't listen! You would rather I marry someone you choose—a man I don't love..., No, I don't even like him. Hell, I hate him, and I refuse to spend another moment around him!"

"You're just nervous about the wedding. I understand that all women experience this, it's natural. You feel this way now, but in a while, you'll come to your senses and agree that this is the best thing for you. Jacob is just that. He's a successful businessman. He makes a fortune, and he will keep you…"

"Wrong again, Daddy! My god, are you blind? He's a controlling egotist. Life with him would be a nightmare. I'd be in fear for my very life!"

"Oh, stop the drama. You always exaggerate. You're making this up hoping I'll change my mind."

"NO! He hit me and hurt me! Then he promised to do it again! He said that once we were married, he could do anything to me that he wanted!"

"What? When?"

"I tried to tell you that day in your office, but Jacob told you that I fell, and you chose to believe him. Once again, you wouldn't hear me. I was bruised and hurt, and you still listened to him!"

"Dixie, I've never seen you like this. Now, get dressed and make that appointment."

"You know, the other day I told Autumn," she began—her voice calm but assured, "that I did not think I could be happy living without money and the things it buys. But in the end, I'm going to try. Rather than marry a man I don't like or respect, I will change."

"I'm sorry he hit you. Truly I am, and I intend to speak to him about it."

"Don't you get it? There is nothing you can say or do to keep him from raping me again."

"Rape! He raped you?" His whole demeanor changed. "He raped you? I… I didn't know that." David's anger swelled. "That son of a bitch! I offered him everything, and this is how he repays me?" He turned and stormed out of the room.

"I look forward to a new life," she said to the empty room. "Please, Don. Watch over me and I won't fail."

David was furious as he stormed down the hall to the guest room. He didn't bother knocking but barged right in. "Jacob!" he shouted, but the room was empty. He checked the bathroom and found it empty too. Exasperated, he left the room.

It was a little after four o'clock when Jacob got to David's study. He walked in and sat his briefcase on the floor. David was finishing his third *Johnny Blue* and looked up when the young man entered. Instantly David charged and slammed the cocktail glass over the man's left ear, showering him with glass chards, liquor, and ice.

"You worthless piece of human flesh!" David bellowed, obviously drunk and somewhat unbalanced. "I bring you into my business, my home, I promise my daughter to you, I introduce you to influential people, and how do you repay me, by raping my daughter?"

Jacob was just recovering from the surprise attack when David sucker-punched him in the gut and knocked him to the floor. When the younger man tried to get up, David kicked him.

"Wait." He stammered, then crab-crawled in an attempt to get away. Blood ran off his face and trickled onto his State & Liberty shirt. David was merciless and kicked him again before he stumbled. Jacob managed to get behind the chair where the older man could not reach him.

"Stop! Let's talk!" He brushed at the stream of blood and *Johnny Blue* smearing his face and hand.

David grabbed the arm of the chair and threw it aside, but Jacob had time to get to his feet and ward off a wild punch. He quickly got the desk between himself and his assailant, but David seized the stapler off the desk and threw it. He was red-faced and weaving. Whether it was the effect of the alcohol or he was out of condition he paused and leaned on the desk.

"You have thirty minutes to pack your things and get out of my house or I will shoot you on the spot!" He was breathing heavily, but his tone left no question as to his intent.

Jacob backed away, and when he was sure David wasn't going after him, he rushed out the door. Even before he reached the stairs, he'd pulled out his cell phone and hit speed dial.

"Hello," came a raspy voice.

"We have to meet; There's a problem."

~ 50 ~

Autumn sat the bags of groceries on the counter. She took out the bread, dinner rolls, and ground coffee and put them in the refrigerator to keep them fresh. She put the cereal, tea, salt, and steak sauce in the pantry.

"Mrs. Wilburn, I ran into that FBI officer that I told you about. We had coffee and talked a while. He's really quite nice. Oh, and I won't be here for dinner."

"Oh?" The eyes of the older woman lit up. "Why is that?" The expression on her face made it obvious that she already knew the answer.

"Well," Autumn hesitated, feeling a little self-conscious. "He asked me to have dinner with him."

"I see." She picked up one of the paper bags and folded it before taking the second. "Coffee in the afternoon and dinner the same night? Hmm..."

"Oh, stop. It's just dinner." Autumn could not hold back a grin. "A dinner with a friend, that's all."

"It's good to have friends to share a meal with."

"Right. Dinner with a friend, that's all."

Just then her cell phone rang. Autumn reached into her purse and pulled it out and hit the green icon. "Hello,"

"Autumn, it's Boatman. Bradshaw was here; he returned Don's personal items. Don kept a journal, like an appointment book. He kept it with him all the time, but Bradshaw never found it. The question came up that the killer might have taken it. The book may have been the reason for the murder."

"Could Don have accidentally left it home?"

"Not likely. He told me once that if people had a clue what was in it there'd be hell to pay. Apparently, he wrote things in it like a diary."

"What can I do?"

"You know a lot of people. If you hear any mention of such a book, will you let me know? Bradshaw knows, and now you know. I believe we're the only ones who do. I don't know how we'll find it if we can't tell anyone. I'm at a loss."

"I know a man who's with the FBI. Would it be all right if I spoke to him about it?"

"Autumn, I trust you. Use your own judgment but be careful. If Don was killed for this book, then it's a very dangerous item."

"I'll be careful."

~ 51 ~

Mrs. Wilburn was dusting the furniture when she saw a car pull into the driveway. She had just enough time to put the cleaning items away before there was a knock at the door.

"Hi, is Autumn at home? I got off work a bit early and thought I'd invite myself over for some coffee, or tea, or whatever you have at this hour." She started to walk to the study but turned back. "Oh, I'm sorry. I'm Carol Tanaka. You must be Mrs. Wilburn. Yes, of course, you are. Sorry, I need to talk to Autumn. Is she busy?"

"Miss Tanaka, it is nice to finally meet you. Yes, Autumn is in her study. Why don't you see if you can pull her away from her computer, and I'll fix you a glass of iced tea."

"Thank you," she said and quickly walked away.

Mrs. Wilburn went to the kitchen and pulled a tray from the cabinet. She collected two napkins, two iced teaspoons, a plate of cookies, and two Villeroy & Bosh tumblers molded to resemble ice cubes. These were placed on the tray. The ice cubes made little tinkling sounds when she dropped them in and then added a lightly sweetened tea. The aroma of banana and orange wafted as she carried it out of the room.

"Oh, Mrs. Wilburn, thank you." Autumn pulled magazines to the side so the tray could be set on the coffee table. "Aren't you going to join us?"

"Thank you, dear. You girls sit and enjoy your drinks. I have a few things to do in the kitchen but let me know if you need anything else." With that, she was gone.

"What a nice surprise, Carol. How did you happen to get off early?"

"Actually, I told them I had a dentist appointment and had to leave early."

"Oh?"

"I was working at the drive-through window when a guy pulled up in his truck and gave me some checks to cash. When I handed him his receipt, I remembered something! I couldn't wait to tell you."

"You seem pretty excited. What is it?"

"Oh my god, how could I have forgotten this? And then to be reminded by the guy's truck. I couldn't get out of the bank fast enough. My mind was racing all the way to your house."

"I guess this is a good thing, right?"

"Oh, you know it! Wait till I tell you!"

"I can't wait..."

"Trust me, it's worth the wait!"

"Carol, tell me!"

"I don't remember exactly when it happened, but it was some months ago. Fran came into the bank to make a deposit. You know how she is—well was—anyway, she was so rude, and I hated waiting on her because you never knew what would come out of her mouth. Anyway, she couldn't find her pen. You know we have one at every station, but she didn't want to use ours. She insisted on using her own, but she couldn't find it in her bag. So, she turned it upside down, dumping the contents. Oh my god, I was so embarrassed, and of course, she was cursing up a storm."

"And you came all this way to tell me this?"

"No, I came all this way to tell you she had Jeff's knife!"

"What!"

"Oh yes. As she was putting everything back, I saw the knife in its scabbard and picked it up. I asked her what it was for, and she said it's just a little thing I picked up. I asked her from whom, and she said this guy gave me a ride in his truck. I asked her what guy, what truck, and she said the truck was just like Jeff's! You know, she never gave you a straight answer.

"But what made you think it was Jeff's?"

"We were out drinking a couple of years ago, and he had it. He said it was a birthday present. He showed me the initials on the blade."

"Oh, Carol. This is the information we need! It proves that Jeff didn't kill Don."

"Of course, Jeff wouldn't kill Don or anybody! Well, not with a weapon. He might drink them to death, but he wouldn't even do that on purpose."

"Do you think Fran killed Don?"

"I don't know that. I never knew her to be physical, but she could sure skin you alive with her foul mouth."

"If she didn't kill him, who'd she give the knife to?'

"The killer..." Carol's eyes were huge as she looked off in space. "And Fran was killed."

"We have to get this information to..." she stopped as another thought came to her. "But to whom? Bradshaw? Carmen?"

~ 52 ~

It rained off and on in the afternoon bringing the humidity up. Thunder bellowed and a light show played in the distance.

David had still not gotten over the day's confrontation. He had planned the next five years: Jacob would marry Dixie, the business would grow two-fold with the young man's contribution, and he could begin to plan his retirement. That had all changed now. Jacob had left and not a word had been heard from him since. Dixie had been so thrilled with David's action that she threw herself into his arms and kissed him on the cheek. He was caught off guard. In spite of all he had given her through the years, she had never responded in that way before. He wished she felt that way all the time. Tonight, he had instructed Mary to make Dixie's favorite meal and set the dining room table for the two of them.

Dixie walked into the room and saw David seated at the head of the table.

"What's all this?" His daughter noticed that the second place-setting was just to her father's right. Normally, her place was at the other end. Normally? Nothing felt normal. Jacob had not been around the house all day. That alone made for a much more pleasant Bedwick Mansion.

"I thought it would be easier for us to talk if we sat closer together. You should know that I *was* listening when we talked this morning. Being a parent is not an easy job, and I've made a lot of mistakes, but I hope to rectify that. Please, sit down."

"What do you want to talk to me about?" She hesitated, but then took her place at the table.

"I was hoping we might talk with one another. No more one-sided conversations."

"Okay." She was skeptical. "What do *we* want to talk about?"

"Oh, our future might be a good way to begin. Have you thought about what you want to do?"

"I intend to change my life."

"That is a good way to start. Have you thought about how?"

"Don't start that same argument about what will I do for money!"

"Actually, I wondered if you had thought about getting a job or taking some classes."

"What are you getting at? So, what if I do take a job? Would that be demeaning or too degrading for a Weinberger?"

"No. What is it you'd like to do?"

"I haven't decided."

"Have you made any decisions? I'm just curious."

"Well, I don't plan to live here much longer, that's for sure!"

"I'm sorry to hear that, but if that's what you want, I won't stand in your way."

"Really?"

"From now on I promise to try not to control you but don't get too upset if I back-slide from time to time. This is a new role for me, you know."

That made her laugh. "I do need to try living without your help. After all, I *am* old enough to make my own decisions, but don't get upset if I back-slide from time to time. This is a new role for me, you know."

They both laughed. David held up his water glass.

"Let's toast our new futures. To trying what we like and keeping our fingers crossed that it works out for us."

"Agreed!" they called in unison—clinking glasses.

"I think I will get my ducks in a row and begin planning my retirement. When I met Jacob, I saw my business grow bigger and better. But that was the old me. Dixie, I'm almost 65. Why do I need to work so hard? I have plenty of money. I own more property than a man needs, and honestly, I'm getting tired. You know, I've always felt that Napoleon should have quit while he was ahead. But he continued to push until he failed miserably. A man should learn from experience."

"I was afraid you and I would end up enemies, but if we stay on this new path, we will become great friends."

David rang the small bell on the table that gave Mary the signal to bring out the food.

~ 53 ~

At exactly 7 pm Mrs. Wilburn heard a knock at the door. "Autumn, your date is here."

"Stop that," she said just above a whisper and grinning. "Would you mind answering that while I finish dressing?"

Mrs. Wilburn went to the door. A charming man with a high forehead, short sandy hair, and dark-framed glasses smiled. "Good evening," he said.

The woman took note of his red and white checked shirt, tan slacks, and loafers—sans socks—and smiled back. She also approved of the simple mustache that sat just above his upper lip. "And to you. I'm Mrs. Wilburn. Autumn is almost ready. Do come in."

Autumn came from the hall placing the second earring. "You're right on time, while it seems I'm always a bit behind. Pierced earrings can be rascals to get on sometimes."

Mrs. Wilburn smiled as she passed Autumn on her way to the kitchen. "Enjoy your dinner."

"Thank you." Larry opened the door for Autumn. "She seems nice. I can see why you like her."

The evening was warm, but the air-conditioned car was most comfortable. They chatted about Mrs. Wilburn, the weather, and how nice it was that the traffic was minimal. Before long they were heading north on Tamiami Trail and passed Oscar Scherer State Park.

"We should plan a day to visit the state park. Have you been there?"

"Richard and I went there years ago, but it would be nice to go again. Are you an outdoors-man?"

"I enjoy fishing and sailing, but I'm really not the rough and rugged, mountain climbing type."

"A golfer, maybe?"

"No, chasing a little ball around is not my idea of fun. I'd rather count sheep than count strokes."

Autumn laughed. "I tried it a couple of times, but I found there are cheaper ways to embarrass myself."

He laughed. "Yes, I can relate to that. So, what do you do for fun?"

"Oh, the usual, I suppose. I read, and of course, I write. Richard and I used to go camping. We weren't the tent-type, more like finding a cottage on a lake where'd we fish and swim. Or find a spot in a forest and walk the trails and photograph the wildlife—that kind of thing." Her tone dropped, and her voice quivered. "But I haven't done anything like that since he... uh, he died."

A long silence filled the car.

"We just crossed Clark Road. Is it much farther? I'm starved."

"Uh... no." She cleared her throat of a sob that threatened to escape. "It isn't far now. It's just past of Constitution Boulevard. There it is, on the right."

They pulled off the highway and parked in front of the rustic restaurant. A young woman gave them menus and directed them to follow her. They passed the bar with a long row of straight back stool under a short blue awning above which was a huge shark.

"Would you like to fish for that?" he asked, pointing.

"I'll catch it if you clean it," she said with a wide grin.

The hostess took them to an oil cloth-covered picnic table sporting a roll of paper towels, a bottle of ketchup, and salt and pepper shakers. The menu cited oysters, lobster, fresh fish, prawns, and dozens of other tasty combos, steam pots, platters, treats, desserts, and beer and wine.

"Shall I take your drink orders while you look at the menu?"

"Yes," said Larry. "I'll have a tall Merlot."

"Um, I think I'd like a blush."

"Very good. I'll get those and be back."

"I know you drink white wine with fish, but I am in the mood for a tall glass of Merlot."

Autumn looked up and shivered.

"Are you cold? I have a sweater in the car."

"No, no. I'm fine. Thank you." She looked at him more closely. What was it about this man? She had met him only this morning, but she felt so comfortable with him.

When the waitress returned with their drinks, they gave her their choices: steamed shrimp dinner with baked potato, and seasonal vegetables for Autumn and Larry chose the fried seafood platter combination that included crab cake, oysters, scallops, shrimp, grouper, and clam strips with fries and coleslaw. Two glasses of wine later their food came, and they ate until they were satisfied. They passed on dessert preferring instead to just relax and enjoy their wine.

"Something happened today that I must share with you. You're in the business to know what I should do with this information. Several weeks ago, a man I know was murdered. He was stabbed to death with a fishing knife. The knife once belonged to my brother. He doesn't remember much about it or how he lost it, but the police figure he is their prime suspect. Today I learned that a woman I knew stole it from him without his knowledge. I'm sure she didn't murder Don, and a few days later she was found murdered. Who would have gotten the knife from her? Whoever it was is probably the culprit."

"Did the two victims know one another?"

"I'm sure they did. Venice is a small town. I doubt they ran around together, but I imagine they had met or at least knew of one another."

"Did either use drugs or have any enemies?"

"Don? I wouldn't think so. Not enemies or drugs. Fran? She might have both. She was extremely rude and foulmouthed. Most people I know avoided her, but kill her? I don't know."

"You need to give this information to the police. It could work on your brother's behalf. Was this Fran ever arrested?"

"I don't know."

"But you think she took drugs."

"I didn't know her well, but I heard she did."

"I'm here investigating a possible drug dealer. If the woman had a habit, she would have a dealer."

Autumn paused—and then continued. "There is one other thing. Don was Boatman's housemate and business partner. Boatman said that when Don's personal items were returned, a journal he had was not among them. Don kept a record of dates, addresses, clients, and thoughts or suspicions in it. He told Boatman it would be dangerous if people learned what was in the book."

"I'll look into things for you. Is Carmen your attorney?"

"Why, yes, how did you know...? Oh, of course. You saw me in her office."

"If you're finished, we can leave. I don't want Mrs. Wilburn putting out an APB because you're out after curfew. Tomorrow I'll explore some ideas I have and let you know."

"Oh, for the first time I feel like there is some hope. Thank you."

Wednesday, June 24, 2020

~ 54 ~

Mary knocked softly on the door of David's bedroom.

"Come in, Mary."

Still balancing the tray on her left hand, she opened the door. "Good morning, Mr. Weinberger. Here's your breakfast."

He was dressed, but his choice of clothes was considerably more casual than the norm. "Um, poached eggs, crisp sausages, toast and butter, orange juice, and coffee—my favorites. Thank you, Mary."

She laughed. "You get the same thing every morning." She laid everything out on the table by the window and went to open the drapes.

"Right you are. And I never tire of it."

"The paper is either late, or I'll find it among the bushes. Whichever, I'll find it and bring it up."

"Thank you." He took a sip of creamed coffee and sighed aloud. "Good from the very first drop," he said.

"You're in a cheerful mood today, Mr. Weinberger."

"Yes, I am, as I hope to be every day from this point on. Dixie and I had a long talk last night, and I think I'm seeing the world differently today."

"This *is* good news, sir."

"We have come up with new plans, Mary. Dixie tells me she wants to get a job and strike out on her own."

"Dixie told you that?"

"She did. And I told her that I'm going to plan my retirement. We have agreed to change our lives. She wants adventure, and I want less stress."

"I don't hear Jacob Crawford's name in either of these plans."

"You're right again, Ms. North. She and I agree that he is no longer in the picture, nor is he ever to return to the house. He has been evicted and fired. I don't ever want to see him again!"

"I'm happy for both of you, sir. Please excuse me. I think I'd better forage in the bushes if I'm ever to find the newspaper." She smiled sweetly—and sincerely—as she slipped out and closed the door behind her.

David ate his breakfast leisurely. There was no need to rush. This would be a day of firsts. He picked up the tethered phone next to his bed and hit speed-dial #1. He waited, and after the third ring he heard the familiar female voice say, "Good morning, Weinberger, Inc."

He smiled and said, "Beth, cancel my appointments and postpone my meetings for today. I have some personal business to take care of."

"Dare I guess, wedding preparations?"

He could hear the inquisitive tone in her voice, which had once annoyed him something awful, but today it was lilting and friendly.

"Another of your assignments today is to locate everyone involved with the wedding. That would be the preacher, florist, catering team, the Ritz Carlton wedding planner—cancel all of them, including the room reservations. Dixie has decided not to marry Jacob Crawford. Also, he should be in shortly to remove his things. He has been terminated, so go with him and make sure he takes only his own personal things. Any pending work of his will remain with us. Do you understand?"

"You mean no files, no computer downloads, no thumb drives, no corporate books or handouts, nothing," she said.

David thought he sensed an approving tone in her voice. "Be sure to get his keys to the front door and his office."

"Should I arrange for a severance check?"

"No. Call security before he arrives. Ask one of them to escort him through the building—in case he tries to give you any trouble."

"Yes, sir. Anything else?"

"Yes, I'll need you to pull all my deeds and have them at the reception desk. I'll pick them up around 11 a.m. Call Copeland and Varzea and make appoints for me as soon as possible. I'll be available on my cell if you need me. If I need anything else, I'll call you."

He hung up the phone with a smile. He hadn't felt like this—jovial—was the word, since the day he met Rosemary, and it was a very good feeling.

~ 55 ~

The day was cloudy, and the humidity hugged the air
like a wet mop. The gray atmosphere didn't help
Jacob's disposition. All morning he had practiced
what he would say to Frog. Frog had been elusive.
Ever since he called from the mansion there had been
no word from the big man. Jacob had left messages
several times to no avail. Then he tried to make an
appointment. Of course, Frog was a busy man. He
dabbled in numerous projects. Normally, Jacob
wouldn't approach him in his office. The Atlanta
fiasco had brought them together, and Frog had kept
him alive and funded his move to Venice. But even if
you didn't owe the man money, Frog was not a man
to cross. He needed to talk to him before he heard it
from someone else. He knew this would not please
the man, but he was confident that the deal was not
yet dead, and Jacob needed to reach him ASAP.

The car pulled into the last available parking place
in the rear of the building and went through the
archway. The office was on the second floor, and the
elevator was on the outside next to the stairs.
Awkward as it was to get to the office, once inside the
reception area had a magnificent view of Venice
Avenue.

"I have an appointment," he told the male
receptionist. "Your name please?"

"Jacob Crawford." He waited as the young man flipped pages of the appointment book.

"I'm sorry. I don't have an appointment for you."

"WHAT! I called early yesterday and was told to come in an hour. Then I got a call saying that was out and to come today!"

"Please don't shout, sir. I can't help it that your name isn't on the list, and he has a full schedule today. I have an opening Friday at 5:46 p.m."

"Friday!" He caught himself. If he made Frog mad, he might never get to see him, and he needed Frog on his side. "Okay. I'm sorry. It's just that it's crucial that I speak to him as soon as possible."

"I understand. Shall I pen you in for Friday, 5:46?"

"Yes, please. If he has a cancellation, could I see him then?"

"I'll do what I can." He wrote the name Jacob Crawford on the timeline and closed the book.

Jacob was fuming when he left the building. "The son of a bitch is stonewalling me. He can't know yet that David kicked me out, so why is he doing this?" He got to his car, got in, and backed out. He swerved enough turning onto Tamiami Trial that the driver in the next lane honked his horn.

"Oh, eat shit, Grandpa!" he yelled, as he flipped him off. "Goddamn gray hairs! If you can't drive defensibly, hang up your keys!"

Jacob was so annoyed at this point that he purposely ran the red light at Tampa Avenue, causing a Ford truck to leave tire tracks when he slammed on his brakes to avoid a collision. He was approaching the North bridge when the light turned red, the red and white arms began to drop down, and the mesh floor began to separate. Jacob floored the accelerator, made it across the split mesh, but broke the long arm on the far side before slamming through the next red light at Venice Bay Drive. When he reached the intersection at Urgent Care he screeched to a stop as a semi and fuel truck raced by heading north. He sat pounding the steering wheel, his left foot on the brake, and gunning the engine.

~ 56 ~

"**G**ood morning, Angel. How did you sleep?" asked the male voice on the phone.

"Very well, thank you," she said and caught his sweet salutation.

"I've had a very interesting morning. I talked to Bradshaw, and he's agreed to work with us on this case."

"Is it normal for local police and the FBI to work together? On TV they always seem to be so competitive."

"That's television for you. Actually, if he'll help me get my guy, I'll let him take credit for anything else."

"That's very nice of you. I take it you're a very giving person."

"Well, if you want to know the truth, it's my way of getting more time with you."

"Really?" She chuckled nervously. "I don't know what to say about that."

"That's okay. You'll like me better when you get to know me."

"Convinced?"

"Confident."

This made her laugh out loud.

"So, are you ready to play detective?"

"If it will help get Jeff out of trouble, I'm all for it. How do you want to begin?

"Let's meet with Bradshaw and compare notes. Shall I pick you up, say, in forty-five minutes? We can include lunch and then lay out a plan. What do you say?"

"I say, let's do it!"

A short time later they walked into the police station. Bradshaw was at the shelf that doubled as a coffee counter. The 18-year old percolator was burping away as it tried to make a decent brew.

"Mr. Bradshaw? I'm Larry Sparks. I called earlier." The two men shook hands. "This is Autumn Mariiweather, Jeff Markison's sister. Where can we talk?"

The detective showed them to his cubicle. "Here we are, my home away from home."

"Nice digs."

"Uh, don't say that too loud. I don't want to make the other guys jealous."

"Got 'cha." Larry put his briefcase on the table and opened it. "My assignment here is to locate and apprehend a drug dealer who we've been chasing for several years. We think he's changed his name and now lives here in Venice. Here's the rap sheet on him."

Bradshaw read it over. "He's been a busy boy. Do you have any pictures?"

"Oh yes. Here he is at 19. He was recruiting high school kids to pawn them off on their friends to create the habit. Once they were hooked, he'd step in and supply them. He served a little time but got out early for good behavior."

"He was a good-looking kid," Autumn said as she studied the picture.

"Yes. He got off easy because of his looks. People couldn't believe such an innocent looking kid could do such awful things. Here he is at 22." Larry handed the picture to Bradshaw, who glanced at it and handed it over to Autumn.

"What a shame." She handed it back to Larry.

"He's thirty in this one. Each time he was released from prison, he'd move, and we wouldn't hear about him for a while." He handed the photo page to Bradshaw. "And this is the last time we caught him. We were investigating a triple homicide and he was part of it."

Bradshaw took the snapshot and looked it over before handing it to Autumn.

"We were taking him from Omaha to Lincoln for processing. A fuel truck was hit by a Holland truck from Fargo, and all hell broke out. The fuel truck blew up, cars were dodging debris, and trying to avoid hitting one another; many failed. It caused a jam that blocked traffic for five hours. We handcuffed him to the post in the car and went to help, but somehow he got away, and we haven't seen him since."

"Oh, my, he changed so much I'd never recognize him."

"That's part of the problem. We figure he changed his name," Larry replied.

"These guys somehow find social security numbers that make them nearly invisible," Bradshaw added.

"That too," Larry replied. "We got an anonymous call that he was in the Venice area. He probably pissed off someone who knew him. That's often how we get these leads."

"I don't know if I can help with that but let me copy that last picture and pass it around. Maybe someone here can get a lead." Bradshaw looked around. "Brian," he called. The young officer responded. "Make 20 copies of this rap sheet and photo for me." He turned back to Larry and Autumn. "I'm sure you're here to help your brother, Ms. Mariiweather. Let me share what we have."

"Don MacKenzie was murdered late Monday night on the 15th of June." Bradshaw pulled the MacKenzie box from the small stack that was collecting in the corner and put it on the desk.

"We have the knife that was used, and as Ms. Mariiweather knows, it has her brother's initials on it. We interviewed a number of people he knew and worked for, but we got nothing from them. On the 20th a woman was stabbed and mutilated. The fact that we seldom have murders in Venice, and both were stabbed made us wonder if the two killings were related. Then we found a clue. A cigar wrapper was found at the woman's crime scene." He pulled out the sealed bag with the item. "The brand is Cuban, and one of the people I interviewed smokes that brand. That's not enough to bring him in, but we are keeping an eye on him."

"That's good news." In her excitement, Autumn reached over and squeezed Larry's hand. This made him smile.

"When I took MacKenzie's personal items to his house, the housemate remembered a journal the man had kept. He said MacKenzie intimated that it would be dangerous if people knew the contents. We're beginning to suspect that might be why he was killed." He turned to Autumn. "It's beginning to look like your brother did not do it."

"Thank God," she said.

"Autumn, tell the detective what you told me."

"We all knew Fran. She was a character. A friend of mine, Carol Tanaka, told me that she saw Fran with the knife. Fran told her that she got it from a guy in a truck—a truck that looked just like Jeff's."

"Ms. Tanaka didn't say anything like that when I questioned her."

"Well, she left work early and rushed to my house to tell me that she just remembered it. I don't believe she would purposely keep it from you."

"She was visibly nervous when we went to talk to her."

"Carol has a brother. He's been in a lot of trouble, and her parents have disowned him. He's in some sort of crime gang." She smiled. "He's her brother, and she worries about him. I imagine she would be nervous to see the police pull up."

"Are you talking about Heru Tanaka? I know him. He's a member of the Yakuza or ninkyō dantai, as they call themselves. It's one of the Japanese crime gangs," Larry said. "The ones I know are in Chicago, but they've been spotted as near as Atlanta."

"Neither Carol nor the family have anything to do with him. Naturally, they're afraid *for* him, but they're also afraid of him."

"Smallwood saw a picture of the knife. He said it looked like one he had, but he said someone stole it. He could have been lying, but he did seem genuinely surprised when he couldn't find it."

"Smallwood? Boatman used to work for him."

"Now he's an interesting character. He tells me he has dreams or something that are like clues." Bradshaw put the items back in their assigned boxes.

"He does," Autumn agreed, "When I ran into him at Dixie's engagement party, he said something bad would happen very soon. He didn't know what or when, but he was noticeably frightened."

"I appreciate your seeing us, Detective. I'm sure we can help one another with these cases. You have my number if you need to reach me, and vice versa."

"Yes, and thank you for sharing this information with us," Bradshaw answered, shaking their hands."

They turned and walked away. Bradshaw went back to the coffee shelf. He picked up the pot to pour himself a cup and found the percolator empty. He rolled his eyes, grabbed his fedora, and headed out the door.

"If anyone needs me, I'll be at Starbucks."

57

"**W**here would you like to go for lunch, Angel?" Larry asked as he opened the car door for her.

"Should we find some place in Venice? Where would you like to go from here?

"I'm thinking we might go look at boats."

"Boats? Seriously?"

"I'd like to meet this Smallwood at the Jaguar Boat and Supply. What better way to talk to the guy than on the pretext of making a purchase?

"In that case, let's go to Anita's in Nokomis."

"Anita's it is."

They drove the short distance and turned at the red-roofed building onto Magnolia Avenue and quickly into the parking lot. Inside the hostess led them to a booth near a window. The room was not over-crowded, and the light from all the windows added to the comfort. Larry smiled as he looked around.

"Autumn, did you see that blue 1957 Chevrolet on the wall above the entrance to the kitchen?"

"It's a real eye-catcher, that's for sure."

When the waitress returned with beverages, they gave her their order.

"I've been thinking. How would you like to do something on Saturday? It would be fun to get away from all this drama."

"What do you have in mind?"

"It's been ages since I've been to a zoo. I understand there's one in Orlando. It would be a nice drive, and we'd be outside, *walking on the wild side*." He laughed and took a drink of his sweet tea."

"You want to go to a zoo?" she gasped.

"Sure, it'd be fun. We'd see Florida Panthers, alligators, wolves, bears, and I understand they have a wonderful selection of birds."

"I don't know..." She was suddenly nervous.

"What is it? Come on, be a kid again. It'll be fun."

"I, uh... I don't think so. I don't think I could..."

"What? What is it, Angel?"

Autumn was visibly shaken. She began wringing her hands, and she started to sweat.

"Excuse me," she said and left the table.

Larry was confused. What had he said to disturb her so much? She was still gone when the waitress delivered their lunch. He was about to ask the waitress to check on her or even go himself when she returned. He could see immediately that she'd been crying. She sat down and opened her napkin. "Larry, I apologize. You must think I'm awful."

"No, I don't think any such thing, but I admit I'm confused."

"I owe you an explanation. I don't like to talk about it or even think about it for that matter. But I feel I should explain, especially after making such a scene." She choked on the words and tears began again. "I'm sorry. Give me a moment."

He reached over and laid his hand on hers. "It's okay. Take your time."

Slowly she began. She told him about the trip to the mountains, how they'd planned it for months. She talked about Richard and how happy they were together. How they'd enjoyed the little cottage on the lake. Then she told him about the day they had gone to the zoo, how they ran into the guards searching for the run-away bear, how Richard died, and how she'd lost all control and killed the bear with the ax.

"I still have flashbacks, and when I do, I'm completely incapacitated."

"Oh, Angel!" He moved to her side of the bench and put his arms around her. This brought more tears and he held her.

"I understand."

He held her until she stopped crying.

"Something like this can stay with us for years. You don't ever have to apologize for it." He lifted her chin. "We can leave if you like, or we can finish our lunch and go look at boats. What do you say?"

She smiled up at him. "Thank you for being so understanding. I'm feeling much better. Let's eat, and then we'll go boat-shopping."

Before long they were heading south on the by-pass. "There it is. Sunset Boulevard will take us right to the marina."

Larry slowed down to make the turn. The road was lined with numerous types of palm trees. Some were young and short, and others towered above giving the area the illusion of dense growth. Nonetheless, here and there were glimpses of the bay and houses accessible by shale driveways.

"Do you know this Smallwood?"

"Not really. I know Boatman worked for him when he came back from Jamaica.

"What's Boatman's story?"

"I have a lot of respect for him. His family is affluent, but he prefers a simpler lifestyle. We've been friends for years. Even while he was away at college, we wrote to one another. He's like a brother."

"I'd like to meet him."

"Oh, you will. This whole melodrama began when Don was killed. They were good friends. Boatman wishes he understood his gift better, so it could be used to help others. The night before Don died, Boatman sensed something, but he didn't know what it was. Now he feels guilty that he couldn't have prevented it."

"So, you don't feel he's faking?"

"Oh, heavens no!"

Before long they spotted the sign: Jaguar Boat and Supply shown prominently against the backdrop of magnolias. Larry noticed that there were four cars present. He pulled into the space nearest the door.

"Are you ready?"

"I am. But of course, I'm only here for the ride. You, Mr. Moneybags, are the one who wants to add a boat to your vast list of rolling stock." They both laughed.

"Keep your eyes open. I'd like to know who might belong to these cars. Obviously, the Jaguar parked in the shaded spot is Smallwood's." Larry said as they headed for the big glass double door entrance.

The showroom was void of people, so the two just walked around studying the models. Each had a thin stand displaying the brand and size of the model.

"What kind of boat are we looking for?" Autumn asked.

"I'm looking for speed, sleeping quarters, and ocean fishing. Preferably something that will sleep at least six."

Just then a teenage girl came into the showroom and approached the couple. She had a way of walking: a little nervous, a little jaunty, a little bit like a dance. She smiled.

"Hello, welcome to Jaguar Boat and Supply company. Have you been in before?" She put her hands behind her back, probably to keep them from shaking and giving away the fact that she was unaccustomed to talking to customers.

Autumn smiled. "No, this is our first time. Are you a saleswoman?"

"Uh, no. Well, not exactly. I'm Suzanne, the cashier. Mr. Smallwood is in a conference at the moment and asked that I speak to anyone who might come in."

"What can you tell us about the models here?" Larry asked.

"Well, as you can see, they are rather... uh, big and expensive." Her expression floundered. "What I mean to say is: you really get your money's worth when you purchase one of Jaguar's boats. Uh—or yachts."

Larry smiled at Autumn, then turned to the girl.

"How long do you expect Mr. Smallwood to be detained?'

"Gee, I don't know. We have a lot of books about boats. Would you like to see some of them?"

"Yes. I would. Could you show me? That might help us make up our minds," Autumn replied.

The girl cha-cha'd to the rack of books and magazines in an alcove with two upholstered chairs and a coffee table. "Please make yourself at home. Read all you like. May I get you a cup of coffee, or a candy bar, or something?"

"Coffee would be nice," Autumn's smile threatened to slip into a titter. She found the girl charming and innocent.

"Do you think *he* would want some?" the girl asked in a conspiratorial tone just above a whisper.

"I don't believe so," Autumn replied in a similar tone.

The girl seemed happy with the response and danced off to get the coffee. Then she stopped and tip-toed back.

"Would you like creamer? It's powdered. Do you need sugar or artificial sweetener?"

"Black will be fine, thank you."

"Oh, good. I won't be long."

Autumn flipped through a couple of books displaying the top of the line of many brands. The choices ran the biggest and best on the market today. She wondered if the owners were single-boat lovers or if they were part of a fleet of the rich and famous. For her taste, she felt that the time she spent on one would never justify the cost.

Suzanne returned with a cup of black coffee and a package of cheesy-crackers on the back of a clipboard as a make-shift tray.

"Do you like the books?" she asked, her hands again held behind her back.

"Everything is lovely," Autumn said. "You are very kind. You'll make a wonderful saleswoman."

"Oh, no, I graduated last month, and I've been accepted at FSU. I'm going to get a degree in mathematics. Math is the language of science, and I'm going to be a physicist." She smiled and danced away.

Autumn pushed the coffee aside, having no intention of drinking it. She thumbed through a few more books and began to wonder what Larry was doing. She laid the magazines on the coffee table and went back into the showroom. She walked around a few of the models looking for him. He was no place to be found. Maybe he was in the men's room.

She wondered for about twenty minutes, and he never came out. She glanced out the glass double doors. The car was still sitting where they'd left it.

"Where are you?" she whispered to herself.

Autumn walked down a hallway that displayed showcases of boating gadgets, which led to a room filled with parts of every shape and size, but no Larry. She went back into the showroom thinking he'd surely be back by now. Just then the door opposite the huge glass entrance opened and two men came out. They were bickering and did not notice her.

"Mr. Black," Nate was enraged. "Why would you pass yourself off as a customer! Instead, you're a loose cannon!"

"I like to know who I'm working for. I told you in the beginning, pay me and I'll do what you want - which I did -   but you don't have an exclusive and you're not my only client, and I also do what *I* want."

"We were never to meet you face to face. I certainly never wanted you to come here!" The big man turned on the other man and poked him in the chest. "Listen, asshole, I've got a good thing here. I've built this business up for four years, and I don't want some son of a bitch coming in and ruining it!

The thin man stepped up nose to nose with the other.
"Touch me again, and I'll cut your fucking finger off and stuff it up your ass!"

Autumn froze. They failed to realize that they were not alone even though she was in plain sight. They only had to turn her way. She looked around—hoping to find a place to hide until they left. A motor yacht cruiser on display in the showroom was less than four feet away. If she could quietly inch that way, it would certainly conceal her. She held her breath and eased toward it.

"The cops have been here twice. I'm taking a hell of a chance with you here! Take your fucking money and get out! Out of town and out of my life!"

"Maybe I like it here, fat man." He brushed his nearly bald head with his hand before putting on his baseball cap and Ray-Ban sunglasses. "You don't want to cross me," he said. "And don't forget it."
These last words were spoken so vehemently Smallwood shivered involuntarily.

Autumn kept her eyes on them and was mere inches away when her foot touched the sign stand for that model yacht. The noise it made was minimal, but both men turned.

"What the...!" exclaimed Smallwood. "Who's in here!"

Autumn didn't hesitate but ran behind the yacht, past another, out the big glass doors, and toward the row of magnolia trees. She didn't look back, but—hearing footfalls behind her—she ran as if her life depended on it—which she was sure it did. She made it into the trees and kept going. Through the branches, she got minute glimpses of the blue water bay. Her mind was racing. What if she ran out of the foliage? She needed a place to hide... what if... suddenly someone grabbed her from behind. She screamed and turned facing him clawing and kicking.

"Sh. Stop, it's me." Larry was holding her wrists to avoid being clawed and dodging the kicks.

It was then that she realized her eyes were closed and opened them. She nearly collapsed as her legs turned to rubber, and he held her close for strength.

"It's all right. He saw me and didn't pursue you. Let's get to the car, and you can tell me what happened."

58

As David poured his second cup of coffee, he called his realtor. The phone was answered on the second ring.

"One moment, Mr. Weinberger, and I'll connect you with Mr. Walker."

There was a small clicking on the line and a cheery male voice answered. "David, what a nice surprise. What can I do for you?"

"I'd like to meet with you this morning for a couple of hours, say about 11:30?"

"All right." David could hear him shuffle papers.

"It looks like I am free at 11:30. Where would you like to meet?"

"Your conference room should work for me, Chad. It's private."

"May I ask—are you thinking of buying or selling?"

"Let's talk when I get there."

"Fair enough. I'll see you soon."

Traffic was light when David pulled off Tamiami Trail North onto the curve at Valentia Boulevard. The landscaped drive was beautifully manicured, and the lush trees blocked much of the oppressive summer heat. He pulled into his parking place and stepped out of his car. The sweet aroma of Jasmine and Camilla wafted through the air. A quick glance around the parking lot indicated that Jacob was not there. David did not wish to run into him and spoil this euphoric spell he was under.

The large beveled glass doors opened automatically to let him enter. On the center of each door was the family crest—a red shield with a left-facing golden eagle. The ribbon across its chest spelled out WEINBERGER.

As David strolled to the reception desk, John Mobley scratched his head. "My goodness, Mr. Weinberger, I had to look twice to realize it was you. Do you have a golf date today?"

"No, John. I'm just taking a day off for a change."

"Good for you. You should treat yourself to a day of rest once in a while. Can't say I ever knew you to do that, and I've been here five years—going on six."

"You know, you're right. I believe I'll take your suggestion from now on."

That made Mobley proud to think such an important man would take his advice, and he stood a little taller.

"Do you have a package for me, John?"

"Oh, yes sir." He reached under the counter and pulled out a box. "Can I help you with that? It's kind of heavy."

"No, I'm good. Thank you."

In a matter of minutes, David was again on the by-pass and heading south. He was remembering what John has said about treating himself more often. Handling the preparations would be easy, for he was an extremely organized person. Putting the five properties on the market would clear his plate and remove the major part of his stress. Keeping the mansion was important for Rosemary, and Dixie if she decided to stay. He'd stay too, of course. David could not see himself in a condo or—god forbid—an apartment! No, he liked the mansion. It had everything he needed.

He would have Bernie work up a plan. The sale of the properties would build his gross profit, and more write-offs would be needed. He'd increase his charities and the trusts for both Rosemary and Dixie. Bernie had once suggested that David purchase an airplane to help with write-offs, but he told the old man that being rich didn't mean one should spend foolishly.

The next step would be to relinquish control of Weinberger, Inc. Good attorneys are worth their weight in gold, and the best around Venice was Carmen Varzea. She'd see that he got the most for his years of labor building the business. She had a brilliant mind, a good heart, and he liked to watch her walk.

David was in his private library considering the conversation he and Dixie had at dinner. Truthfully, he had not considered what he would do once he was out from under everything. He had answered her question with whatever popped into his head at the time, but now that he'd said it, he felt it was a pretty damn good idea.

He found himself thumbing through one of the books about the life of Napoleon, who was born on the island of Corsica in 1769. He figured that would be a good place to start—at the beginning. He found a map of Corsica and followed it through his early years. This would be an exciting trip. With no deadlines to interfere, he could go wherever he wanted and stay as long as he liked. The more he read, the more excited he became.

The sun had gone down in a burst of color changing the gray clouds to pink, orange, and lavender washes—and finally, it grew dark. In the dining room, Dixie again joined David for dinner.

"Is this becoming a habit, the two of us having dinner together?"

"I hope so," said David.

Dixie sat down and pulled her chair up to the table. So, what's for dinner?" She took a sip of her Beaujolais.

"I believe it's pork chops and kidney beans, potatoes au gratin, applesauce, and a fine chocolate mousse for dessert."

She tittered. "Who came up with that one, Daddy?"

"Actually, my dear, that was the first meal your mother cooked when we got married. The pork meal was the only thing she knew how to cook, the potatoes came from a box, and she told me that pork simply *had* to be accompanied by applesauce." They both chuckled. "So, for the next week or so we had it every night." This brought laughter.

"When did you hire Mary?"

"It was about a week or so after we were married." This brought more laughter.

Mary brought in biscuits and two Caesar salads and laid them before David and Dixie as they sat at the corner of the long dining room table.

"Is anyone ready for coffee?"

Dixie shook her head.

"Maybe after dinner. Thank you, Mary." He reached for a biscuit and began buttering it. "How was your day?"

"It went quite well. I went to Job Finders and signed up."

"Oh, looking for a job? Good for you."

"It was a bit stressful. They asked me all kinds of questions like, did I type, what computer software did I use, and what previous experience did I have?"

"And what did you say?"

"Well, I was honest. I told her that I took typing in high school and that I was very good on Facebook. The *experience* question stumped me. I've had a lot of experiences, but which one did she want to hear about?"

David smiled at this. "Is she going to help you find work?"

"Oh, yes. There is an opening at Kohls on Central Sarasota Parkway. I will start Monday."

He noted the excitement in her voice. "In which department?"

"I will walk around the store and show people the latest perfume. Tomorrow I think I'll start looking for an apartment."

"So, you're really going to move out of the house?"

"It's your house, Daddy. I want to be on my own, and that means I cannot live in your house. You understand, don't you?"

"But you're my daughter. I have always taken care of you, darling."

"Exactly. Don't you see, if I continue to live here, you will continue to take care of me."

He didn't answer. Instead, he took a drink of his Johnny Blue and let silence fill the room. He was surprised to find that he could overlook things she said that a few days ago would have set him off.

"I love you, Daddy. But I *am* a woman, and I must learn to be self-sufficient." She took another sip of her wine. "Okay, it's your turn. What did you do today?"

He forced a smile. They'd made a pact, and he didn't want to spoil it. For the first time in many years, they were getting along. They had even laughed together. He took a deep breath and looked at her. "I began planning my retirement."

"Really!"

"Oh yes. I put all the properties up for sale. Not Bedwick, of course, but all the others. Bernard is working on the finances. A lot will change, especially the taxes. And our attorney is handling the restructuring of the business. I will stay on in an advisory capacity, but I'm leaving the day-to-day running of the business to those younger who can handle the stress."

"Are you going to be comfortable relinquishing all that? Whatever will you do with all the time on your hands?"

He paused a long moment before responding. "Travel, I think. Italy and France call to me. Napoleon was born in Corsica and later became a French statesman and military leader. He was prominent during the French Revolution and led several successful campaigns during those wars. I would enjoy seeing those places first-hand."

"It sounds like you've put a lot of thought into this. I hope it will make you happy."

"I hope so, too. The key to happiness is change, but the keyhole is often hard to find. I've always been a hard worker—creating, commanding, controlling, enforcing, and making things run to my satisfaction. Now it's time to relax and enjoy the bounty of all that hard work."

The door to the kitchen opened, and Mary came out pushing a cart with their dinner.

"Happiness is change," She paused. "I've never thought about that before. Change can be devastating, but hopefully, in time, when we can see clearly again, we'll find that things are better."

~ 59 ~

That night, the moon was nearly full as wispy clouds skidded by, hiding and then peeking down at Autumn as she rested on a chaise longue beside the pool. She was thinking about Larry and his attempt to teach her how to defend herself. She couldn't take it seriously; all this talk about killing and defending. She'd never been physically hurt. Even as a child, she'd never fallen from a tree or been bitten by a dog. That kind of thing might happen to other people, but never to her. Those people were probably just in the wrong place at the wrong time. She took a sip of the cool blush wine that sat on the stand beside her. Larry was just worrying unnecessarily. She took a deep breath and sighed.

"What a sweet guy."

Just then her cell phone rang. She had left it on the shelf near the sliding glass doors that lead to the kitchen. "Hello."

There was a long silence, and she suspected it was Larry. What a darling tease he had turned out to be.

"You'd better talk to me, or I'll hang up," she said, with a coy chuckle.

"Hello," said the male voice on the line.

She didn't think it sounded like Larry, but he might change his voice if he was playing. "You called me. What do you want?"

"I want to suck you all over. I'm going to strip you of that blue swimming suit you're wearing, and..."

She threw the phone down and backed away. Who was this, and how did he know she was wearing a blue bathing suit? My god, could he see her! She looked in all directions but couldn't see anything in the darkness. She grabbed her towel and covered herself. The voice was still droning—although she couldn't make out the words as she turned and ran into the house.

Thursday, June 25, 2020

60

The lounge chairs were in the shade of the oak tree just outside the fence, and the gentle breeze on their wet suits was cool and refreshing.

"I have to tell you, Larry. He frightened me out of my wits. He must have been able to see me to know I was wearing my blue swimsuit."

"This is the very thing I was afraid of. You have no security around your house. Anyone could walk from the beach onto your property and hide in the shrubs. If he wore black, he could easily get close enough to see you by the pool. Maybe you should get a gun."

"I'd be more likely to throw it at him then shoot him."

Larry looked over at her and smiled.

She caught the look. "What?" she asked as if she could read his mind.

That was the opening he was looking for. "Angel, I've been thinking about what you told me—the experience with Richard in the mountains, and more recently the situation at the marina. You surely realize that you were just damn lucky in both instances. Both events could so easily have gone the other way." He threw his legs over the side of the chair, so his feet touched the deck. "My feelings for you are growing, and I don't want anything to happen to you."

"Don't tell me you want me to have a gun. I can't stand guns. I wouldn't know what to do with it. I can't imagine shooting someone!"

"Angel, I do understand that. What I'd like to do is teach you self-defense, so you can protect yourself."

"Self-defense?"

"Yes."

"What do you mean—fight someone?" She laughed, and he picked up the cynicism in it.

"It isn't fighting. That's the sport of boxing. This is defending yourself—keeping someone from hurting you."

"I don't know..."

"Come here. Let me show you."

They both stood and stepped closer. "Okay, punch me in the face."

She backed away. "I WILL NOT!" Her hands went on her hips and she looked at him defiantly.

"Okay, I'll punch you."

He took a step closer, but she turned and walked away.

"Larry, stop it. I don't like this," she said, but there was a little laughter in her words.

"Okay, come on. I won't hurt you."

She stepped closer, and he grabbed her arm and twisted it behind her back. When she reached out with the other hand to push him away, he pulled that arm behind her. She squirmed but he only held her tighter.

She laughed. "Okay, you got me. You can let go now."

Instead, he clasped both wrists with one hand and pulled her hair back with the other exposing her fragile white throat. She shrieked, but he still held her. He let go of her hair but continued to hold her arms. When she looked at him, he could see the anger in her eyes and the tears that were building. He let go of her wrists and held her tenderly.

"You can imagine all the things a man could do to you—held like that. I would never hurt you, but I wanted you to understand the danger when you can't defend yourself."

There was a long quiet moment and he knew better than to break that silence. Finally, she whispered, "Okay, show me."

"Place your feet apart; it will help you stay balanced. Now, punch me in the face."

She hesitated, but finally lunged at him. He reacted swiftly. First, he brought his straight arm down hard blocking the punch and thrusting his open hand with straight fingers straight to her eye.

"Oh my god, you could put someone's eye out that way!" She scolded stepping away.

"That's the idea, Angel. Women usually have long nails, and a move like that, if done seriously, can badly scratch or even put an eye out. When your life is in danger, there's no time for politeness. It's kill or be killed.

"Let's try another one. We'll go very slowly 'til you get the hang of it. Come at me like you're going to grab me by the throat."

She moved toward him with her arms out and hands coming together. Slowly he grabbed her left arm, swung around putting his shoulder under her armpit, and jerked her off balance. She shrieked again, and he caught her before she hit the ground.

"How do you expect me to ever learn to do that!" she shouted—brushing herself off.

"With practice."

"Humph," was all she said and walked away.

"Aw, come on. You can do this." He reached for her to comfort and reassure her.

She grabbed his outstretched arm, whirled around until her shoulder was in his armpit, jerked him off balance, and pulled him over her back. He landed hard, and she walked away brushing the dust from her hands as if to say, *well done, girl.*

Friday, June 26, 2020

61

The day was gray and somber. Those attending the funeral were mostly friends in their late 20s and early 30s. The mass was quick and the eulogy even quicker, but no one seemed to mind. They were lost in memories of happier times. Boatman had asked Jeff to be one of the six pallbearers and they carried the casket to the waiting hearse for the final trip. The crowd milled around momentarily before the procession to the cemetery and then slipped quickly to their cars in a sea of black umbrellas.

The hearse took the lead carrying their friend and flanked by police motorcycles to assist when moving through red lights. Larry, Autumn, Boatman, and Jeff came next. In the third car were the remaining four pallbearers. David drove his car with Dixie, and the others followed in line. The prayers, moods, and pace all culminated in the gloomy atmosphere.

"Whoever set the scene for Don's funeral certainly got it right. This miserable rainy day is right out of an old black and white movie." Boatman sat in the back seat of Larry's rental car, his elbow resting on the window, his chin resting on his closed fist.

"I'm surprised his family didn't show up," said Autumn, looking back at him.

"They're caring enough, but I get the impression they do not travel much. Janie Davenport is the only one I talked to. She said the twins are still in Scotland. She thinks they're taking bagpipe lessons."

"How old are they?"

"Fifteen, I believe, she said. She also mentioned that they have traded their jeans for kilts and have burned all their underwear."

"She's his younger sister, right?" Autumn asked.

"Yes. Mrs. Frankenwalter is the older sister. She couldn't make it because she's suffering from rheumatism. No, wait. That was last week. This week it's gout. Janie apologized—saying she couldn't make it either. Seeing him dead would be too sad to bear. She's going to reframe his high school graduation picture and put it on their living room wall so she can remember him that way."

"I was surprised to see Mr. Weinberger there, but I suppose he didn't know of Dixie's relationship to Don." Boatman shook his head.

"Well, it makes sense. Don was his gardener for some time," Autumn said. "Dixie says they're getting along surprisingly well. She says they have dinner together every night. That in itself is a real turn around. Driving Jacob out of the house was the turning point in their relationship. She said it was wonderful having a real father."

"Autumn, I'd like you to meet the movie producer we talked about. I finished reading the script. It's a sure winner." Jeff had moved forward and rested his arms on the back of her seat. "Will you have time this week?"

"I think that's a good idea, Honey. If I'm going to invest in his project, I should at least meet him."

"Yes!" he exclaimed and sat back again.

"Boatman, how is the chartering business?"

"Truthfully, I haven't done anything. My heart just isn't in it. No one has called, and I haven't put any time into getting clients."

"Well, if this is a slow time, maybe I could take you up on your offer to check out locations?"

"Sure, if you want."

"If I want! Of course, I *want*. You know, it might be a good thing for you, too. I understand that working without Don is not something you would look forward to, but if you do it with friends, that old love for the work will return."

"Maybe you're right. It will be good to get out."

"Good. We'll make it a picnic, say Friday? It'll be fun."

"Which do you prefer, beer or wine?" Larry asked.

"Beer," said Boatman.

"Wine," said Autumn in unison.

"Okay, I'll bring both!" They all laughed.

"And I'll call and make an appointment to see the producer.

62

Gray clouds were stationary in the sky above Venice, and Jacob prayed they wouldn't last forever. He feared they might be a harbinger of things to come. Despite the several calls he'd placed, and the two appointments he'd made, he had yet to connect with Frog. This was not a good sign. He had to convince Frog that the plan could still be saved. But to do that he had to see him face to face.

The car pulled into the now empty parking lot behind the building, and he jumped out. His watch read 5:43. There was no way he would miss this appointment, and to be on the safe side he took the stairs two at a time rather than risk any delays on the elevator. At the top of the stairs, he turned right running and stopped in front of #206 Electra Enterprises. He tried the door, but it was locked. The sign underneath read,

Mon - Fri 9 – 5:30
Closed Sat-Sun

"Son of a bitch!" Jacob pounded on the door. There was no response, so he pounded again. When there was still no response, he kicked the door. Furious, he spun around, hands on hips, and stared down onto Venice Avenue. "I'll be a goddamn son of a bitch; he's done it again!" Few cars were parked on the street at this hour, and none were Frog's.

Just then the door opened. It was the male receptionist.

"I knocked, and you didn't answer!" Jacob barked as he brushed past the young man.

"You're right on time," he said pointing at the clock on the waiting room wall.

Jacob was still pissed but didn't say anything.

"He will see you now," said the young man with a flick of his wrist. He opened the door to the office and allowed Jacob to enter before shutting the door again.

The suite was four rooms deep. The receptionist area had a half bath, and the office had its own bathroom. The latter included a glassed-in white marble shower with Dresden double-sinks, bidet, and toilet. The office was painted gray with chrome filing cabinets, bookcases, and a desk cluttered with a computer, printer, a six-line phone, and stacks of manuscripts and papers. The ultra-modern light fixtures were outshone by the picture window displaying the southern view of beautiful, historical downtown Venice.

Jacob thought for a moment that no one was there until he saw smoke rise from the large desk chair facing the window.

"You didn't answer my calls," he said as he took a few steps forward.

"I was busy. What do you want?"

"I need to talk to you," he said. Jacob realized that his palms were sweating.

"Are you here to let me know the wedding has taken place and you're happily married and ready to put our game into play?"

Jacob hesitated for a moment as he carefully considered his next words. "There's been a glitz." He hesitated for only a second—until he saw three smoke rings rise from the chair. "But it's nothing. David has become impossible, but I have a backup plan. I'll convince Dixie to marry me and work around him. Then I can get rid of him and the field will be open to continue as we wanted."

"Convince her, you say; does that mean she's against the marriage?"

"Oh, no. No, that was a poor choice of words. You're making me nervous. Can't you turn around and face me?"

The chair turned slowly, and Frog laid the cigar in the lead-glass ashtray and sat forward in his chair. "Are you comfortable now? I hope so because I want you to hear me clearly. I want my money. I'll say it again. I want my money, and I want it in a week. I've given you months to come up with it, and all I get are plans and stalls and excuses. Now get out! I don't want to see you or hear your voice again until you hand over what you owe me." He concluded—picking up the smoking cigar and turning back to the window.

Jacob was sweating when he left the office. He took the elevator down and got into his car. His mind was racing like a chipmunk on a treadmill.

He drove out to the beach. A walk in the sand had always helped him think. He heard the surf pounding on the shore and sliding back to meet the next rushing wave. Seabirds were calling, and the pelicans were grouping. Time passed, and the sun was quickly approaching the horizon, but nothing, no viable ideas came to him.

"I've got to quit pussy-footing around! Frog means what he says without a doubt. I need a plan!" he said aloud in desperation. He smacked his forehead repeatedly with the palm of his hand as if that might help. "Son of a bitch! What am I going to do? Think, man!"

As the sun slipped silently out of sight, he got an idea. "But of course!" Jacob pulled out his cell phone, hit speed dial, and waited while it rang.

"Hello," a female voice said.

"Dixie, Sweetheart, I called to apologize. I am so sorry."

"You've got to be kidding me! You have got a lot of gall!"

"Please, I've been on this medication... I know that is no excuse. I told the doctor I thought I was losing my mind, he said it was a side affect. I stopped taking it immediately! How can I possibly make it up to you? I'll do anything you say. Please forgive me. From the bottom of my heart..."

"Anything I say? Seriously?"

"Honey, you know I mean it. May I come over so we can talk?"

"We have nothing to say to one another, now or ever!"

"Dixie, I love you."

"How can you say that? You don't even know the meaning of the word. You never will." Her voice cracked as she fought back the tears.

"I know you have feelings for me. Please, let me make it up to you. Let me show you how sorry I am."

"The feelings I had were never for you."

You whiny little bitch! When I get my hands on you, I'll make you pay for all this groveling. "Dixie, you're breaking my heart. I had such plans for us. I was planning a honeymoon you'd never forget. First, we would fly to Hawaii for a week, then China, and Scotland, and back to New York, and all the while we'd shop for furniture and other things for the new house I plan to building for us."

"Jacob, I don't know how to make it any clearer. It's never going to happen. The feelings I have for you are loathing and disgust. I want you completely out of my life!" The connection was broken and "call ended" appeared on the screen.

"Damn!" He thought for a moment. "Well, if the kid won't cooperate, maybe the old man will." He hit another button and waited as the phone rang.

David was still thinking about the possibility of traveling the path of the emperor. He was skimming through *The Life of Napoleon* when the phone rang.

"Hello."

"David, we need to talk. Could I stop by for a few minutes?"

"No," David answered the caller. "Was there something in my tone the last time we spoke that made you think I was not serious?"

"Please, you didn't let me explain. You need to hear my side of this. Five minutes. That's all I'm asking for. Please..."

"I'm hanging up now, and if you choose to come anyway, I'll set the dogs on you."

"Dogs?"

David hung up. "Damn! How could I have been so wrong about him? Well, it ends here! Tomorrow I'll take care of him, once and for all."

The Queensway Tambour clock on the shelf chimed nine. David sighed. "Tomorrow is another day."

Saturday, June 27, 2020

63

Morning came bright and clean. The rain had stopped, and Venice was already growing hot. Autumn's long blond hair fell to her shoulders as she poured her second cup of coffee and turned the page of the *Herald Tribune*. Mrs. Wilburn, also in her robe and nightclothes, took a Danish pastry from the plate, cut it in half, and drizzled honey on it before taking a bite.

"Anything interesting this morning?"

"Schools are out, graduation ceremonies across the city are over, no more rain predicted for a week, and the new Publix in Osprey will celebrate their second anniversary tomorrow with big sales and free samples. I take it all is well in paradise," said Autumn as she skimmed the news.

Mrs. Wilburn scoffed. "Wish that could be said of the world news." She licked her thin lips and took another bite.

Autumn nodded in agreement and laid the paper aside. "I haven't accomplished much writing, so I hope to finish the next chapter of my book today."

"I think you needed a day off to let your creative juices brew."

"Sometimes I think you should be a writer, Mrs. Wilburn. You certainly have a way with words."

-

"Me? Write! Oh no. I wouldn't know how to begin," she answered as she got up and began to clear the table. "Would you like anything else, dear?" The old woman took the pair of French presses to the sink and rinsed them. "You work on your mystery world, and I'll take care of this world. Laundry is the title of my chapter today."

"You're right. Duty calls." Autumn took her plate of half-eaten Danish and her coffee cup to the sink. She re-tied her robe and headed for her room. "You know where I'll be if you need me."

Autumn walked down the hall and stepped into the walk-in closet that doubled as a dressing room just off her bedroom. Minutes later she reappeared in slacks, flats, and a lime green Chico tank top with matching earrings.

She was just sitting down to work when she heard a gentle knock.

"Come in, Mrs. Wilburn."

"I didn't want to bother you but there's a package for you. I just found it on the doorstep. Funny thing, it's too early for the mailman."

"Oh, I wonder what it is," she said, as she picked up the letter-opener and cut through the tape that sealed the package. "Curious, there's no return address."

"It's probably some advertising item soliciting money."

"You're may be right," she said as she lifted the lid. The item was wrapped in tissue paper, and she lifted it out. "It is very light."

"Probably something made in China from paper or a cheap piece of plastic."

"Hmm..." She carefully peeled the tissue away and revealed the item. "What is it?"

Autumn lifted it higher so Mrs. Wilburn could look at it more closely. "I'm not sure, but it smells awful."

It was then that Autumn noticed the smell. "Oh, you're right. It smells like dead meat."

"Autumn, it looks like a tongue."

The younger woman dropped the item on the desk and stepped away. "Oh my god! Who would send me something like this?"

"I think you should call the police.

~ 64 ~

Bradshaw used a pen to turn the piece of decaying flesh around in the box of tissue Autumn and Larry had brought in. "It's a tongue, all right. We can do a DNA testing to be sure, but I suspect it was once in the mouth of Fran Major."

"What!" Autumn's hand went involuntarily to her mouth to cover it, or maybe it was the smell that seemed to get worse by the moment.

"We never told anyone that her tongue had been cut out, just that she was mutilated."

"Oh, poor Fran. Nobody deserves to be treated that way."

"It's my guess that the sender kept it frozen all this time. It appears only now to have begun to decompose."

"Detective, what do you think? If this is Fran's, then the obvious question would be why did her killer send it to Autumn? Does he target women? Maybe blondes; they're both blond."

"No, I doubt that she's simply being targeted. This seems like a warning of some kind."

"Of course! We went to the marina to see what we could dig up on Smallwood. He was with a man, and we didn't get to talk to him. However, Autumn was caught listening to them argue. One of them chased her."

"Spying? Did you learn anything?"

"The two men were talking about some job. The fat one had hired the thin one to do it. He said he did it, but he wasn't working exclusively for him. I just got bits and pieces. It didn't make a lot of sense at the time. The fat one didn't like it that the other was in his place of work. He said something about the police had been there and this guy could ruin everything."

"Was there anything else?" Bradshaw asked.

Autumn tried to remember. "The fat one wanted the other to take the money and leave town, but he didn't want to."

"The fat one was undoubtedly Smallwood. What did the other one look like?"

"He had really short hair that he covered with a black baseball cap. He wore all black, as I remember. Oh yes, and dark sunglasses."

"It doesn't ring a bell with me. But if Nate wanted him to leave, he is probably not from around here."

"Not much to go on. The thin guy with very short hair could be anyone," Larry noted.

"I'm sorry, I'm not much help."

"On the contrary, we have suspected Smallwood all along, but we now know he has an accomplice. Why don't you two run-along? Kincaid and I need to pay another visit to the fat man. Kincaid," he called. "See if you can find some formaldehyde to improve the fragrance of this stinking thing."

As Bradshaw neared the marina on Dona Bay, he could see the vehicles parked there. "Let's wait here and see who belongs to that battered truck." He pulled off the road among a cluster of palm trees and scrubs.

"What have you got in mind?"

"Well, we know we won't get much from Smallwood. I suspect the owner of that truck is not a customer."

"You think? What gave it away, boss?"

"Nobody likes a smartass, college boy."

"Maybe he's a handy-man come to fix the shitter."

"Maybe. We'll know soon enough. I believe that's him coming out now."

Matt Crawley hurried out the showroom door and rushed to his truck, his stiff arms flapping. The engine choked to life, backed out of the parking space, and pulled away in a cloud of smoke.

Before the truck reached the second crossroad, blue lights and a siren sounded. The driver pulled off the road and turned off the motor.

"May I see your driver's license and registration?" Bradshaw asked as Kincaid approached the truck from the other side.

"Shur-nuff, Sheriff." He shuffled through the glove compartment tossing maps, napkins, small car parts of some sort, and candy bar wrappers until he found the items in a plastic envelope that at one time had been clear enough to read through.

"Would you step out of the truck, Mr. Crawley?"

"Ya want me ta get out, Sheriff?"

"Yes. Please step out of the truck, Mr. Crawley."

"Shur-nuff. I'll do as ya say. I'm a law abidin' citizen."

Matt climbed out and stood beside the rusty facsimile of a 1992 GMC truck that had not aged well. Despite the Florida heat, he wore bib overalls, but no shirt.

"Mr. Crawley. Do you know a Nate Smallwood?"

"Uh... Smallwood. Hmm... Smallwood?" He tapped his chin and looked around as if thinking. "Smallwood, you say?"

"Mr. Crawley, I should probably warn you that I am an E.G.O. T.S. Ta Co. S.B. That is the superior branch of the Florida State Police, and I can spot a liar a mile away. Now if you choose to lie to me, I can take you off in handcuffs to the Federal Bastille for habitual deceivers. The guards there are all of the canine variety."

Crawley's eyes grew to the size of saucers.

"You don't want that, do you?"

"No, sir. I shur don't."

"Now that we're clear on that point, I'll ask again. Do you know a Nate Smallwood?"

"Yes, Sheriff. I do.

"How do you know him?"

"I work fer him from time to time."

"Tell me more."

"I pick up and deliver thin's."

"What kind of things?"

"If he needs a cord'a firewood, or supplies, or Blue Bayou."

"I'm not familiar with that last one. What is Blue Bayou?"

"Well, d'at's what Nate calls it. Ever'one else calls it Purple Drank."

"Have you ever used Blue Bayou?"

"Oh no, Sheriff. I take care of my body. It's d'a only one I got."

"Where does Smallwood sell this stuff?"

"He knows lots of folks."

"Does he sell other drugs?"

"Oh yea, Sheriff. He's got Mary Jane, en crak-co-cain, but I don't use none of d'em."

"When you pick up the drugs where do you go?"

"It's differ'nt ever time. He gives me a bag to take to an address, en I brin' back a differ'nt bag."

"Tell you what, Mr. Crawley. I won't tell him we talked. I don't want you to get into trouble with him. But you must give me your word that when he sends you again, you'll stop and show me first. Is that a deal?"

"Yes sir, Sheriff. D'ats real nice of ya."

"You won't forget, will you?"

"Oh no, sir. I'll remember."

"Okay then, Mr. Crawley. You're free to go. Be careful now; watch your speed."

"Yes, sir," he answered as he got back into his truck and drove off in a cloud of smoke—waving good-bye.

Bradshaw got into the car and turned off the blue lights. Kincaid got in and put on his seat belt.

"Easiest interview I've ever experienced."

"Well, sir. There's no fixing stupid, even with duct tape."

65

Dixie pulled the car into the garage and closed the overhead door. After taking the packages from the car, she dropped the key on its assigned hook and went into the house. As she passed the wine room, she reached for the bottle of Beaujolais, reconsidered, and put it back. She went into the kitchen and poured herself a tall glass of sweet tea with ice and headed for her bedroom.

The day of shopping had been hot and exhausting. She wrapped her long hair in a towel and took a quick shower. After towel-drying she took the glass of tea to the bedroom and began laying out her purchases.

One bag held a darling one-piece swimsuit of a draped aqua fabric and a matching sarong cover-up. Another held a two-piece bathing suit. The top was a high neck tankini in a mock leopard skin material that formed a V hemline in the front. It fit over a high waist, full bottom style pant. The matching leopard fabric cover-up doubled as an oversize scarf rolled and worn around the neck or opened fully to wrap around the shoulders or waist. The third was a simple black one-piece suit with a gathered bodice, full back, and a Venetian lace, mini-length casual fit cover-up in black.

"Eeny, meeny, miny, mo...," she said pointing to each ensemble. "Okay, the black one wins."

She quickly changed and headed down the hall. As she got to the beveled glass sliding doors to the pool, she saw David reading in the shade of the fringe-covered pergola.

"I don't believe my eyes!" she said as she joined him. "Who would ever have thought that my Dad owned a bathing suit?"

"Of course, I do. I only choose to wear it in the sunlight. And look at you. Aren't you pretty? What happened to the old peek-a-boo cutaway outfits you usually wear?"

"Oh, do you like it?" She spun casually to give him the whole 365-degree view.

"I do."

"This is part of the new me. My brand is the updated, subtly sophisticated, career woman-look. I'm throwing out the old In-Your-Face, *JBF* fashion style."

"Dixie, you are amazing."

"I take it that's a good thing?"

"Oh, my dear. That is a very *good* thing." He motioned to the chair beside him at the table cluttered with his books and brochures. "Come sit with me a minute and let me show you the places I plan to visit soon."

She smiled. "I would love to, Daddy."

66

Boatman went to the kitchen and pulled a beer out of the refrigerator. He sighed, twisted the cap, and returned to Don's bedroom. He had spent the whole morning going through his closet and bureau, packing items to give to friends and things to donate. Originally, he had hoped to find Don's journal tucked away safely somewhere. But as time passed, it became clear that it was not here.

Bit by bit he ran across significant objects he thought friends and family would like to keep, so he brought boxes from the garage and began the sad work of removing Don's physical items from the house.

In a drawer, he found two small framed pictures of his sisters. He would mail these to Mrs. Davenport, and she could pass the one to Mrs. Frankenwalter. Later he found the *Complete List of Ailments, Symptoms, and Remedies.* When he opened the cover, he was not surprised to find the inscription "To Donny, from Mary Ellen."

Don had been an avid records keeper. In a shoebox, he found bits of papers and miscellaneous items. A dried rose with a tag stated: "April 14, 2018—kissed Dixie in the rose garden." A clip of hair marked "a souvenir of our first time together, taken while she slept" was next. Following were a wine cork marked "Dixie's favorite," a braided grass bracelet "from Dixie," a small cluster of pine needles tied with string and marked "our adventure in the pine grove," and many more items. All were dated. He closed the box gently. No question who'd want this.

Boatman looked around the room. Everything was packed and ready to mail off or deliver. He stacked as many boxes as he could carry and took them to the garage and put them in the truck. It only took four trips to get it all.

He was closing the garage when he heard the phone ring. He caught it on the fourth ring—just in time.

"What do you want, Nate?"

"Is that any way to talk to an old friend?"

"I don't have time to talk right now." He started to push the end button.

"I just wanted to apologize. I couldn't make it to the funeral."

"No one was expecting you."

"You're a cold fish, Boatman. Here I am, making nice and how do you treat me?"

He knew Nate was drunk and that this conversation would eventually go bad. But something compelled him to keep the fat man talking.

"Well, it rained all day, and it was gloomy. Otherwise, it was a decent funeral."

"I know, it's always tough sending a friend to the hereafter, and I know how close you were."

Boatman thought, here it comes, but to his surprise, it didn't.

"I have never had a really close friend," Nate said, "but it's probably because I work all the time."

Boatman wondered how much he'd had to drink. Was he sincere or setting him up for a fall? "Yes, you are a very hard worker. I don't know how you do it, Nate."

"That's true. I should take more time for myself."

"When have you ever taken a vacation? There were none that I knew of."

B'man wondered if he could get any information while the fat man was in such a genial mood.

"You're smart to keep to yourself. I've always admired you for that."

"You have?"

"Oh, yeah. This business with Don has been hard on me. Today I had to clean all his stuff out of his room. You can imagine how much work that was."

"Yeah. That would be."

"You wouldn't believe all the shit he had."

"I can imagine."

"You can't imagine all the stuff I took out. I guess I'll just take it to the Restore. I don't know what else to do with it."

"Probably."

Boatman heard him take another drink. It was now or never. "The one thing I didn't find was his journal. He kept the names of all our clients in it."

There was silence on the other end.

"Nate, are you there?"

He heard him take another drink, and then he choked. He realized he wasn't choking; he was stifling a laugh. Then he couldn't hold it in any longer and burst into a drunken laughing fit. Boatman pushed the red button ending the call.

Sunday, June 28, 2020

67

The night was alive with chirps, caws, crooning, and hoots of nocturnal creatures. David stood on the end of the diving board, paused a moment, then dove into the refreshingly cool water. He stayed low until he could feel the pool bottom with his fingertips, then rose to the surface, where one more stroke took him to the far wall. There he pushed off and swam back again. He preferred to swim with only the underwater light on. He could turn onto his back, quietly float and pick out a number of constellations in the star-filled sky. For the first time, in longer than he could remember, he was at peace with the world. Jacob was simply an inconvenience, and that too would end tomorrow.

The stress of planning the wedding was gone. He had even paid a visit to Rosemary on the third floor. She smiled when she saw him, but she obviously didn't recognize him. He looked at her sitting there in her wheelchair and tangled gray hair, fussing with her fingers and glancing around the room as if she had never seen it before and again took on that perpetual expression of wonder.

How different it would have been if she had never gotten sick - the loneliness was unbearable - I wouldn't have buried myself in my work. I wouldn't have done a lot of things I did to build the business.

He chuckled to himself. *I might have actually earned that Businessman of the Year title.*

Dixie was born in 1985, and shortly afterward Rosemary had changed. Instead of the romantic, fun-loving young woman, she became forgetful and moody. She began losing things and couldn't remember the names of the servants and grounds people. She left one day to pick up a few things from a nearby grocery and did not return. The police brought her home after midnight. She had been walking alone in the dark. She'd left the car at the grocery, started walking, and got lost in the neighborhood she had lived in for years. He felt his throat lock up as he kissed her on the forehead. He said good-bye to the day nurses and hurried away. The feeling of sadness that came over him with each visit was almost more than he could bear.

David rolled over in the water and did ten speed-laps before exhaustion took over and camouflaged the pain of the memory. He swam to the ladder, pulled himself out of the water, and picked up a towel.

How I wished Dixie had joined me, but she wanted to get to bed early. Nail and hair appointments have been scheduled in the morning, and she is eager to get an early start at her first job. He began toweling off. *How I've enjoyed these past few days. Why couldn't we have had this closeness all along? I just couldn't have juggled all I do and been there for her at the same time. I wish... but it's too late now. She's going to move out and I'm going to miss her.*

David studied the stars and wondered how different the constellations would be in France and Italy. The accommodations for the trip were nearly complete, and next week he would arrange the flights. He was excited to finalize the alterations of the company, but he had confidence that Carmen would notify him when the legalities of the conversion were complete.

I am going to miss Dixie, but it's probably all for the best. She's a grown woman and needs to be on her own. At any rate...

Just then a shot rang out. He gasped and looked down to see blood on his chest. He felt no pain, but confusion enveloped him. What was the blood from? He took a step, lost his balance, and fell. As he lay on the concrete, he noticed it was still warm from the heat of the day. He thought he should probably get help, but instead, he closed his eyes.

Maybe it was a wisp of wind that sent a chill through his body and made him look up. Someone was moving toward him, but his vision was cloudy and all he could make out was a apparition. He blinked and uttered a startled cry.

"Rosemary! Oh, my darling..."

She was as beautiful as the day they had married. She knelt beside him and gently stroked his cheek. Her white lace tea-length dress fluttered in the breeze and she wore the white tulle wedding hat. The diamond and pearl ear drops that he'd given her reflected the light from the pool. Her hair was no longer gray, but burgundy again, and she wore it pinned up and back, as the style had been back then. He had so many questions, and he wanted to tell her how beautiful she was, but the words caught in his throat.

She didn't speak, but a single tear slipped down her cheek. David ached to hold her, to tell her how much he'd missed her, but breathing was difficult, his arms felt heavy, and he shivered from the chill.

Suddenly, the scene pulled away, like a photograph on a black background. The vision ebbed, becoming smaller and smaller until it was just a pinpoint, before disappearing completely.

David tried to call to her, but no words came, just an anguished cry. Tears filled his eyes as he struggled to speak. He choked with the effort as blood filled his throat, and the harder he tried to get air the more he realized it was futile. For a second, he almost panicked, but then a relaxed smile took shape and a moment later he closed his eyes for the last time.

68

Bradshaw and Kincaid came up the now familiar walk to the front door of the Bedwick Mansion and rang the bell. Mary North opened the door. The detective saw immediately that she had been crying. Her hair did not have the neat appearance that he had seen on their previous visit. He felt that it had been a rough morning for her.

"Detectives, they're in the pool area. Follow me, please."

"Thank you, Miss North."

They went through the grand foyer, living room and atrium, turning right onto the veranda and passing the beveled glass sliding doors, and then to the pergola. Someone had placed a 10'x10' gazebo tent over the body.

"It's another murder, Syl. Shot from that direction," Coroner Fred Gilbert said—pointing. "It happened around 11 p.m. last night. The single shot woke the daughter. She rushed down and got the housekeeper, and they found him as you see him now. The daughter, Dixie, covered the body to protect it from the hot rays of the sun. That strikes me as a very caring woman. She called 911, and we were called."

-

"Fred, I'm concerned. This is the third murder in two weeks. I can't tell whether or not they are related. We've found clues, but it remains a puzzle."

"Two knives and one high-powered gun—are we talking about three killers?"

"Could be, but I sure as hell hope this isn't a crime spree. I'd prefer to think it's one perp with an arsenal."

"Kincaid, call the CSI team and have them check the perimeter. I'm going to speak to the daughter."

"Right, boss."

"I'll get back to you with my report, Syl."

Inside Bradshaw found Dixie sitting at one end of the dining room table, the seat that had previously been David's. "Miss Weinberger, I'm Detective Sylvan Bradshaw. I'm sorry for your loss. Do you mind speaking to me now? I can wait if it's inconvenient at this time."

"No, sir. Now is a good time. I want my father's killer found and punished."

"Did your father have any enemies?"

"Detective, my father was a successful and strong businessman. I'm sure he did. I don't know who might do something like this, however," she said glancing in the direction of the swimming pool. "Who would kill him?" She paused again. "One that comes to mind is Jacob Crawford, my former fiancé, and my father's employee. Until last week he lived with us, but my father discovered he was untrustworthy. He was fired and kicked out of the house."

"Miss Weinberger, did you know a Donald MacKenzie?"

"Yes." She took a deep breath as if bolstering herself for what was to come. "He was our gardener for several years... and a dear friend."

"I understand. Your father's death must be extremely hard, especially on top of the recent death of your close friend."

"Yes, thank you."

"You say Mr. Crawford lived here. Was he living here when MacKenzie was killed?"

She cocked her head thinking and frowned. "Yes, he was," she whispered as if remembering. "Do you think he might have...?"

"I'm just trying to get a clear picture. He's not a suspect at the moment. This Crawford—is he a sportsman? You know—a fisherman or hunter?"

"No, not that I know of. He is much like my father in that he focuses primarily on his work."

"And, his work would be...?"

"Daddy said he was an investment broker."

"Broker, huh. Was he a kind, considerate man? Were you disappointed when he left the house?"

"Crawford is a mean and cruel person. He enjoys hurting people."

"Did he hurt you?"

"Yes, that's why Daddy got rid of him."

"Were you and your father close?"

"Not until recently. When he got rid of Jacob, everything changed. For the first time, we could talk. He was different, he listened, and he shared ideas and plans with me. I might say that we have become friends." She answered—tears welling up. "Very good friends, Detective. I will miss him terribly."

"I think I have what I need for now." He rose to leave. "Miss Weinberger, I am so sorry for your loss—both of them.

~ 69 ~

Everyone was gone by noon and the silence in the house was palpable. Mary tried to get Dixie to eat something, but she couldn't stomach the thought. She told Mary that she was going to take a nap, but instead, she went to David's bedroom and closed the door.

"Oh, Daddy, how could this happen just when we were beginning to understand one another?"

She went into the private library. A 40" beveled glass-top sat above a Lalique base fashioned like a three-arm cactus. Several books about Emperor Napoleon lay open along with maps of Italy and France. Dixie walked slowly around the table—her finger sliding over each item in her wake.

Tears streamed down her cheeks, but she did not bother to wipe them away. In the 1980s David had walnut bookcases built into the room. She went to the wall of books and studied the titles of many. One whole section was dedicated to his foreign idle. Some books were on business strategy, creating a competitive advantage, and building on cost leadership. Another section seemed to focus on classic crimes.

"I can't say I'm surprised. You weren't the type to read Zane Grey or Larry McMurtry." She smiled through her tears.

As she walked around the room, she came to a shelf covered with framed photos. One was Rosemary in her wedding dress posed angelically against a stained-glass window and holding a large bouquet of white lilies, baby's breath, and long satin ribbons. A cap with white pearls topped the white fingertip veil. Other photos showed Rosemary at the beach and Rosemary holding Dixie.

"She was beautiful. I wish I had known her before she got sick."

There was one of Dixie's first steps and one of David as the 2008 Businessman of the Year.

"It makes me sad that the pictures you cherished were from so long ago. Wasn't there anything current to treasure?"

A wave of sadness washed over her. She sat on the floor as she had done so many times in her youth. She just wanted to be near him. Mother was only the old woman upstairs who didn't know her. Daddy was her parent, but he never had time for her. She ached to have him put his arms around her and hold her close, or maybe kiss her from time to time. Instead, he would pat her head or touch her shoulder as he guided her out of the room, so he could get back to work.

As she grew older, he'd give her money to go shopping to get her out of his hair. For birthdays and Christmas, he'd lavish her with gifts, when all she really wanted was for him to spend time with her. He seldom traveled, but when he did it was always for business and she was never invited. Nonetheless, when he returned, he always brought her gifts.

She looked at the picture of David receiving the Businessman of the Year award and remembered the times he would be on the phone shouting angrily at the person on the other end. He never shouted at her, but he was stern. He never swore at her, even when he was angry.

She got up, blew her nose, wiped away the tears, and sighed. "Daddy would say, Dixie, stop feeling sorry for yourself. There's work to be done." She smiled. "That's just what he'd say."

The girl continued her review of the library. She admired how he had organized so many books. They were all laid out by subject, then in alphabetical order by title. She came across a drawer fitted into the bookcase. "What's this?" She pulled on the handle, but it was locked.

"My goodness. Daddy had secrets." She knelt on the beige Berber carpet and inspected the small keyhole. "That doesn't look too complicated." Dixie found a letter opener on the table with a few pieces of mail. She returned to the drawer and peered into the lock, then poked the letter opener into the hole and gently turned it. Nothing happened. She tried several times before it clicked, and she was able to pull the drawer open. Inside was a small ledger. She thumbed through it; page after page of numbers and symbols that made absolutely no sense.

SN $2,500 0920UG1725 <
SN $5000 0820EM1809 < /12
KB $3,000 0920GY0616 >/6
MC $1,500 0419NS9812 *
SN $5,000 0620DM2015 <
MC $1,500 0519NS9816 *
KB $2,000 20JW1726 >/12
KB $1,500 0620BW0618 <>
KB $$1,500 0220ER1708-0-

"Okay. This is a waste of time." She set the ledger aside and rummaged through the drawer. There were receipts for things he had purchased over the years.

Theobald's—Indianapolis, Indiana. April 17, 1984. $68,000. Lalique table.

Jon L. Rodkers Diamonds—Venice, Florida. 1984. $1,800. Diamond and pearl ear drops.

"My gosh, Daddy. You must have saved the receipt from every purchase you ever made! Why?" She chuckled. "I guess he was a hoarder in this respect."

She reached in and pulled out piles of such receipts. It was then that she noticed another keyhole. With the drawer empty, she could see that the back had a hidden compartment.

She tried to pick the lock to no avail.

"There's a key to this somewhere, but I'm in no hurry. I'll find it eventually." She put everything back in the drawer and left.

70

"Have a seat, Mr. Copeland."

"Your officer came to my house and told me to accompany him to the police station for questioning. What is this all about?"

"We're investigating the murders that have taken place over the past couple of weeks."

"What does this have to do with me?"

"That remains to be seen but right now, we're looking for information." Bradshaw sat back in his chair. "Mr. Copeland, what is your profession?"

"I'm an independent CPA."

"You keep the books for various business owners. Is that right?"

"Yes, sir."

"How many businesses do you work for?"

"At the moment I have five clients."

"And they are?"

"Let's see, there's Billy Wilkenson's auto body shop, Mark Stroud's pool hall, Jim Johnson's Tavern and Grill to name a few."

"Do you keep the books for Nate Smallwood?"

"Well, yes."

"How long have you been working with these businesses?"

"I moved to Venice in 2007. As you can imagine, clients come and go. Businesses grow and others fail. I can't remember how long I've been with each."

"Smallwood has been in business for four years. Have you been with him all that time?"

"Yes, I believe he contacted me shortly after the building went up."

"Then you are familiar with his finances, right?"

"Well, I suppose I am. You aren't going to question me about confidential matters, are you? I don't believe it is prudent to reveal..."

"Mr. Copeland, this is a murder investigation, and it would be quite prudent to answer my questions." Bradshaw sat up and rested his arms on the desk. "How much would you say he makes a year?"

"I don't know. I don't have any paperwork with me."

"Give me a ballpark figure."

"I... I don't know..."

"Would you say the figure is around $100,000 annually?"

"Well, I..."

"Would you say it's more around $500,000?"

Mr. Copeland looked around as if he wanted to run. "I guess it's around the $500,000 mark. But it has dropped recently." He took out a handkerchief, removed his wire-rimmed glasses, and wiped his brow.

"I understand that he had a partner or someone working with him."

"Mr. Smallwood has several employees, but no partners."

"It could have been a salesman. What I want to know is when that person left—did it make a noticeable difference financially?"

"A salesman did quit a short while ago."

"Mr. Copeland, did his leaving affect sales?"

"Uh, well... Yes, sir. Actually, it did."

"Do you like working for Smallwood?"

"I need the money, Detective. I'm not getting any younger. In my day I had as many as 15 client companies, but I just couldn't keep up the pace. One of my clients passed away this week. Things can't get much more dismal for me."

"The client who passed away—who was that?"

"David Weinberger. He was my first client when I moved to Venice."

"Do you go by Bernard or Bernie?"

"It depends who you're talking to. Mr. Weinberger always called me Bernie."

"I have to ask you this, and I want a straight answer. Do you keep all Smallwood's books?"

Copeland wiped his brow again. "I don't know what you mean?"

Bradshaw rubbed his itching ear. "I think you do, sir."

"I can't afford to lose another client, Detective."

"If he's involved in illegal activities, I'm going to find out, and when I do, he won't need a bookkeeper; he'll be in prison."

Bernie slumped back in his chair as if all the air in his body had just deflated.

"One of these days I will bring a search warrant and collect both sets of books and more. If you don't want to follow your employer to the lock-up, you will not reveal this conversation, and you will keep everything intact. Do you understand what I'm saying, Mr. Copeland? Working with us is your best option."

Tuesday, June 30, 2020

71

Nate was sitting on the throne reading the paper when he heard the alarm that sounded in the back rooms when the large double doors opened or closed.

"Shit! Can't a man have a minute of privacy!" He clumsily folded the newspaper and laid it aside. He used a wad of toilet paper and pulled up his pants still mumbling to himself. He went to the sink and growled when he found the soap dispenser was empty. He dampened his hands under the cold water and went to grab a paper towel, but that dispenser was also empty. He put his hands in his pockets to dry them before he went out to meet his potential customer.

Much to his displeasure, he found Bradshaw, Kincaid, Larry, and five uniformed officers milling around the showroom.

"You're not here to sell me tickets to the policeman's ball, so why are you here?"

Bradshaw turned at the sound of Nate's voice and walked over to him. "Good morning, Mr. Smallwood." He reached into his pocket and pulled out a neatly folded paper and handed it to the fat man.

"What's this?" he asked, unfolding the paper.

"It's a warrant to search your facility."

"You're what! Why?"

-

"We believe you have a regular schedule of receiving and selling street drugs and related items and work out of this building."

"I don't know where you got your information, but it's all lies. I run a legitimate business here. You have no right to search my place!"

"Mr. Smallwood, the paper in your hand gives me that right." He turned to the team of officers. "Spread out, you know what to look for. Sparks, Kincaid, start with his office. Mr. Smallwood, you'll want to open your safe for these gentlemen."

"I will not!"

"Okay. I figured you'd say that, so we brought a blowtorch. Kincaid can handle that job."

Kincaid and the two of the officers went outside and returned with dogs and a torch.

"Smallwood, why don't you and I go to your break room? I have more questions for you."

Suzanne, the cashier came out to see what was happening. "Is there a problem, sir?"

"You are free to leave, Miss. When we finish, we will be shutting down the business indefinitely."

"What are you saying? You can't shut me down!"

"Go ahead, Miss."

She looked shocked, faltered a moment, then returned to her window and gathered her things. As she passed them, she stopped. "Excuse me, Mr. Smallwood. You can call me when you get this all worked out."

The two men went into the small room—an oversize closet that housed a chipped Mr. Coffee pot in which the bottom ¼ was stained from repeatedly burned coffee. The counter was cluttered with powdered cream, used plastic spoons, and an array of unwashed, mismatched cups. Bradshaw hesitated to sit on any of the old plastic straight-back chairs. Nate sat, and his chair swayed threateningly. Bradshaw reasoned that if the chairs could hold Nate, who was easily 70 pounds heavier, he was safe.

To Nate's surprise, Bradshaw pulled out a four-page rap sheet. Under the photos the names were different, but they were all Nate.

~ 72 ~

Dixie spent the morning in her father's study. She found his accounting records, a financial statement that recorded his income, expenses, and equity. There were IRS tax records and returns. In another ledger, he had listed all those who worked for him, but there were no jobs assigned to them; nor was there any indication of what they did for him. Jacob's name was not included in this list, and he'd worked for him for about six months.

One folder was titled "Rental Properties" and included packets for each property he owned. "I thought he owned five properties, which he told me he had put on the market recently. There must be twenty packets in this folder. And why are they here and not at the office? Oh, Daddy. What is this all about?"

She suddenly felt overwhelmed, put the folder down, and left the room. The house felt so quiet it made her shiver.

"Mary, is it about time for lunch? I'm starving," she asked as she entered the Morning Room.

Mary was putting away freshly washed linens in the bureau and looked up to see Dixie enter. "I made a Caesar salad and some baked chicken. Does that sound good?"

"Oh yes," she said, stretching her neck and arms before taking a seat at the table. She took a deep breath and let it out slowly. "I've been going through Daddy's things in his study. I cannot imagine how he handled everything. He's got books and ledgers of records in the study and other things in his library. And we must not forget his office on the by-pass. How did he keep everything straight?"

"I don't have a clue, my dear. He was an amazing man."

"It will take me a while, but I intend to take over his business. But first, I'll have to learn just what all he did."

~ 73 ~

The earlier 90-degree temperature of the day had cooled to a muggy 84 degrees as the red 2013 Miata convertible turned right from Honore onto Laurel and headed west. The breeze blowing Jacob's hair was invigorating.

"David is dead. David is dead!" he chuckled out loud.

"That's one pain in the ass I will never have to contend with again." He broke into joyful laughter.

He reached down and turned on the radio to 97.5, then sat back humming the tune to the music that was playing. Traffic was zero when he reached US 41, ran the red light, and continued on. Up ahead he saw a sign: *Buckle Up. It's The Law.*

"Fuck it!" He said cheerfully, flipped it the bird, and sped up. "Fuck them all! Even if this turns out to be Atlanta all over again, I'm better off. No one will ever find the millions I have stashed away in the Bahamas. Frog, you old fart! Thanks for the help. You're as good as any U.S. Marshal assigned with forging me a new identity. In time I'll add to my wealth and disappear again.

He chuckled to himself as he thought about Dixie. *David had been nuts when he thought I would lose everything.*

"I couldn't decide which I'd enjoy more, handling David or handling Dixie. I wouldn't really want to hurt or disfigure her, but there are ways to make her scream. I love it when women scream."

Just thinking about it made his cock hard. He pictured her naked, wrists tied, and hanging from the overhead bar in his room. When he bought the little house on the Intracoastal, he had done a bit of *redecorating* with just this kind of thing in mind. Until now he hadn't had a chance to use it. He'd constructed a *safe room* you might call it, constructed of 16-gauge square galvanized steel. No woman or man could break out of it.

"I wish I had put David in there and just left him for a few weeks. It would have been good to see how the son of a bitch would act then. I'd love to have seen him beg for his life. Fuck him. Let him rot!"

He passed a sign that read, Speed Limit 30 mph. He jammed the accelerator till it read 85. Speeding along listening to Billie Eilish singing "Bad Guy" and lost in thought, he didn't see the cable strung across the road—even when it reflected in his headlights. Suddenly the car hit it, driving the cable through the fiberglass body, into the engine and stalling the vehicle. Jacob was hurled into the air like a rag doll. He cleared 30 feet before slamming into the branches of an oak tree, where he came to rest—draped and lifeless.

Wednesday, July 1, 2020

Autumn and Larry turned from Harbor Drive onto Airport Road heading for Boatman's house.

"What did he say?"

"Just that he needed to talk to me," Autumn said.

"He didn't mention what it was about?"

"No, but I could tell he was nervous."

They turned left onto Avenida Del Circo. "That sounds ominous."

"I agree. Perhaps he's found something, a clue maybe."

When they reached US 41, Larry asked. "Do I turn here?"

"No, go straight. The street name changes to Amora Avenue and then turn onto Golf Drive."

When they pulled onto his driveway, Boatman met them at the door.

"I'm glad you came so quickly. Please, come in."

"What is it? You sound worried," Autumn said. "This is Larry, the guy I mentioned to you. He's teaching me *sleuthing*."

"And..." Larry said.

"Oh yes, self-defense."

"Good," he said to Autumn and shook Larry's hand. "Larry, it's good to meet you. I'm afraid she's going to need protection."

"Why, what happened?

-

"I had a vision. Oh yeah, I'm one of those crackpots who gets messages from the spirit world or underworld, or God knows where. The damn things drive me crazy, and lately, I've been having wacky-world marathons. I'm getting a beer, would you two like anything?"

"It's almost noon; sure, I'll have one," Larry said with a grin.

"And you?" he asked Autumn.

"It's only 10:15. I'll have a diet Coke if you have one."

They took their drinks into the living room and sat down.

"I'm not sure where to begin. These things used to happen once every quarter or so, but now they come almost daily. I believe the first one came the day before Don died. I saw a fisherman cleaning a fish. If you've ever cleaned a fish, you usually cut off the head and gut it before removing the scales. In my dream, the fisherman stabbed the fish pushing the knife into its brain and twisting it. The background turned red, and the fish's eye became that of a human. There was an explosion of stuff that hid the fish from view."

"Stuff?" Autumn asked.

"Yes, beer cans, fishing plugs, a fishing hat, a book, and confetti, that kind of thing. Anyway, none of this meant anything until later, although I had a feeling of dread that I couldn't explain. But now I believe it was a premonition of Don's murder."

"The blade was pushed into its brain. That's what happened to Don, right?" asked Autumn.

"I didn't know that then, but I do now. The next one came after Don died. I entered a building that I knew from my time in Barbados. It represented a safe place to visit when meditating. Inside I found a knife. It was a birch handled fishing knife, Jeff's Rapala®. Blood flowed from the blade, covered the glass top table, and spilled onto the floor. Shortly after that, Jeff was accused of Don's murder."

"Oh my gosh, Boatman, why didn't you go to the police?"

"I thought it was just a dream. I didn't realize it was important until it happened. Then I got the connection. You see, that's the problem. I can't tell a prophetic vision from a dream," he told her.

"You indicated that there were more," Larry reminded him.

"Oh, yes. The next one came after Bradshaw returned Don's things. I found myself in a dark room, and yet I could see my way around. There were large pictures of boats on the walls and a bright flickering light coming from the next room. When I got to the next room, the light increased in brightness. Like the sun, it was too bright to look at. Then came the scream. It went on and on until I couldn't bear it any longer and I screamed too. Suddenly it went silent. With the silence, the light began to dim, and I could see there were no windows or furniture in the room, nothing, except a book hanging open in midair. The light was coming from the book. The book slowly closed and as it did the light inside dimmed. I could see the book's leather cover was etched with symbols. The light inside went out as the book closed."

"You think the book in your vision is Don's journal," Autumn figured.

"I do. I gave that book to Simka, my roommate at Cave Hill. Someone sent it back to me after he died. He'd never used it, so I gave it to Don," he chuckled.

"Don must have been the world's greatest records keeper. He noted everything in it."

"Did you recognize the symbols in your vision?" Larry asked. "Do you know what they represent?"

"No, I remember one symbol looked like an egg standing vertically. There were primitive animals on it. Another was a circle with knives and spears and that one also had words, but I'm not familiar with what the words stood for."

"Are we talking Voodoo or Obeah?" Larry asked.

"They are similar, but Simka was drawn to Voodoo." Talking about Simka brought a painful nostalgia. "I had my truck with me then and we traveled from Christ Church to St. Lucy on most every decent road, and some not so decent. After college, we traveled a lot. Simka was my best friend." He smiled and took a few swallows of beer before continuing. "We went to Belize, Grenada, Jamaica, Trinidad, Tobago, and the Virgin Islands. Simka wanted to learn all he could, to *master* Voodoo." Boatman took a long drink. "I watched Simka become more and more obsessed with voodoo and how it could be used to control people. We met Malavad, a voodoo priest, in Trinidad. The two men immediately disliked one another and became rivals. "I wanted to leave Trinidad for I sensed danger brewing. I tried to convince Simka to leave, but he was fixated. I couldn't sleep nights because of horrific nightmares, and during the day I suffered from frightening visions of voodoo sacrifices. No amount of pleading or threats swayed him, and I eventually came home alone." He lifted the beer bottle to his lips and downed all that remained. "I later learned that Simka challenged the priest to undergo a secret cleansing ritual. I suspect Simka's plan was to kill his rival, but Simka was the one who died. When I learned that my nightmares and visions stopped. I swore never again to practice any of the dark arts."

Autumn got to her feet and went to him. "Oh, how awful," She put her arms around Boatman. "I am so sorry."

"It was hard losing such a friend, but there was nothing I could do."

"I know exactly how you feel, believe me."

"This gift I have is more of a curse." He took Autumn's shoulders and held her back so he could look into her eyes. "It's more of a curse because I cannot turn off these visions, and I cannot seem to prevent what they appear to be telling me."

"You've had another vision, haven't you, Boatman?" Larry asked as he got to his feet, his voice demonstrating concern.

"Yes."

Autumn looked questioningly from one man to the other. "Oh my God, Boatman, this new vision, it's about me, isn't it? Tell me."

Boatman looked at Larry for support but of course, he couldn't.

"Please, Boatman." She took his arm. "Tell me."

He walked away and then turned back. "Please, both of you, sit down." He paced a moment—working up the courage or maybe choosing the right words—then began.

"Three of us were on my boat. We were searching for a location that you could use in your new book. We found the island. It seemed perfect, and you were very excited. The sun was setting, so we decided to spend the night on the island and explore it in the morning.

"During the night we heard a woman scream and discovered that Autumn was gone. The sound of screams turned to monkeys screaming. Larry, you must have been the other man who was with us. I now realize it had to have been you. Autumn had mentioned you, but I hadn't met you yet. We split up to save time. I looked around the campsite and beach, and you went off alone. There was another scream, and I thought I knew where it came from. When I got there, I saw a body, but it wasn't Autumn, it was a man. I turned him over..." Boatman stopped and took a deep breath. "He was dead. He wasn't breathing and his skin was blue, but then he opened his eyes and looked at me. He said, 'you couldn't save me. You can't save her.'"

"It was Larry?" she suspected.

"No... No, it was Simka."

"I was afraid and ran; I had to find you. There was a path through the undergrowth, I took it—knowing that it would take me to you, but the ground turned to mud, and I couldn't pull my feet out. I heard gasping and looked around. The other man, Larry, was buried up to his neck and slowly sinking. That's when I realized I was sinking too. I fought but couldn't break free. The mud--or quicksand—was up to my chin, I didn't want it in my mouth. Then I saw you running away from a man with a knife... I shut my mouth. The man grabbed you; he raised the knife... I held my breath as the mud reached my nose. I heard your scream die out as I beneath the muck."

No one spoke. The silence lasted indefinitely as each tried to make sense of what they'd heard.

Finally, Larry spoke. "Did this vision feel any different than the others?"

"It was more like a dream. Except for the monkeys, there was less symbolism. I'm not sure. What are you thinking?"

"Am I correct, your visions are more Peter Max, you know, more avant-garde than dream-like?"

"Boatman, did you know that I got a perverted phone call last night?"

"No."

"I'll bet you dimes to doughnuts it was the man with the knife in your dream," Larry added.

"What makes you say that? Do you know him?" Boatman was confused.

"Larry and I went to the Jaguar Boat and Supply to see Nate and learn what we could, but he was in a conference and we were only able to look around."

"Autumn was in the showroom when he and this *Mr. Black* came out of his office. They were talking about a job Black had done," Larry added.

"Nate told him to take the money and get out, but this Mr. Black said he liked it here. Nate was afraid it'd cause trouble if they were seen together."

"There was no mention of the book though?" Boatman rubbed the spot between his eyes thinking. I don't know, maybe he doesn't have the book."

"The book in your vision, any clue that might help..."

"Well, the bright light emitted from the book." He paused—thinking. "I don't know what it could mean."

"Didn't you mention a book in an earlier vision?" Larry asked.

"Oh, yes! In the first one—the fish and the explosion! Yes, there was a book in that one," Autumn reminded them.

"The way the fish was killed was very much like how Don was killed, and a book was one of the things in the explosion!" Boatman remembered.

"Oh my gosh, that's got to be it," Autumn said, clapping her hands.

"If that's the case, is there a link in the vision with the bright light coming from the book?" Larry sat back and crossed his legs. "We're missing something, Boatman."

"I don't think so. There was nothing live in that vision. The fish's eye became human in the first, but there was nothing like that in the book vision."

"Tell us the book vision again," Autumn suggested.

Boatman thought about it and retold the vision step by step, but nothing clicked with the group.

Autumn frowned. "No, something is missing. Think, Boatman. I agree you said nothing was in the second room, but you've left something out of the first room."

He thought about it. "It was dark, but I could see to get around. Wait! Pictures on the wall. That's it! They were pictures of boats. Not artsy pictures, more like posters."

"Could they be pictures like those advertising boats a person might buy? Pictures like Smallwood might use at the marina?"

Larry nodded, "That's got to be the connection."

"I don't know. These visions are just snippets of unrelated thoughts. There's no rhyme or reason to any of them," Boatmen said, shaking his head.

"My dear friend, you have a wonderful gift, but you don't have the confidence to trust yourself. You need to take each one at face value and trust that the clues you get will reveal themselves," Autumn smiled. "I believe in you, and I'm confident that in time you will believe in yourself."

~ 75 ~

The red Porsche convertible backed out of the garage, did a 180-degree turn, and drove off the property. At Honore, she turned left and headed for town. The call from Opel Hemmings had requested that she come to the office at 9:30 am for the reading of the will. Dixie was a little peeved that the call was from the receptionist and not Carmen directly. But she told herself that the new, more sophisticated businesswoman wasn't bothered with such minor occurrences. As she planned to take over her father's business, there would be many opportunities to establish the ground rules with Carmen.

Honore became Pinebrook at the light, and she continued to Venice Avenue, where she turned right and headed for town.

Over the past three days, she had been able to get a feel for what it would take to learn the business. It wouldn't be easy. The office had key people to run the business as her father had, but the secrets, the codes, and hidden things at the house were another story altogether. She would have to decipher the codes in the ledger. The drawer of receipts would be easy to collate chronologically to learn if there was any reason for keeping them. As for the books in the private library, she had already decided to sell them at a New York auction house specializing in books. She had also decided to move into David's bedroom suite and had called the top designer in Sarasota to do the remodel. Her bedroom would become the guest room, and Jacob's old room would become a galleria for David's collection of three-dimensional art pieces; many of which were stored in the attic on the third floor. The gym would also be rearranged, repainted, and different mirrors added. She intended to remove any trace of Jacob having been there.

The convertible crossed the Venice by-pass, drove over the Venice Avenue Bridge, and turned left onto Business 41. Within minutes it pulled onto the driveway of the Tandem Building and into a parking space near the door.

Dixie entered the reception area.

"Oh, Ms. Weinberger, Carmen asked me to take you in as soon as you arrived," Opel smiled as she got up from her chair behind the desk and led Dixie to the conference room at the end of the hall. Dixie entered the room, and Opel closed the door behind her and returned to her desk.

Dixie was surprised to see Mary North and a man she didn't know.

"Dixie, welcome. Please, take a seat, and we will begin."

"This is the will of David T. (Thaddeus) Weinberger, being of sound mind and..." Carmen began.

Dixie was only half listening as her mind was focused on who this man might be. *I've never seen him before, and why would he be at the reading of Daddy's will?*

Carmen continued reading. "To my only child and daughter, I leave Bedwick Mansion and all its contents and all five of the properties I personally own. Should these properties be sold, she will receive all the revenues from them."

A frown formed on her brow. *What about the business?*

"To my dear wife, Rosemary, I leave a trust of $100,000 a year for her care and needs and the stipulation that she remain in Bedwick Mansion with two to three personal nurses attending her 24-hours a day, until her passing.

"As for Weinberger, Inc., arrangements have been made for the restructuring to begin for the control and running of the business. Each current employee will receive a $5,000 bonus at the end of every fiscal year that he/she remains with the company. This does not extend to anyone hired after my death. If an employee quits, his bonus ends and cannot be reclaimed at a later date.

"To my faithful agent Kevin Bond, I leave the house on Pemberton Street, for its use as he sees fit. He will also receive an annual bonus of $200,000 for his loyalty and continued help in running that facet of the business as long as he is capable or until his passing."

Dixie was confused. *What was this guy to my father that he got such a generous settlement in Daddy's will?*

"To my ever-faithful caretaker and friend, I leave Mary North a raise in salary of 20% a year—effective immediately—as well as her residence in Bedwick Mansion, along with a $50,000 bonus for remodeling it to her pleasure. If and when Bedwick Mansion should be sold, she will receive a $200,000 severance fee." Carmen sat the papers down. "Are there any questions?"

Dixie raised her hand.

"Dixie, please stay a moment. Ms. North and Mr. Bond, Opel has some papers for you to sign. Thank you for coming."

"Carmen, I assumed that I would be taking over the running of Weinberger, Inc."

"David and I talked on Friday. He said he knew you would want to follow him in the business. He said that he was so proud of you making a new life for yourself. He did not want you burdened with the corporation, though. Because of it, he never had time to be a real father to you. Instead, it had made him hard and aggressive; and he didn't want that for you. He told me that he loved you very much and hoped you'd understand."

"I wish he had told me that."

"You must remember, he thought this would be read down the road, ten or maybe twenty years from now. He expected that by then you would have a loving husband and a couple of children."

"I think I understand, Carmen." she started to leave—but then turned back. "Carmen, tell me—who is this Kevin Bond? I've never heard of him."

"I don't know, but your father obviously wanted him to continue working in the future."

"Yes, thank you. Good-bye." Dixie thought she'd catch him in the outer office and ask him herself, but he had already left.

"Peaches, I don't know what to say. I never expected he'd leave me with anything. After all, I'm just a..."

"Oh hush, dear. From the very beginning, you were there when he needed you. You were more help than you will ever know." She put an arm around Mary, and they walked to the door. "Why don't you think about how you'd like to remodel your rooms?

I'd be happy to help if you like. It will be so much fun."

"Why do you suppose he did it?"

"Because I imagine he loved you as much as I do, and I want you to be with me forever."

Jeff and Autumn sat in the waiting room of #206 Electra Enterprises awaiting their turn to meet with the producer of the upcoming movie that Jeff would be a part of.

"I am so excited, Autumn. This is the opportunity of a lifetime. Imagine me, a fireman turned movie producer! I will be rubbing elbows with this marvelous director and the cream of Hollywood talents."

"I hope this works out for you, Honey. But try not to get your hopes up. I understand these deals come and go like a puff smoke from a candle."

"What? You sound like you don't want this for me."

"No, it's just that so many people are involved in these projects that anything can happen to kill the deal. I just want you to look at it reasonably, that's all. And honestly, this is a lot of money to risk so casually."

Just then the male receptionist spoke up. "He'll see you now. You may go in." He led them to the door and opened it to let them pass.

As the pair entered the room, Frog looked up and smiled. He took the cigar out of his mouth and laid it on the ashtray. When he saw Autumn, he broke into a salacious smile and rose from his chair.

Jeff took this as a cue to approach the desk, and charged, his hand extended to shake hands with the older man.

"It's so good of you to see us, sir. I'm Jeff Markison, we spoke earlier."

Frog seemed to see him for the first time and did not return the gesture.

Jeff nervously withdrew his hand. "This is my sister, Autumn Mariiweather. She is my, uh... financial partner."

Frog's hand went up immediately toward the woman, who gently shook it, then withdraw it just as quickly. She had noticed his slight toward her brother and was quickly sizing him up.

"Please, have a seat," he croaked to Autumn. She looked over at her brother. When Jeff sat down, she sat. Frog sat then, never taking him eyes off her. "What can I do for you?" he asked her.

"I understand that you talked to my brother about investing in an upcoming movie. We are here to discuss the details."

He looked at the young man. "Refresh my memory, Jim. I have a number of projects pending."

"It was a couple of weeks ago, sir. We met at the Stage Right bar. We talked about a movie called *JAZZ*. You gave me a copy of the manuscript and said you were looking for funding."

"Funding? Oh, yes. Of course, I remember, Jim." He reached into a drawer and pulled out a contract. Here you go." He picked up a pen and handed both to Jeff. "Just sign here, and here, and here. Press hard, each page is in duplicate."

Jeff took the paperwork and pen with a Cheshire grin. He laid the papers on the desk and clicked the pen.

"May I look at that? Autumn asked.

Jeff agreeably handed it to her.

"Nothing to worry about. It's just a simple agreement used in the business." Frog smiled at Autumn.

"I'm sure it is," she said. She began skimming the legal contract.

"May I get you anything, Autumn?

She looked up, "no, thank you, I'm fine," and continued reading.

"Are you sure? Maybe a soft drink or iced tea?"

"I'm fine," she answered as she continued reading.

"I take it this is your first venture into film producing."

She didn't respond.

"Yes, this is the first time for both of us," Jeff said, becoming annoyed at being left out.

"I can always spot a newcomer to the business, Jim," he said, finally looking at the young man.

"It's Jeff, sir."

"Whatever," the man answered.

Autumn had had enough with his rudeness and spoke up. "We appreciate the opportunity you've given us, sir. It looks like a workable arrangement. However, I will need to read this over carefully, and I don't wish to take any more of your time. I know you're a busy man." She stood, "With your permission, I'll take this home and finish it there. Do you have any objections?"

"Of course not, Autumn. Take all the time you need. Call for an appointment when you're ready. I do look forward to our next meeting." He stood again, and they shook hands, although he held on just long enough to get her attention.

From the look on his face, it was clear that Jeff was confused. They left the office and got to the elevator before he spoke.

"What's going on? I had the pen in my hand ready to sign. You may have squelched the whole deal! Why would you do that?"

"First lesson in business: have an attorney look over any and all contracts. It's for your own protection. Didn't you notice what a sleazeball he is?"

"Come on, Autumn. He's just a Hollywood type."

"There's no such thing as 'a Hollywood type.' The people you mentioned being interested in making this film, they are 'Hollywood types' you want to work with. I'm sure they have to deal with people like this man a lot."

"So, it's a dead deal, right?"

"Not necessarily. Let's have Carmen look at this. If she thinks it's worthwhile, we can pursue it." She could see he still didn't get it. "Carmen will know what has been left out. You will want this investment to have the best chance of succeeding. The first step is to have a valid contract.

Thursday, July 2, 2020

-

~ 77 ~

Dixie sat in the morning room looking out onto the Veranda and beyond to the swimming pool—the glass of orange juice poised in her right hand. In her mind, she was imagining David as he swam laps that night. When he left the pool and dried off, he would have been silhouetted against the blue of the pool light. He would have taken a few steps and then *BANG!* She gasped as though she heard a shot. She sat the glass down and looked away, but the picture in her head wouldn't stop. She imagined looking to the right, the direction of the shooter. She saw a man standing in the dark, the gun in his hand still smoking, and that smug expression.

Just then, Mary entered from the Gallery.

"It's Detective Bradshaw, Peaches. He would like to speak to you."

"Good. I want to talk to him. Where is he?"

"He's waiting in the living room."

Dixie went through the Gallery and turned left into the living room. "Good morning, Detective."

"Miss Weinberger." He stood holding his fedora. "I hate to disturb you this morning, but I have more bad news."

She smiled. "I can't imagine anything being worse than your last visit."

"I'm sure you're right."

-

"What news do you have?"

"There's been an accident. Your fiancé was killed."

"What!" Her shock was not that of a caring soul but that of... well, shock. "Really?"

"Most likely, he was driving home the night before last. He was thrown from his car and died on the spot."

Dixie fought to keep from smiling. "You know, Detective. I suspect he is the one who murdered my father."

"Yes, ma'am, I thought you did. We still don't have any proof, but he was a serious contender. How are you holding up?"

"It's a day-to-day process, but I will rest easier knowing Jacob is no longer in the picture. Thank you for asking."

"I understand." He smiled at her. "I'll show myself out."

"No, please. Let me walk with you." She took his arm, and they started out. "My father was so caught up in his work that he never had time for me. But when he kicked Jacob out, everything changed. For the last week or so we talked. He listened. We shared thoughts and ideas. That short period made up for all the past misunderstandings. Maybe that wouldn't have happened if not for Jacob, I'll never know." She opened the front door, and he stepped out. "Thank you for coming today."

He smiled, put the fedora on his head, and left.

Dixie had put off going through David's things. It felt like such an invasion of privacy, but she also knew that the longer she put it off the harder it would become. She was in the study deciding which books to keep and which to get rid of when one caught her eye. *A Place No One Should Go* by DL Havlin—the eye-catching cover with its emerald green, the snake's head, and the silhouette of two men rowing a boat.

"Daddy, you were slipping." This book was certainly not a study in business law or anything to do with business. She took the book down and began thumbing through it when something fell out. She got on her hands and knees to look for it. It had bounced once and ended under the desk. It was a key. She picked it up and looked more closely. After putting the book back where it had been, she took the key to his private library. She opened the drawer in the bookcase, removed the ledger and piles of receipts. She was pleased to see that the key fit the little door, and she opened it. Inside was a hand-tooled, leather-bound book with a wrap-around cover that was arrayed with exotic symbols.

She sat on the floor and opened the book. It looked like a diary. She began thumbing through the handwritten pages with simple dates and snippets of information.

8/14 Heru Tanaka and the ninkyō dantai, hung him off the roof of a building in Atlanta, GA. They didn't kill him, but he's marked for life and barely has a voice. Ironically, they call him "Frog."

8/16 B went to work at a new marina on Dona Bay.

9/16 I got a job gardening at Bedwick Mansion.

10/16 I met the most beautiful woman I've ever seen. Her name is Dixie.

Her heart almost stopped when she realized what she was holding. She read more.

9/19 Learned today DW and NS are partners. DW funds it; NS pushes it.

1/20 DW hired JC today. I suspect he has something else planned for him.

3/20 B quit NS. Does he know about NS's other job?

12/19 DW's mistress found dead today. Rumor is it was no accident.

3/20 As I thought, DW wants to marry Dixie off to JC! My god, what is he thinking!

5/20 SN, a known cut-throat, has been hired by DW.

5/20 I cut a lock of her hair while she slept. God, I love her. One day soon I will whisk her away from the criminal and this psychopath.

This could only be Don's book!

Dixie had spent the whole day sifting through the ledger and receipts in the drawer. Comparing them with the initials in Don's book, she was able to somewhat translate the ledger. She determined the dollar figures were payments, but she wasn't sure who everyone was. SN was still a mystery, but KB had to be Kevin Bond, the loyal agent David had named in his will. The symbols could have represented the jobs done, but what those jobs were, was still unclear. She looked over the list one more time and stopped dead as one line stood out from the others.

MC $5,500 0120NS1612 *
MC $5,500 0520NS1616 *
MC $5,500 1020NS1607 *
KB $1,500 0620BW1618 <>
KB $3,000 0920GY1616 >/6
KB $$1,500 0220ER1708-0-
KB $2,000 0820JW1726 >/12
SN $2,500 0920LN1925 <
SN $2,000 1120FM1909 < /12
SN $5,000 0620<u>DM</u>2015 <
SN $2,000 0620JC2030??

She grabbed a pen and note pad and began transcribing the ledger.

DM-Don MacKenzie $5,000   < (killed)
06202015 (June 15, 2020)

"SN was the killer!" She jumped to her feet. She would call Bradshaw right away and tell him what she'd found. This was positive proof that would surely hang the son of a bitch! But then she stopped.

"Oh, my god, Daddy! *You* had him killed? Why!" She was instantly furious. "You goddamn, son of a bitch! How could you do that? I loved him, wanted to marry him." She burst into tears. Her grief was overwhelming. She picked up a straight back chair and threw it into the bookcase, shattering one of the back legs of the chair. She screamed in agony and pulled handfuls of books from the neatly organized sections and threw them in every direction. Books went flying as she kicked them out of the way as she reached for more. Lamps, figurines, and furniture were thrown or overturned. She brushed everything off the Lalique table until exhausted, she dropped to the floor. Uncontrollable sobs continued until she could no longer catch her breath. She closed her eyes and forced herself to breathe. In time, she grew quiet but still she laid there, thinking.

Why! Daddy, did you hate me so much? Did you hate him? No, if he'd known about us, he would have paid him off—but never killed him because of me. Daddy was never cruel. Not to me."

She got to her feet and with shaky hands began picking up books and setting them haphazardly on the shelves. *He didn't know about us. If it wasn't because of me—then why? Why!"*

Dixie paused, thinking. Her expression changed as she searched through the scattered mess on the floor. *For the book, of course.* She picked it up and thumbed through the pages.

"How could he have known about the book? I didn't know about it." Dixie closed her eyes, thinking. "Daddy must have found out somehow. Of course, it's a tell-all, and "DW" is mentioned throughout." Then she remembered what Don had said, *We could buy a little house someplace where no one knows us. It will be all right.*"

Dixie pressed the book to her heart. "Don's book."

He wanted to get me out of the danger he saw all around me. "Stupid, stupid me; I didn't get it."

She laid the book on the Lalique table and gathered the ledger and all the receipts.

"Bradshaw will find and prosecute SN and all the other sleazy culprits outlined here." She sighed deeply. *He can no longer arrest or punish DW for his crimes.* She smiled at that, but then the smile faded. "My God, it would ruin the family name and we would no doubt lose the business." *The employees would lose their jobs, not to mention their hefty bonuses. And Mother, Mother would spend her last days in a cheap assisted-living facility. Mary would lose her home and inheritance, and me... I couldn't live here, I'd have to leave, where would I go?* Her hand went to her mouth as if to prevent the thoughts from becoming words. Tears filled her eyes as she whispered "and all the misery it would bring, none of this, nothing would bring Don back.

Dixie dropped the ledger and receipts on the table and took Don's book back to the drawer in the bookcase. She returned it to the hidden safe and locked it. She tossed in the receipts, laid the ledger on top, and shut the door. She put the key back into the book *A Place No One Should Go* and put it back on the shelf that had kept it hidden all this time.

As she left the personal library in the Bedwick Mansion she uttered, "Daddy, I won't take over the business, but I will keep your secrets from the rest of the world."

Friday, July 3, 2020

July 3 began with a show of morning colors. The golden glow of sunshine peeked over the horizon with the promise of a warm and wonderful day, until the clouds rolled in and changed it all to rainbow pastels that morphed into shades of vermilion and cadmium red. But it was Friday, and the day they had planned included the adventure of finding the perfect spot for a picnic and a day free of worry.

"Are you ready," Larry called as he burst into the back door. "Hope you brought a bathing suit. The tide's up and water is inviting."

"Hi," Autumn said as she slipped off her apron. "I'm almost ready."

He sidled up to her and gave her a quick kiss on the lips. "Um, you taste like peanut butter."

"Mrs. Wilburn and I had a small breakfast with our coffee," she grinned. "I made fried egg sandwiches, peanut butter stuffed celery, sweetened iced tea, diced watermelon, Macadamia nut and white chocolate cookies."

"Yum, and she bakes!"

"No, she buys; the gals at Walmart bake."

"That works, and it leaves you more time to spend with me."

Mrs. Wilburn hurried in with a beach bag full of sunscreen, towels, a beach umbrella, and a blanket.

-

"You two had better be off. My arthritis tells me it's going to rain. Here, take this, too," she offered—holding out an umbrella.

"Oh no, there will be no raining on our parade today, my dear Mrs. Wilburn. I checked the weather, and there's only a 20% chance of rain today."

"Well, young man, I'll bet my bones against your weatherman any day."

He grabbed the bag and gave her a quick kiss on the cheek. She grinned. "Have fun. I'll see you tonight," and waved them good-bye.

They stowed the items in the back of Larry's Jeep Grand Cherokee, and they were on their way.

"Have you talked to Boatman?" Larry reached over and slid Autumn a little closer.

"Yes, he's not as excited about this adventure as we are. He's so worried that there'll be trouble, but I just can't see it."

"Maybe he needs to get away for a while," Larry offered.

"I hope so. He's been so bogged down with all that's happened, and he feels somehow responsible."

"Responsible?"

"Well, he thinks he should have been able to prevent all that's happened."

"No way."

"I know, but that's how he is. He's quite sensitive."

A short 20 minutes later they arrived at the Osprey Marina. Boatman rushed down the pier to greet them.

"Hey," Autumn waved when she saw him.

"Let me help you with that," he said taking the picnic basket, while Larry handled the cooler, and Autumn grabbed the noodles and beach bag.

"This is your boat? Wow! I'm impressed, Mr."

"This is it. The *Able Seaman.*"

"It really is nice. Must have cost you a pretty penny," Larry noted.

"We got a good price. My years with Nate taught me a lot, and I met some great people. It's a 2016 Viking. The guy that bought it from me back then is downsizing. He made us a heck of a deal."

"It looks in pretty good shape."

"Yes, it is. It's a Cummins engine and uses diesel fuel."

"It's huge. I guess I was thinking of a party boat."

"It's 42 feet. Not big, but perfect for our needs."

"It looks bigger than that."

"Well, the extras help. It has the tuna tower, Eskimo chipper, Rapp outriggers, a faux transom, Skyhook feature, and much more. It's cherry."

"I'd say so," Larry added.

"Let me give you a quick tour. Larry, set the cooler on the deck. Step carefully until you get your sea-legs. Here is the galley on the port side." Autumn sat the picnic basket down.

"Here's the head," Boatman gestured. "The guest stateroom is aft, and you can use it for changing and storing your things."

"Wow, Boatman. I could live here!" Autumn crooned. "Where do I plug in my computer?"

He grinned knowing she thought that would be a challenge. "Nice try, young lady. There will be no computer work done on this vessel today. This trip is strictly for fun in the sun and a location finder, emphasis on *fun*. If you two would like to settle in, I'll get us out of here."

"Aye, aye, Captain," Autumn said with a quick salute.

They pulled out of the Osprey Marina and headed out to sea. The water was calm and the winds mild. The cumulus clouds were beautiful against the cerulean sky. Autumn changed into her bathing suit, grabbed a towel, and headed for the deck. Larry was already preparing drinks. As she laid her towel on one of the tan seats, Larry handed her a glass of wine.

"I bought this especially for you. It's *Whispering Angel 2018 Rose* Cote De Provence."

"Are you trying to make points with me?"

"Does it show?"

"It does, indeed," she said, glancing at him from under her eyelashes. And I am impressed."

"Then I have succeeded."

"I admire the unbreakable plastic wine glasses, too"

"The unbreakable glasses were a requirement of the captain of this vessel."

"A wise man, indeed." She leaned forward and kissed him on the cheek.

"If I'd known I'd get a reaction like that I'd have spent more money on them."

"Less is often more."

"Ah, a wise woman of taste."

Autumn un-wrapped a tray of baby Swiss cheese with crackers, apple wedges, and seedless red grapes. She fixed a selection on a clear acrylic plate and took it into the cockpit for Boatman.

"So, Captain," she began, handing him the tidbits. "What is our ETA?"

"It won't be long. I have a spot in mind. It's a little north of Sarasota. Don and I ran across this hidden lagoon by accident. It's amazing. Once inside you would never know we were still in Florida. It's a natural, untouched island. I can't imagine how the public, especially investors, have not discovered it."

"Ooo, I can't wait."

"You're going to like it, I'm sure. It's densely covered with scrub, but there are paths. I think they were made by deer because we found tracks. There are a variety of palms, crepe myrtle, and oak trees. It's amazingly beautiful."

"Are you going to be tethered to the wheel while Larry and I enjoy the trip?"

"We'll be there soon, and then I'll be free to join you."

"Would you like a glass of wine?"

"Beer is my drug of choice. A lite if you have it."

"I can accommodate you, sir. Be back in a minute."

Larry had thought of everything in the choice of libations. He opened the cooler and pulled a can out of the bin of crushed ice. "Once you serve the Captain, Wench, join me on the aft deck."

"You're cute," she said, taking the brew from him.

"I try," he said coyly.

In no time the *Able Seaman* reached the location. Overhead, the cumulus clouds continued to grow in height. Boatman pulled into what appeared to be a small bay. He inched the boat to a perfect spot and dropped anchor. From there they portaged to the shore. Autumn donned a hooded swimsuit cover and slippers. They brought the cooler with beverages, beach bag, and the picnic basket. They found a small meadow just out of sight of the boat and dropped their items.

"Let's eat. I'm starved," Autumn suggested.

"That works for me." Boatmen chortled. "I haven't eaten since dinner last night."

They laid out the blanket, but the beach umbrella wasn't necessary as there was plenty of shade. They passed around the food.

"Fried egg sandwiches? I would never have thought of that," Boatman lifted the lettuce and inspected the cold egg and mayonnaise.

"Actually, it was Mrs. Wilburn's idea. She said that when she was growing up a picnic wasn't complete without them. The trio talked about picnics when they were kids, their favorite foods, and shared stories until they had eaten their fill. After stowing the rest of the food, they policed the area.

"Let's scout the area. I'm eager to show you the spot that made me suggest this to you," Boatman said." He led them along a narrow path into a darkened area. The canopy was so dense in many places that little light could get through and with no breeze, the air was still and added to the heat. The area took on a dark and mysterious feeling, almost threatening.

"My gosh, Boatman, this is spooky," Autumn said, pulling the hood of her coverup as if for protection.

"I knew you'd love it," he said, in a soft, almost reverent whisper.

They walked slowly observing their surroundings. Further up the trail, the space opened, the trees thinned, and the air was filled with chirping birds and insects, and the earthy scent of the forest.

Autumn gasped as a black snake slithered across the path and disappeared in the undergrowth near her.

"What?" Larry inquired.

"Snake; sorry, it startled me."

The path narrowed again, forcing the group to walk single file. Larry followed Autumn as Boatman took the lead. The leaves above them rustled as a breeze built indicating that the wind was picking up. They pushed through low-hanging vines and small branches. As they walked along the canopy thickened and thinned. Occasionally the three could spot clouds and rays of sunshine.

"I keep expecting to hear monkeys laughing and calling to one another," Larry whispered.

Boatman smiled. "Right atmosphere; wrong country."

"Good. Snakes don't bother me, monkeys... Ugh," Autumn shivered.

"What wildlife do you suppose lives here?" Larry asked.

"I haven't done a study or anything like that, but I would imagine deer, opossum, rabbits, and rats. With all this foliage I'd imagine all kinds of birds. There are swampy areas around here, so turtles and alligators would be a safe bet."

Just then they heard a familiar cry in the distance.

"And panthers," Autumn added, with a nervous chuckle.

"There are certainly scorpions and spiders," Boatman added.

"I could have gone all day without hearing that!"

Both men laughed.

"I wonder if I can use this location in my book. It's very tight."

"We have to be careful, too. These paths narrow and widen and converge. It would be easy to get lost.

They walked in silence for a bit. The smell of decaying leaves and mold added to the forest's mystique. Suddenly, they heard a muffled sound unlike their surroundings.

"That was strange," Autumn noted aloud as they continued on.

The path widened and walking became easier. "This is much better," Autumn said, turning around to say something. "Larry. Larry?"

Boatman turned and saw that the man was no longer with them. "I wonder if he missed the path and got turned around? LARRY!" he called. No answer. "Why don't we backtrack? We'll find him," he assured her.

They weren't concerned until they'd gone about a quarter of a mile. Boatman stopped and scratched his head. "We must have missed a path or something. We should have caught up with him before now."

"Oh my gosh. How will we ever find him if he's lost? We can't see more than five feet in any direction. What are we going to do?"

"You're right. He may have gotten off the path and couldn't find his way back. We may not be able to see far, but he can certainly hear us. Once he realizes he's alone he'll most likely backtrack in hopes of finding us. Let's go back."

They took turns calling out. Autumn noticed that even though Boatman was telling her to stay calm he was becoming agitated. They were nearly back to the spot where they realized he was gone when they heard a sound.

"Did you hear that?"

"It sounded like a moan. It came from over there." Boatman pushed through the philodendron and ferns. In the mass of green foliage, he could just make out Larry's tropical shirt. He reached down and pulled the man to a sitting position, but Larry was out cold.

"Autumn, help me get him back to the path."

It was a struggle moving the dead weight a mere six feet through the foliage, but then they were able to look him over.

"There's no blood or bruises. What could have happened to him?"

"What are we going to do? There's no way we can carry him back to the boat."

"We could make a travois. We'd need two long poles; maybe use vines for rope... but we'd need sturdy tools. He reached into his pocket. All I have is a small pocketknife."

"Boatman, let's be practical. You can find your way back to the boat. You should go for help. I'll stay here with Larry."

"I can't leave you here alone!"

"Do you have a better suggestion?"

Boatman paused. "No, I guess not. Before we do this, you need to realize, it will take me time to get back to the boat, and then go for help. I can call the Coast Guard to meet me, but you'll still be out here with no food, no water, and no way to communicate. There could be any number of delays." He was still thinking. "What if I'm not back by dark? It's hard enough to find the way in daylight, I've never tried after dark. No, Autumn, there must be another way."

"Please, there's not a minute to waste. If you don't leave right away, it will be dark before you get back."

"But I don't want to leave you." He brushed his fingers through his hair moist from the heat. I was afraid something like this might happen. This trip wasn't a good idea, and now this..."

"Seriously, you must go. I'll be all right."

"But..."

"Boatman! Go, go, go!"

"All right." He stripped off his shirt and handed it to her. "You may need this."

"For what?"

"I don't know—sun, wind, rain, bugs? Oh," and he handed her the knife. "Here."

"What's that for?"

"You may need it."

"For what, skinning deer?"

"You never know," he grinned. "I'll go, but I'll feel better if you have it." He turned and quickly dashed out of sight.

Autumn looked around. "Why did I even question him? He's the one who has visions." She sighed deeply. "Well, he's right about me needing the shirt," she said out loud—as she spread the shirt beside Larry and sat down on it.

Boatman ran along the path taking in anything that might be a landmark in case his return trip was in the dark. He timed the distance running from the spot where he'd left Larry and Autumn. As he passed their picnic area, he grabbed a beer from the cooler. Even so, he felt guilty that he had access to refreshments, and they didn't.

It took him 25 minutes to run the distance. He had to slow down and stopped twice to catch his breath. He hit the water running and the cool water was invigorating. Once onboard the boat, he started the engines and backed away from the shore. It was then he noticed a speedboat tied up about 70 yards away. It was nearly invisible under low hanging vines.

~ 80 ~

Boatman quickly turned seaward, pulled down the VHF marine radio, and switched to channel 16.

"MAYDAY, MAYDAY, MAYDAY. This is the *Able Seaman* out of Osprey, Florida, *Able Seaman*— Osprey, Florida, the *Able Seaman* out of Osprey, Florida." He gave his call letters and waited for a response—all the while pushing the Viking as fast as it would go.

In a matter of minutes, he received contact from the Sarasota Coast Guard suggesting they switch to channel 68.

Boatman quickly introduced himself and relayed the emergency to the officer. He explained that they didn't know the cause of the man's condition and suggested they bring a doctor. He described the dense foliage on the island, the distance, and the need for transporting the man off the island. "One more thing," Boatman added, "When I headed out, I saw a speedboat hidden among the trees a short distance from us. I have a bad feeling. You'll want to come prepared for trouble."

"Got it, Boatman. You should also know the weather has taken a turn for the worst. The temperature is dropping, and the wind is picking up. Storm cells are converging—bringing with them thunderstorms. It's going to be a bad one."

"And that is going to make the rescue even harder. May I give you the coordinates and wait for you on the island? I'm eager to get back and check on the woman staying with the injured party. But I'll wait for you and guide you through the jungle."

Boatman made a wide sweep and headed back to the island as storm clouds began to form in the southwest.

~ 81 ~

As time drug on with little to do but sit and wait, Autumn stood up and stretched. Her neck ached, and her bottom was numb from sitting so long on the hard ground.

She walked around the small area. It was free of shrubs and vines and they were lucky to have found it so quickly. It had been a struggle carrying Larry the short distance, and it had taken both of them to accomplish it.

Overhead the canopy of trees offered occasional views of the sky. The rich blue had been replaced by a ceiling of gray clouds. She noticed that the wind had also picked up as the upper-most branches were agitated. The birds were quiet, but the insects flitted by frequently.

She looked at her bare wrist that usually held a watch. None of them had worn watches. The plan had been to picnic, tour the island, swim, and enjoy the day without computers, phones, or watches. Without them, and no view of the sun, it was impossible to tell how much time had passed.

She looked down at Larry. He hadn't moved or uttered a sound since they found him.

"How could this happen? What caused it?" She asked aloud. She leaned close to see if he was breathing and took his pulse. It was slow. "I wish there were something I could do," her tone came from frustration rather than anger. She picked up Boatman's shirt and shook it out. Bits of leaves and moss fluttered about. Then she spread it out again and laid down beside Larry. She nestled up against him and smiled to herself. It had been a long time since she had been this close to a man. That man had been Richard. Oh, how she missed him. She yawned and closed her eyes, and before long she was asleep.

In the distance, thunder sounded, and lightning flashed overhead. There was no rain, but that could change at any time. Autumn found herself walking in a forest of palms and pine trees. She was searching for something or someone.

"Richard!" she called."

"This is a nice island; so close, and yet so far away. I never knew it was here."

In the mist of the dream, Autumn looked around. "Richard? Where are you?"

"I'm right here."

"Where?" Everywhere she looked the colorful meadow was filled with patches of wildflowers. A long-eared rabbit skipped by, but nothing else moved. "I can't see you. Richard!" She called a third time, but she could feel the dream world slipping away."

"I'm right here. Open your eyes."

The day was hot, and although a slight breeze could now be felt, the ground level air stifling. She brushed strands of wet hair from her face. Her eyelids were heavy. She didn't want to leave. She wanted to find him, but it was no use. The last remnants of sleep drifted off, and she opened her eyes.

A man, naked but for a short loincloth, crouched beside her. He was tattooed from the middle of his chest, around and all the way to his neck including both arms. He was clean-shaven with a high forehead, shaved eyebrows, and a buzz cut. He looked familiar, but she didn't know him. She shook her head, blinked away the last of the dream, and then frowned.

"Did you think I'd forget you?" He reached over and pulled her bathing suit cover gently to the side. Oh, I see you're wearing your blue swimsuit."

Suddenly, wide-eyed, she sat up.

"Oh, I see you remember me. Good," He said.

He hated bars. He'd always hated them. He wasn't claustrophobic, or anything as prissy as that. But from the first, he didn't like being confined. Here he was again, sitting alone, in yet another interrogation area, waiting for a cop to come in and question him.

"Questions, questions! What a fucking, boring job that must be. Jazus Cryst! They probably have a book in the back where all cops can choose what questions to ask!"

Nate Smallwood stood up so quickly the chair slid two feet behind him.   "I've been here four days, and I'm going flat fucking frustrated. This has to be the curse Fran put on me when she gave me that knife. If I ever get out of this building, I'll disappear, and those assholes will never find me again!" He paused in his tirade. "Damn. I'll have to give up the Jag," he realized.

Well, you stupid ox, you're going to lose it anyway when they bus you off to the big house, the voice in his head replied.

"Great, now I'm arguing with myself."

Just then the door opened, and Bradshaw walked in with a note pad and a cup of coffee.

"Good afternoon, Mr. Smallwood. How's your day going?"

"Don't be a smart ass, Smart Ass."

"I see you're in a good mood, as usual."

"What do you want from me?"

"I just have a few questions."

"Why do I even ask?" He went back, picked up the chair, and sat down at the table again.

"I have a list of what was found at the marina. Do you care to hear it?"

"Why do you want to tell me something I already know? What? You're out of questions?"

Bradshaw didn't understand that remark and moved right along. "As you will recall, you were arraigned, and the judge advised you of the charges."

"Blah, blah, blah." Nate rolled his eyes and shook his head. "He pissed me off when he refused to set bail!"

"Are you kidding? You're a major flight risk. No judge worth his salt would give you another chance to skip out."

"What am I supposed to do? You want me to just sit around here till December 10th?"

"No, you'll be transferred to the Sarasota lock up until your trial date. We're just waiting for Larry Sparks to return. He's going to be your shadow for a while."

"Great."

"Aw, cheer up. Sarasota is Club Med compared to us. They have books, TVs, tennis courts, swimming pools, and hot and cold running women. You're going to love it."

"Fuck you,"

"Actually, you probably won't get to go there either. That will be up to Sparks.

~ 83 ~

In an instant Autumn was on her feet pulling her cover more securely around her.

"You don't need that thing. Here, let me take it off for you."

She sidestepped to avoid his touch. "Stay away from me!"

"Don't be silly. Here we are all alone on this secluded island. No one will see or hear us."

She glanced down at Larry.

"You don't have to worry about him. I took care of that." He took a step closer.

"Stop right there!" she ordered—her palm raised to hold him off. "What did you do to him?"

"Oh, it's just one of many ways I have of getting rid of pests. I figured the other one would go for help, and with this one out of the way, you and I would be all alone." He grinned and licked his lips. "That night I saw you, wearing that bathing suit, the suit you're wearing now, I've had fantasies." He rubbed the bulge that grew in his loincloth.

Autumn felt a shiver despite the heat. "But, but what did you do to him?"

"It's something I learned from some friends in Africa. I have a special concoction that will disable a man... or woman for quite a while. I didn't make it strong enough to kill him, but he won't bother anyone for a couple of days, and when he does come around, he'll have one hell of a hangover." He moved toward her, but she stepped away.

"You're lying. He was behind me one minute and gone the next. You didn't have time to drug him." She hoped that if she kept him talking, she might find a chance to get away.

"Why would I lie? You aren't going to live long enough to tell anyone."

"What! Why would you kill me? What have I done to you?"

"You overheard me talking to the fat man. You heard us discussing our business. In my line of work, there's no room for witnesses."

"I heard him tell you to take the money and leave. That's all."

"Nice try, Sweetheart."

Thunder sounded in the distance and she looked up.

He lunged forward grabbing her wrist preventing her from getting away.

"I can't let you live. You might suddenly remember a little more of that conversation."

He pulled her to him with such force that she might have fallen instead of colliding into him.

Autumn gasped, now she could smell him, like a dog after a hard run. She tried to pull away, but he held tight. As she struggled something in her pocket bumped against her leg. The knife. Her mind raced with notions of how to break free and get away; he would not take her so easily. One hand clenched her wrist and the other held her so tightly she could barely breathe. She tried to push him away but found it impossible. He leaned in and kissed her on the mouth, his tongue searching for an opening.

Her free hand reached into the pocket and withdrew the knife, and without the slightest hesitation, she plunged it into his kidney. He let her go as his hands went automatically to the wound. When he saw the blood on his hand, his whole persona changed. His teeth locked and she saw the muscle in his temple tighten, his eyes narrowed angrily, and his hands became steel fists.

"You're right. Forget the foreplay. Let's get down to business," he growled.

Just then a loud clap of thunder sounded close by. Before he had even finished the sentence, she had dropped the knife back in her pocket and was running. She tore back along the path. If she could stay out of reach, she might run into Boatman returning, but could she out-run this madman? She heard footfalls pounding the ground behind her. He was barefooted and she prayed that would slow him. Speeding along the path she recognized a few trees and bushes they'd passed earlier but the forest was dense, and the path narrowed and broadened. She was too afraid to turn to see how close the man was. She could see the path ahead narrowing. Grasses and shrubs bit at her legs as she raced just ahead of the stomping feet behind her. She brushed the perspiration that seemed to flow from every pore. Her legs ached. Her chest hurt, but she could not slow down. The flats she wore were flimsy, but they protected her feet from the bits of rubble on the forest floor. The shoes surely gave her an advantage. She hoped that the two weekly trips to the gym would give her the stamina required to win this footrace with Satan.

Just then a bolt of lightning sent rays through openings of the forest's canopy—immediately followed by thunder so loud that she instinctively cried out and covered her ears, but she kept running. Her thighs felt like they were on fire, but to slow down would mean certain death. She could still hear the man behind her. Was it her imagination or was he gaining on her?

Rain began to fall with loud splats on the leaves overhead. Lightning and thunder were very close, but Autumn was more concerned about her assailant.

A flash of lightning cut through the forest near them, and the moss and dead leaves on the forest's floor were becoming slippery. Lightning and thunder had to be close for there was little time between them and the rain quickly built to a deluge.

Autumn's mind was racing. She dared not slip or fall. She must keep going. Just then she heard the man cry out in frustration; not with words, but a deep guttural sound like that of a bear. Instantly her thoughts went back to Richard trapped under the bear and fighting for his life. She had watched the crazed animal slash her husband to death while she cowered back and did nothing. If she had acted sooner, she might have saved him.

It was happening again. While Larry laid unconscious and helpless, although still alive – she, his only hope - was running away in fear.

Have I been given a second chance? Hot tears mingled with the cold rain. *My God, if I live through this there will be a second regret tearing at my soul. But what can I do?*

She was weakening. Her chest hurt so badly she could hardly breathe, her muscles ached, and she knew she couldn't go much longer. Suddenly, a hand grabbed her shoulder, tearing the cloth covering and pulling her off balance. As she fell, she remembered the knife. She hit the ground hard and rolled over fumbling for it.

A blinding flash, a splintering burst, the smell of ozone, as thunder simultaneously filled the air. She shrieked. The man swung at her and she dropped the knife. He lunged. She knew he meant to choke her. The last thing she would see would be the hideous sneer pasted on his face as he watched with pleasure seeing her die.

Exhausted and terrified, panic took over. She grabbed his outstretched arm, whirled around until her shoulder was in his armpit, she jerked him off balance, and pulled him over her back. He landed like a stone and lay there, wheezing.

Autumn gasping for breath, quickly grabbed the knife and held it ready to use. Her hands shook so badly she feared she might drop it, but the man did not get up. He laid there in the mud and moss fighting for air.

"I see you're as tired as I am," she told him in a shaky voice.

His eyes were huge. Frantically, he looked around His mouth moved as if trying to say something, but it was all he could do to breathe. He flailed his arm over his shoulder, and struggled as the rain splashed the blood dripping from his nose and mouth. His movements began to slow. Then, the only sound was the falling rain, a burbling gasp, another, then he relaxed, and his arm fell away. It was raining hard and his eyes were wide open, but he did not blink.

She forced herself to take a step closer, but staying out his reach.

"Oh my god, he's dead." When she moved around the body, she saw it. A long splinter had pierced his back, and the fall she'd caused had driven it deeper.

Suddenly, her legs turned to spaghetti. She collapsed, and began shaking all over, and she burst into tears. The rain fell and lightning flashed, as the thunder was moving away.

~ 84 ~

It was still light out, and the storm was finally moving off to the northeast when the rescue team reached the island. Two Coast Guard officers, two EMS responders, and Doctor Coons, who had answered the emergency call and agreed to go with them, rushed along the path as Boatman took the lead.

They hustled the stretcher needed to move the victim. But they were not prepared to find Samuel Nolen where he had fallen and died. The EMS people took the body back to the boat and returned with the stretcher

They found Autumn and Larry side by side with Boatman's shirt covering their heads.

"It made it easier for Larry to breathe, and I was cold," she said as if they had asked her to explain. "By the way, Boatman, here's your knife. Thank you. Sorry, it has blood on it."

They returned to the Coast Guard facility in Bradenton, where the police took their statements, Nolen was sent to the Sarasota Coroner's office where Gilbert would do the autopsy. Sparks was sent to Sarasota Memorial for the treatment of a chemical overdose.

"The doctor was able to relieve Larry's symptoms. They'll keep him a few nights, and he should be released on Sunday."

"Well, this was not the restful get-away that we had planned," Boatman said, as he accepted the shirt that Autumn handed him.

"True, but it had a much better ending than your most recent vision. We can be thankful for that. We will both feel better once we get home, have a meal and some well-needed rest."

Saturday, July 4, 2020

"I can't stand this delay, Sojoe. I have the feeling Autumn is stalling for some reason. Maybe she thinks I'll just forget about it, and she won't be without her money. I don't know. It all just seems fishy to me."

He took a left on Tamiami Trail, made a right on Miami and pulled into the parking lot.

"That's kind of strange. There are hardly any cars here. Are all these businesses closed on Saturdays?"

"Well, it is July 4th, Jeff. Some people consider that to be a holiday."

"I don't care. I'm going up and find out how we can move this along. I'll get back with you." He hit the red icon that ended the call.

Jeff looked into the windows on the ground-level businesses. They were all closed. He took the stairs to the second floor and looked over the balcony onto Venice Avenue. There were lawn chairs and blankets lining the street in preparation for the parade scheduled for later.

"Damn! Sojoe's right. He will be out for the holiday. I am going to try anyway." He turned at the door just in time to see the receptionist coming out carrying a box.

"Hey, man. What's happening? I came to see Frog. Is he in the office?"

"No. The cocksucker left."

"Will he be back later today?"

"No, man. I'm telling you; he's gone! Audios! Hasta la vista!" He shifted the weighty box to his shoulder."

"But we had a deal pending."

"Tough turkey! He left owing me two-weeks salary! No note, no forwarding address, nothing! I got nothing! I took that slab's abuse all this time and he shorts me $900! If I could find him, I'd kill him!" He brushed by Jeff with a flip of the wrist signaling for him to get out of the way. Jeff stood there in shock.

The dream of a lifetime had just melted away like ice on a summer's day. He noticed the guy had not pulled the door closed. He slipped inside.

The reception room was empty. No desk, no chairs, no pictures on the walls. He went across the carpet to the other room. That room had also been stripped. No furniture, no computer, nothing. All that was left were the carpets and the paint on the walls. Even the light fixtures had been removed. Then, he saw a couple of scraps of paper on the floor behind the door. He picked them up and saw that it was a photograph torn in half. He matched the edges. It was a picture of a wrecked car—a 2013 red Miata convertible.

Jeff tossed it aside and left the building.

Sunday, July 5, 2020

~ 86 ~

Autumn drove to Sarasota Memorial Hospital around nine a.m. to pick Larry up when he was released. The doctor had been confident that there would be few repercussions from the drugs. They had antidotes that had not been available a few years ago. The doctor found a prick on Larry's back that confirmed that the drug had been administered by a blowgun. Autumn confirmed that the tattooed man had said he learned this method in Africa.

They bid the doctor good-bye and headed for Larry's car. "Thanks for letting me take your car. It would have been a long walk home."

"You know, of course, I was out of my mind at the time. You could have taken anything, and I wouldn't have said a word."

"You must be feeling better; you're talking non-stop this morning."

"It has to do with being so well-rested. After all, I slept over twenty-four hours straight.

"Did you have breakfast?"

"Boy, did I! Eggs, bacon, toast, hash browns, orange juice, tomato juice, milk with cereal, and coffee."

"You must have been starved!"

-

"Doc said that in some circles they'd call it 'the munchies'!"

They took the Trail south and turned onto Business 41. "We're not headed home?"

"Actually, I thought we'd stop to see Boatman. He was pretty shaken up when he heard all that had happened in his absence."

"He's a nice guy - a worrier - but nice. It's funny he didn't sense anything all that time we were on the island."

"He thinks they come over him when it's quiet. I think he was so stressed with all that had happened that no messages could get through."

They drove through town and headed toward the Circus Bridge. Autumn turned left onto Amora Avenue and then made a quick left onto Golf and in minutes they pulled onto Boatman's driveway.

"Happy to see you survived your ordeal, Larry. It looked like touch and go for a while there."

"No, I just needed a twenty-four-hour nap. Now, I'm good as new and doing a little 'soft shoe'," he said gaily, demonstrating a sort of tap dance.

"Who's up for a beer?"

"Sounds good," Larry grinned.

"Oh, okay. I don't want to be a party-pooper. I'll have one too."

The three sat in the living room discussing all that had happened. Everyone had a different take on it, and they found it fascinating how each had experienced it differently.

"You were so worried about that vision you had of the island."

"We definitely had a problem, but not exactly as I saw it."

"Nonetheless, isn't it ironic that your visions reveal so much? It's almost as if someone was dropping clues for you to find in order to reveal the truth." Autumn smiled and kissed Boatman on the cheek. Then a thought struck her. "Oh my gosh, you don't suppose..."

"What?" Boatman frowned, thinking.

"It seems so obvious I can't believe I didn't think of it before.

"What?" Boatman squinted; not sure she wasn't playing with his mind.

"Boatman, think... the visions, the messages, the book! Who would be able to do this? Who'd have the knowledge?"

"What?"

"Yeah, what?" Larry was confused.

Autumn covered her mouth as if to hide the smile she couldn't help but reveal. "Think about it. The book... who's book?"

"Oh, no way." He thought for a long moment and watched her smile broaden. "No just that couldn't be."

"I'll bet it is, Boatman."

"What?" Larry asked, looking from Autumn to Boatman.

"Don't mediums have spirit guides that educate and help them?" Autumn suggested.

"Simka?" Boatman asked.

"Sure. You were close friends all those years. You did everything together. You even warned him to get away from the danger he was risking. You gave him the book that he carried with him. The book was the connection. Why, he was probably guiding Don to write down all those things. He may have even tried to warn him, but Don didn't have the gift. He might have gotten an inkling, but he would probably have blown it off."

"I don't know... This is all one big mystery to me. It reminds me of a cave in the West Indies. From the inside looking out—it looks like a huge keyhole. But search as I might, I couldn't find the key to its secrets.

"Trust me, if Simka is your spirit guide wouldn't you be more apt to listen to him? I think *he* is the key, and all you have to do is to be open to him."

"She has a point there, Pal."

"Okay, I'll keep an open mind," Boatman said, with a reluctant grin.

"I've never met a fortune-teller before."

"I'm not a fortune teller, *Pal!*"

Larry laughed. "I'm sorry, it's just that you have these visions that lead to important things, and I was wondering if you've had any of Autumn, you know, falling in love with a tall, brown-haired, bespectacled, FBI agent?"

The other two laughed.

"That is something only time will tell," said Autumn, as she took his arm. "But maybe I should practice what I preach."

"What do you mean?" Larry had that quizzical expression that he'd shown so frequently lately.

"I mean I'll keep an open mind," Autumn smiled and winked at Boatman.

-o-o-

Made in the USA
Columbia, SC
02 October 2020